LP F Wal Walter, Elizabeth

A season of goodwill

DATE DUE

JE 10 '87	AG 30 '91	MY 14 '09	OR
JE 22 '87		JUL 08 2010	
SE 8 '87	MY 25 '96		
DE 14 '87			
DE 30 '87	SE 27 '98		
AP 12 '88	OC 26 '98		
JY 22 '88			
	MY 03 '03		
NO 25 '89	JE 11 '04		
SE 6 '90			
NO 30 '90	AP 05 '06		
FE 6 '91	JY 25 '06		
JY 3 '96	NO 15 '07		

42397

BLAIR PUBLIC LIBRARY
Blair, Nebraska

A SEASON OF GOODWILL

A SEASON OF GOODWILL

ELIZABETH WALTER

THORNDIKE PRESS • THORNDIKE, MAINE

F
WAL
L.P.

Library of Congress Cataloging-in-Publication Data
Walter, Elizabeth.
A season of goodwill.

Reprint. Originally published: New York: Charles Scribner's Sons, c1986.
1. Large type books. I. Title.
[PR6073.A4285S33 1987] 823'.914 87-1900
ISBN 0-89621-796-5 (lg. print: alk. paper)

Copyright © 1986 by Elizabeth Walter. All rights reserved.

This novel is a work of fiction. Names, characters, places, and incidents are either the product of the author's imagination or are used fictitiously. Any resemblance to actual events or locales or persons, living or dead, is entirely coincidental.

Cover design by Lesia Sochor.

A SEASON OF GOODWILL

42397

CHAPTER 1

The train shrieked in triumph as it broke free of the tunnel. Roddy, standing at the window, rubbed vainly at the glass obscured by steam and smoke. Beatrix, sitting bolt upright in the middle of the long bench seat, her back to the engine, asked for the tenth time, 'Mama, are we nearly there?'

Emily North consulted the gold fob watch hanging from the lapel of her navy blue travelling costume. 'Yes,' she said tightly.

She hadn't wanted to come to Amberley for this Christmas of 1907 – London was much more fun, although the invitation to the St Devereuxs' fancy dress ball sounded promising – but Maud had written to invite them (no doubt with as much enthusiasm, Emily thought, as she herself had felt in accepting), and George had added a PS in his own hand – George who never put pen to paper if he could help it. Moreover, Harry's last letter had said yet again how much he hoped she would accept his brother's invitation. 'It will be good for the children to get to know their cousins,' he had written, 'and it'll give the Mater no end of a thrill to have all her grandchildren under one roof.'

It probably would, Emily reflected. At sixty-five the widowed Fanny North held undiminished sway over her eldest son and his wife, their children, dogs, servants, and the village of Croft Amberley. It was 'Madam' who visited the sick and needy, gave prizes to good scholars at the village school, interviewed the relatives of unmarried girls found to be in an interesting condition and saw to it that the girls were respectably married off. It was Madam who would catechize Roddy and Beatrix about their life in London; and it was Madam's report which would eventually be read by Major Henry North of the 9th Cawnpore Lancers – read and implicitly believed.

She's never liked me, Emily thought resentfully. She always wanted Harry to marry some girl whose parents she already knew. As if you married the parents, for heaven's sake. When Harry had first brought her home – she had been wearing her best grey alpaca with a darling little hat in pink, as demure as you please – her prospective mother-in-law had questioned her, politely, kindly and insistently, until

Emily felt as though every last fact of her life, parentage and personality had been ascertained, weighed in the balance and found wanting. For the first time she began to have doubts about her swift engagement. It was flattering to be swept off your feet, but when your feet again touched ground . . . She had supposed the head of the family to be Colonel George North, Harry's elder brother, but you didn't need to spend long at Amberley to know where the real power lay. A glance at Maud, George's depressed-looking wife, heavily pregnant, had decided Emily to spend as little time as possible under the North family roof, and to be thankful that her fiancé was in the Indian Army and only a second son.

'Will Uncle George meet us, Mama?' Beatrix asked.

'I don't suppose he'll come himself, but he'll have sent the carriage.'

Only important guests were met by George, and his sister-in-law suspected she would not count among them.

'Does Uncle George look like Father?' Roddy asked.

'Well, yes – and no. He's dark, like him, and about the same height, but stockier. Not so good-looking as your father.' And certainly not so good-looking as the youngest brother, James.

'Uncle George is married to Aunt Maud,' Roddy went on, thinking aloud, 'and they've got Alice and Rose and Louisa.'

And three stillborn sons, the last as recently as this past summer, and half a dozen miscarriages, Emily supplied mentally. Poor old Maud. Aloud she said, 'That's right. Your Cousin Alice comes between you two in age and Rose is four years younger.'

'And Louisa?'

'Lulu's still a baby. We shan't see much of her.'

'Will the ayah look after her?' Beatrix asked.

'Certainly not. Nanny Cardew will. You must remember, Bea, you're not in India any more.'

I wish I was, Bea thought, missing poignantly the wide-verandahed, low, cool bungalow; the soft-footed, dark-faced servants; her narrow white bed with its shroud of mosquito netting. She had been in England for a month now, a month of confusion and discomfort in a dreary Earl's Court flat and a series of dreary visits to even drearier prospective boarding-schools. Her predominant impression of the country was one of damp: a chill grey damp exhaled by the paving stones, exuded by the walls, and precipitated from the chill grey skies. Even in rooms where fires burned it made everything cold to the touch. She was tired of perching politely on glacial chintz while Mama and potential headmistresses interviewed each other, and she was embarrassed by the unfavourable assessments of her educational attainments (No French? No music? No embroidery?). The last headmistress, the patrician-voiced Miss Fortescue, had addressed her throughout as Beatrice, and when, despite Mama's warning glances, she had at last burst out, 'It's Beatrix, Miss Fortescue,' the lady had inclined her head graciously, said 'I beg your pardon, Beatrix,' and then to Mama: 'It seems Beatrice is a perfectionist.' Afterwards Mama had been angry: 'She may decide not to take an awkward little girl like you, and she's much cheaper than most of the others.' But Miss Fortescue did accept Beatrix (she got it right in the letter), and in January Bea would start at The Limes.

'I don't want to go to The Limes,' she said mutinously to Roddy, but her brother had problems of his own. 'At my school I won't even be Roderick,' he pointed out. 'I'll just be North, R.'

But at least there was no argument about Roddy's schooling. He would go to Bradwell House like his father and uncles before him, though a little late, for he was already ten. Beyond that loomed public school. Secretly he dreaded all of it, though his father had assured him school was not so bad. 'Grim at first, of course,' the Major had conceded, 'but you'll come through it all right. We did.'

Roddy did not share his father's optimism, but there was no one he could tell. His mother and sister were unsuitable recipients for that sort of confidence. Already he felt himself engulfed by the world of men, with its mysterious masculine code of conduct, its taboos, its fraternity, not yet experienced but atavistically familiar. The first barrier between him and Bea had already gone up.

Bea was not yet aware of it. The two children had always been close, and though she recognized that from now on their paths must diverge, their experience of life differ, she supposed that this would enrich them both. Through Roddy, she was part of a man's world; through her, the sisterhood of women welcomed him. Hand in hand, they would cross and re-cross the lines drawn up between the sexes as if for battle, inseparable and therefore invulnerable.

The rhythm of the train had altered, the first intimation of slowing down. Through the window now free of steam and smoke the children saw a landscape in which the once-distant hills of the Cotswolds had suddenly closed in. Trees covered their flanks; their feet were firmly planted in ploughed fields, in one of which a flock of black and white birds were feeding.

'Lapwings,' Mama said.

Bea repeated the name under her breath: lapwings.

'Why lapwings?' she asked.

'Heavens, child, I don't know. It's what your father called them.'

Emily had not thought of lapwings since, but now she recalled vividly that first train ride, with Harry pointing out every landmark, giving her potted histories of local families, incomprehensible anecdotes of the chase, information on trees, birds, animals, until her town-bred head under its pretty pink hat spun like a whipping-top. Subsequent visits had never effaced that first one. She had not realized the extent to which this present visit, made so much later, would seem a repetition, only then she had had Harry to lean on, whereas now she came alone, flanked by her children, trying to feel secure in her position as mother of the heir.

The last of the flock of lapwings vanished as the train negotiated a curve. Bea, glued to the window, watched the unrolling of a landscape such as she had never seen. Neat hedges criss-crossed the fields. Here and there, from cottage, farmhouse, gentleman's residence, a plume of smoke rose in the evening air. The sun, a disc of bright red flannel, was sinking in a grey and woolly west, so that even as she watched Bea saw a field turn ashen and the windows of a house blaze with reflected light.

She was getting used to these English winter evenings, their mistiness, their imperceptible deepening into night, cold sun and colder moon counter-balanced in a single arc of sky; but the climate had so far denied her that culmination of Christmas bliss depicted on the cards that so incongruously bedecked their home in Cossipore each December.

Beatrix turned pleadingly to her mother: 'Mama, is it going to snow?'

Busily adjusting her veil in the carriage's speckled mirror, Emily North looked down in astonishment. 'Snow? I certainly hope not. To be snowed up at Amberley – that would really be the last straw.' Then, seeing her daughter's disappointment, she added more gently: 'I think it's too cold to snow. We've had hard frost for almost a week now. No snowballing, but perhaps you'll be able to go skating on the lake at Mawby Hall.'

Roddy hugged himself at the thought. He had never seen people skating, although in the book Grandmama had sent him last Christmas, entitled *The Fur Trappers*, there was a picture of a man on skates being pursued by wolves. Bea always said she hoped the wolves won because they looked so hungry, and certainly their teeth were bared, but that was just Bea, whose kindness to animals was such that she had even been caught putting out a saucer of milk for the snake she claimed to have seen on the verandah. That night, Father had kept watch and been obliged to kill a deadly king cobra. In the circumstances Bea had not been punished.

The train had slowed perceptibly, and Mama was buttoning her gloves and asking Bea to hold the tickets. She reached down the holdall from the net luggage-rack, adjusted Bea's tam-o'-shanter and Roddy's cap, and took up position at the window, the long leather strap in her hands. 'We shall want a porter to help with the luggage from the guard's van,' she said over her shoulder. 'When we get out at Barford, Roddy, you can run down to the van and tell him which cases are ours. Be sure to tell him to be careful with the green dress-box. It's my costume for the St Devereuxs' fancy dress ball.'

Lapped now in folds of tissue paper, the costume flattered her, no doubt of that. Mary Queen of Scots's jewelled cap with its widow's peak, her stand-up lace collar, emphasized the fragility of Emily's neck; the sweeping velvet skirt was held out from her body, displaying her tiny waist. The best theatrical costumier in

Covent Garden had been hideously expensive, but it was not an expense Emily grudged. She seldom grudged what was spent on herself, and it wasn't every day that she was a guest at a ball given by titled people. Besides – and this was the ball's chief attraction – Jimmy North might be there.

Roddy, listening to her instructions, swelled with ten-year-old pride. This was what it meant to be the man of the party. Later he would take charge of tickets, look up timetables, give instructions about luggage just as he had seen his father do, but this was a step in the right direction. He said, 'Yes, Mama,' very dutifully, and suddenly the train stopped with a slight jerk. A huge sign, white letters on black, said 'Barford', steam was rising in clouds, Mama let down the window with a bang as the strap slipped through her fingers, reached out to grasp the brass door-handle, and gave a delighted cry of 'George'.

The children had barely time to take in the dark stocky figure with their father's blue eyes and a moustache that tickled when he kissed them, before he was giving orders to a porter with a trolley, supervising the removal of their luggage, ('Enough for a month,' he was to grumble later to Maud), and leading the way to the gate marked 'Exit', which a man with a

Christmas tree under his arm was negotiating with difficulty.

Behind them doors slammed, the guard blew his whistle, and out of the corner of her eye Bea saw him wave his green flag, but her attention was concentrated on the enamel advertisements affixed to the railings: Palethorpe's Sausages; Mazzawattee Tea; and a great blue-black splash of Stephens Ink. The hissing gaslight illuminated Sir John Millais's 'Bubbles' looking down from a Pears Soap poster upon a notice in which the Great Western Railway Company disclaimed responsibility for almost everything. She was so busy looking that she mislaid the tickets in her muff, while three hampers, a Gladstone bag, a roll of walking sticks and umbrellas, and another Christmas tree queued up behind them and stamped with impatience.

Uncle George and Mama were talking: '. . . a good journey . . . How is Maud? . . . a letter last week from Harry . . . the Mater looking forward no end . . .' There were several carriages outside the station and a little crowd of people. It was towards this that Uncle George made his way, so resplendent in fur coat, checked scarf, cap and goggles, that the bystanders instinctively stepped back. Before the astonished eyes of Emily North and her children a bright yellow horseless carriage stood revealed.

Uncle George patted it proudly.

'Well, you three, care for a spin?'

They were going up the hill out of Barford at fifteen miles per hour.

'She does twenty-five on the flat,' Uncle George yelled. His sister-in-law put her hand to her hat in mock horror; the other hand clutched the side of the motor-car. Oh, but this was exciting. She had never travelled in one before, never imagined that George might own one. He always seemed so staid. Now if it had been Jimmy she'd have expected it, except that motor-cars were expensive and Jimmy was always broke. But he was a daredevil in his way. Would he be at Amberley for Christmas? It would be – interesting – to see him again. But perhaps he preferred to stay in London. It was a city where a bachelor with a modest income could have an agreeable time. Theatres, clubs, concerts, exhibitions, little restaurants where one could dine *à deux*. Jimmy might have a job in that boring old lawyer's office, but his evenings were surely his own. An occasional invitation to his sister-in-law was no more than courtesy. It troubled her that since she arrived in England Jimmy hadn't been in touch. When she'd written to say she was bringing the children home she'd taken care to mention that letters care of Cox's and King's would reach her until she'd found a more permanent address. Could her own letter have gone astray? It sometimes happened, though she'd sent it to him at his club. Considering that he'd spent three months with them in India last year when he was wandering the world after his South African débâcle, she was beginning to be irked by his silence. There was such a thing as the return of hospitality . . .

'You all right?' George roared.

She smiled and nodded.

'What about the children? Can't take my eye off the road.'

She turned gingerly to Roddy and Bea in the dicky-seat.

'Are you all right in there?'

Roddy nodded enthusiastically, for the wind ripped words away. Bea's nod was more cautious: she was feeling a little sick, partly from fright (like her mother, she had never before been in a horseless carriage), partly from their rattling, bumpy progress, partly from the smell of the petrol itself. A great cloud of fumes rose behind them, and every now and then she caught a whiff of these. Horses sometimes smelt, but at least sweat and wind were recognizable animal odours. How did you stop a car?

To start it, Uncle George had gone round to the front and swung a handle until the car juddered into life, and stood there snorting and trembling like a horse exhausted before it had even set out. Now it had the bit between its teeth and it would be no use shouting 'Whoa!' or pulling on the reins, any more than if your horse had bolted. What happened if a motor-car left the road? It would presumably be confronted by fences or other obstructions, and she had never heard that motor-cars could jump. At fifteen miles per hour no one would be able to catch up with it, even supposing anyone dared to try. They were trapped in an unstoppable machine that would never weary and would soon be travelling at twenty-five miles per hour.

Twenty-five miles per hour! Roddy could scarcely believe it. Already the outskirts of Barford had raced by. He had glimpsed houses, a church, two men trying to hold a horse which snorted and reared at their passing, a woman flattening her children protectively against a wall. A cacophony of barking accompanied them, not to mention the dogs, afraid to bite because the panting yellow beast had no obvious throat to go for, but intent on harassment. Roddy wished the drive could go on for ever. If only it were forty miles to Croft Amberley instead of four. If only he could travel by motor-car every day, or better still, if he could drive one. When I grow up, he promised himself, I'm going to have a car.

He had never thought seriously about growing up before. It was something that happened automatically the day you became twenty-one. Father had explained that the banishment about to be imposed on him was a necessary step towards that end. Mama too had been at pains to explain that the children weren't being sent home to school because they were unwanted, but because it was Best For Them. And of course they wouldn't be alone in the holidays: there would be Uncle George and Aunt Maud and Grandmama and their cousins, and possibly Uncle Jimmy as well.

Roddy hoped there would be Uncle Jimmy. His father's younger brother was not like any other grown-up he knew. When he had stayed with them last year in India, the two of them had gone for long walks and rides and held long conversations as if they were contemporaries. Mama hadn't like it much – he knew from the way she looked reproachful and said, 'I thought you two had got lost,' whenever they returned from one of their expeditions, but she never said he mustn't go. Uncle Jimmy was like a big brother, or how Roddy imagined a big brother would be. For the first time he found Bea's company insufficient, and he envied his father whose childhood had been enlivened by the presence of Jimmy and George.

'Couldn't I have a brother?' he had asked his father.

Major North had laughed unamusedly, 'Better ask your mother, old chap.' Something in the way he said it had decided Roddy to do no such thing.

And now here he was in a motor-car driven by Father's elder brother, the never-before-encountered Uncle George, who spoke with Father's voice, and walked like Father, and looked at him with Father's eyes. The broad fur-coated back rose before him like the back of some huge animal, but a friendly animal. Roddy thought he might be going to like Uncle George.

George North thought he might be going to like Roddy. The boy had Harry's eyes. He'd always got on well with his second brother. It wasn't his son's fault that he stood to inherit Amberley. The estate descended in the male line, and nothing Maud could say would alter that. Alice and Rose and Lulu couldn't inherit, and their baby brothers hadn't lived. If only Maud would give him a son. There was still time; she wasn't much more than thirty-five and Dr. Paget had said there was no reason why the girls survived and the boys didn't; it was just the luck of the game. But Paget had also taken him aside and talked about 'restraint'. There was nothing wrong with Mrs North, oh no, but constant pregnancies, psychological effect, etcetera. He knew he needn't spell it out to a considerate husband. One was a gentlemen, after all.

It was because he was a gentleman that George had insisted on inviting his brother's family for Christmas. Maud had said it was because the Mater wanted it and had accused him of being 'under his mother's thumb, as usual', but that had nothing to do with it. George's concept of duty might have been narrow, but it was stern. If Roddy was some day going to be squire of Amberley, he must learn to love the place as George did himself, and he had overridden all Maud's efforts to keep Emily and her brood at bay.

'It's bad enough that that horrible little boy will inherit the girls' home, their birthright,' she had sobbed. 'Do we have to have him here in advance? What sort of a Christmas will it be for me with Emily going round gloating?'

'The same as it'll be for me,' George said.

He was deeply sorry for his wife. He put a hand on her shoulder and felt it stiffen. Defeated, he withdrew his hand.

'It won't be too bad,' he said, more heartily

than he intended. 'It's the season of goodwill. Besides, they're the Mater's grandchildren just as much as our three are.'

'Do you have to remind me?' Maud said bitterly.

'Come on, old girl, they're only children. No good taking it out on them.'

'I am not taking it out on anyone, George. I hope I am Christian enough for that. But you must admit we have a heavy cross laid on us.'

Heavier than you know, George thought. He hadn't said anything to her about the debts. That would keep till later, till after the New Year, at least. Perhaps 1908 would bring with it a miracle, but he couldn't see it yet. He couldn't see further than Christmas week itself, and that was grim enough, for sooner or later he was going to have to tell not only Maud but Harry and Jimmy and the Mater that Amberley would have to be sold. That poor little devil in the dicky-seat would never inherit. It was quixotry on his part that had brought the children here. He wanted them to have something to remember, and their first Christmas in the home of their fathers would also be their last.

George pressed more heavily on the car's accelerator. Twenty-five miles per hour. There was something intoxicating about speed. He liked to imagine that if he could go far enough fast enough he would leave all his troubles behind. Of course the purchase of a motor-car had been crazy for a man already in debt, but damn it, he was entitled to some pleasure before the débâcle, and if a man couldn't even enjoy his own wife . . . And young Dick Sparrow at the blacksmith's had been ecstatic over the car. He was developing quite a nice sideline as a mechanic. Deep inside, George envied him. Land, estates, a house like Amberley – were they part of the past? The thought was treachery, and as if to remind him of it he saw the entrance to his driveway on the other side of the road.

He swung the wheel sharply and the car turned in through pillared gateposts, skirted the lawn edged with white stone markers, and drew up in front of the house. The front door was already open, and Maud's pugs, Homer and Virgil, and his own retriever, Rastus, came barking and spilling out. In the background he could see Jarvis the butler smiling. He turned to help Emily down. Alice and Rose had appeared and stood clapping their hands in excitement as their cousins scrambled out of the dicky-seat.

George, suddenly shy, said, 'Welcome to Amberley,' and felt pompous and awkward. And then mercifully Maud was there, issuing from the hall, hands outstretched, with all the graciousness and insincerity that fifteen years as the Squire's lady had taught her as her voice rang out in the frosty evening air:

'My dears! How lovely to see you at Amberley. A Merry Christmas to us all.'

CHAPTER 2

Amberley was a stone-built gentleman's residence dating from 1748. It reflected the sense of stability of the English middle classes after Bonnie Prince Charlie's final defeat, with the Hanoverians securely on the throne, the Church of England firmly established, and the various elements of society unprotestingly pigeonholed. It was comfortable, more than a little shabby, and pleasant rather than beautiful; most people found it welcoming.

I never did, Emily thought, sipping tea in the drawing-room with Maud, George having disappeared as soon as possible to put the car away and see to some estate matters. She remembered all too well her first visit in the best grey alpaca and the little pink hat. 'Madam is expecting you both in the drawing-room, Mr Harry,' said Jarvis. And a moment later, Harry, having darted forward to greet the grey-haired lady who sat with her back to the door, was saying: 'Mater, may I present Miss Emily Fanshaw, who has done me the honour of consenting to be my wife.'

Afterwards, sitting opposite her prospective mother-in-law, Emily realized that Mrs North's position had been carefully chosen, for her face remained in shadow whereas that of her interviewee – there was no other word for it – caught the light. At the end of the interview Emily had been left with the feeling that she was somehow not up to standard. The feeling had persisted ever since. Even now, when she sat smoothing the folds of her navy blue travelling costume opposite poor, dull, dowdy Maud, she was conscious of a sense of inferiority, although she, not Maud, was the mother of the heir.

She took another sip of tea and said politely: 'I see you've made some changes to this room.'

Since she was last here, the room had been repapered in a pleasantly patterned shade of green. The panels on the cream-painted doors and dado were picked out in gold, and the chairs had been re-covered in a summery floral linen, though the carpet and heavy winter curtains were still old.

Maud surveyed her chairs, her William Morris wallpaper, and looked pleased. 'Yes. With Madam at the Dower House . . .'

Her presence made more potent by her absence, Emily suspected. And said: 'I suppose there were difficulties.'

'Difficulties!' Maud controlled herself. It would be a mistake to talk to Emily – yet. Her sister-in-law's prolonged absence meant that she was a stranger, not an ally. And between them stood a small boy.

The children had been dispatched to have tea with Nanny Cardew in the nursery. For a little while the ladies were alone, while the December day closed in around them and the curtains remained undrawn. It was Maud's favorite time of day, her hour of respite from household and maternal cares. George seldom joined her for tea, and alone in what had been her mother-in-law's drawing-room but was now stamped as her own, with the gentle hissing of the gas lamps, the crackle of the fire, the singing of the tea-kettle on its methylated spirit stove, Maud recaptured in some measure the peace and serenity of her scholarly father's study, which had been her idea of heaven as a child.

Maud had been the younger daughter of a country vicar whose living had not been fat. She could never quite believe that the neatly turned and darned Maud Hunsdon had become Mrs George North of Amberley. Or rather, Mrs George, as everyone called her, for Madam was still Mrs North. I seem fated never to be known by my own surname, Maud thought, for when we were girls it was always Lilias who was Miss Hunsdon and I as the younger sister was known simply as Miss Maud. How she had hated being the addendum on her mother's visiting cards: Mrs Stephen Hunsdon, Miss Hunsdon, Miss Maud Hunsdon. It was as well there had been no further daughters, for the card wouldn't have had room for more. But if George returned to her bed there might be several more North daughters. How would her own visiting card look ten years from now?

Mrs George North, Amberley, Croft Amberley, Near Barford. It was what people called a good address. Shops were only too willing to take orders and deliver. She was part of the carriage trade. She might not have Emily's dashing way of dressing (dashing ways too, she had no doubt), but in her own world she was still a lady of consequence, though only a moon to Madam's sun.

Madam had indicated that she would wait until tomorrow to welcome her second son's wife and children. Maud was both resentful and relieved: relieved to be spared that powerful, upstaging presence, resentful that the upheaval of arrival was to be prolonged. When four years ago Madam had moved of her own accord to what was now known as the Dower House, though it had originally been built as the lodge, Maud had believed for a heady moment that she would at last be mistress in her own home. It hadn't worked out like that. Madam was still Madam in the village, and still the Mater to her eldest son. Between them, squire and villagers maintained her in position; Maud remained somewhere in between.

So when Emily said she supposed there had been difficulties, it was all Maud could do not to elaborate. Instead, she forced herself to be charitable, and, having admitted the difficulties, added: 'But at sixty-five what can you expect?'

Not much, Emily thought. Old age terrified her. What did you have left when you no longer had looks and health, a body worth dressing, worth loving, the assurance that sprang from seeing desire flicker in men's eyes? She had tried once to explain her fears, but Harry hadn't understood, murmuring that to him she would always be the girl who stole his heart the first time he saw her, and the mother of Roddy and Bea. It was strange how men thought children made such a difference. She couldn't see it herself. She had nothing against her own, but having given Harry the son that all men wanted, she felt entitled to desist. Could Maud be pregnant again? It would account for why she looked so pasty, and she was just the sort to believe that constant pregnancies were what God intended. Emily smoothed the skirt of her travelling costume over her own slim hips. The hand of the handsome second officer aboard the SS *Jaipur* had sometimes lingered there when he danced with her at ship's dances. He had reminded her of Jimmy North.

Why hadn't Jimmy got in touch during the month they had been in London? Earl's Court and Pimlico where he had lodgings were not that far apart. She was the more hurt because she had actually believed his avowals of affection. He had arrived home a bare six months before her. Surely in that time a man could not forget those rides and walks under the pine trees of Simla, those evenings on the verandah in the resin-scented dark because a light attracted insects, despite the allegedly repellent effect of gentlemen's cigars and cigarettes. Suddenly Emily was homesick. It was absurd to call this dismal country Home. Already one-third of her life had been spent in India. By the time Harry retired it would be nearer two-thirds. Both her children had been born there. What did England mean to them? Bea's distress at damp and dirt and dinginess was something her mother shared. For the next few years the children would be exiles in their own country.

Would Miss Fortescue be kind to Bea? Would she remember not to call her Beatrice? How would Roddy fare at Bradwell House? And what would holidays be like spent at Amberley? Suppose the cousins did not get on?

She had tried in the train to prepare Roddy for the idea that Amberley would some day be his.

He had looked at her blankly. 'But I want to go into the army like Father. I don't want to be a squire.'

Parroting Harry, she had murmured something about duty.

'Why can't Father be the next squire?'

'He will be if Uncle George doesn't outlive him –' there were dangers in a soldier's life – 'but we thought it would be more sensible for you to take over.'

'I don't want to.'

'You can't always have what you want.'

She did not add that she had found you could have most of it if you played your cards aright, and with more determination than other people. Emily played every game to win.

'I want to be a soldier,' Roddy repeated.

'Well, perhaps you'll get your wish.'

George ought to be good for a few years yet, and there was always the possibility that Maud might at last present him with a living son.

Meanwhile Amberley would provide a convenient haven when Bradwell House and The Limes were closed.

She said impulsively to her sister-in-law, 'Maud, it's good of you and George to give our two a home during school holidays.'

Maud looked at her. 'What else could we do?'

If Emily only knew how she hated the thought of these interlopers, in particular this boy who would some day call Amberley his. But it was her Christian duty to receive them, and duty was something Maud had never shirked. She had none of her elder sister's brilliance and beauty; she could not dazzle and charm; but she knew where her duty lay and discharged her obligations. It was her duty to give George sons, to endure the discomforts of pregnancy, the misery of miscarriages and stillbirths, the disappointment of holding another daughter in her arms. It was six months now since her last stillbirth. Any time now George might return to her bed. Perhaps at Christmas? Maud felt her body stir in anticipation and hated it for its failure to gratify George's desire for a son. The heirs of a man's body. Legitimate issue. These phrases had a meaning where an estate like Amberley was concerned. And it wasn't only George who desired a son: she herself longed passionately for a male child who would unlock for her the world of boyhood, the years of her husband's life which she could never share. Not even to herself could Maud admit the emotion which every thought of George aroused. Since he had first come courting Lilias she had adored him. She could never quite believe that he was hers.

It was as much incredulity as piety that sent her to church each Sunday, not only to give thanks but to expunge her guilt. If Lilias had lived it was she who would have been mistress of Amberley; she who would have been Mrs George North. Plain, loving, homely Maud would have been bridesmaid at her sister's wedding, and her husband's sister-in-law. After Lilias's death Maud had replaced her in George's affections by some miracle she did not understand, and had stood beside him at the altar to exchange vows and receive a blessing at her father's trembling hand. She had taken George from Lilias, even though God had taken Lilias first. For that she owed God; and Maud's God was like a money-lender who reclaimed his principal with interest and would demand repayment in full. Meanwhile she propitiated him with little offerings. The acceptance of Emily's children was one.

She said: 'I hope the children will learn to love Amberley as we do.'

Emily said, suppressing her doubts about Roddy, 'I'm perfectly certain they will.'

At that moment Roddy and Bea were far from loving Amberley. Tea was in progress in the nursery and they were making the acquaintance of seed cake. Nanny Cardew said it was wholesome, but the children would have described it differently. Alice and Rose munched politely and seemed not to notice, but Bea found the cake had disintegrated to a mush in her mouth which she could not force herself to swallow. She took a sip of tea to help it down.

'Miss Bea, don't drink with your mouth full.'

Nanny Cardew had eyes in the back of her head. Even while feeding two-year-old Lulu, she knew what was going on.

'Why shouldn't she drink with her mouth full?' Roddy demanded, springing to his sister's defence.

His cousin Alice answered for the Establishment. 'Because it's rude.'

'Why is it rude?'

Dark-haired Alice lifted thin but shapely shoulders that would some day emerge stunningly from a gown. The ways of grown-up people and their world had always been incomprehensible. You put up with them and changed them where you could. Her father was more reasonable than her mother, admitting that he too did not always understand, that there was no reason why a woman should be considered less important when it came to education, for instance, except that she would probably marry and have no need of it.

'Suppose she doesn't marry?' Alice said.

Her father regarded his eldest daughter with affection. Alice would marry, he was sure. She was her Aunt Lilias over again, and Lilias . . . The pain still wrenched him, though less since she had been restored to him. That she should be so in the person of his own child, the daughter whose survival had been such a disappointment when her two baby brothers had died, was still to him a source of wonder such as his other daughters did not arouse. The whole household knew that Alice was her father's favourite, though only her mother understood why, listening as if mesmerized to a familiar voice expounding familiar doctrines. Lilias had been a rebel too.

Nanny Cardew, however, had a short way with rebels. She believed Miss Alice should be sent away to school. Discipline, not education, was what that young lady needed, and the governess she shared with Miss Rose was far too soft. She might speak French with a Parisian accent and know the names of all Europe's capitals, but Miss Alice needed someone to see she did the things she didn't like doing and didn't slide out of them with one of her dazzling smiles. Perhaps now that Miss Bea was going to school they'd send Miss Alice. It was always the wrong ones who went. Miss Bea now, there was a child anyone could see was brought up properly. Look at her struggling with that cake.

'You can leave the rest of your seed cake if you don't like it, dear,' she said kindly, 'seeing as it's your first day and you're probably tired with the journey, but don't let me see you drinking tea with it again. And it's rude to drink when you're eating,' she answered Roddy, 'because it might make you choke.'

'My father says if someone chokes you slap him on the back,' Roddy informed her. 'If he chokes really bad you have to hold him upside down.'

'I can't see you holding Miss Alice upside down, Master Roddy. She's taller than you by a head.'

'I could stand on a chair.'

'You could hold me upside down, Roddy,' Rose suggested. 'You're ever so much bigger than me.'

Roddy eyed her. 'So I am. I say, let's try it. It'll be something to do after tea.'

'You'll do no such thing,' Nanny interposed firmly. 'It isn't good to hold people upside down. If the Lord had meant us to have our heads below our stomachs, he'd have made us walk on our hands.'

'If he'd meant us to walk on our hands they'd be a different shape,' Alice objected.

'That's just what I'm saying, dear. Besides, we can't have Miss Rose showing her underclothes, can we? Not in front of a little gentleman.'

'My father sees Mama's underclothes,' Roddy said. 'He helps her lace her stays when the amah's played truant. I've seen him.'

'It's different in hot countries,' Nanny said. 'And besides, your mother and father are married.'

'Well, when I grow up I shall marry Rose.'

The idea had been burgeoning in Roddy ever since they started tea. He knew few little girls, and none as pink and white and golden as his cousin. He was in process of losing his heart. The sensation was one his father would have recognized. From the moment he had seen Emily Fanshaw alighting from a knife-board omnibus and had shadowed her to Miss Lang's Secretarial College for Ladies, Harry North had not owned his own most vital organ and could only follow it helplessly.

He was home on leave, and would shortly be gazetted captain; marriage was a possibility. In the junior ranks of the British Army of India it was frowned on by commanding officers, who believed in subalterns sowing wild oats. But by the time a man attained his captaincy and the ripe old age of twenty-eight or -nine, he was expected to be past calf-love for the girl next door, and the more sophisticated excitements offered by the whorehouses of Calcutta and Bombay. Young officers began to receive invitations from the colonel's lady if there were marriageable daughters, and from the wives of other superior officers whose sisters, cousins, nieces out from Home on a visit, were in need of an establishment. Harry North had had his quota of invitations, done his share of duty squiring, and had narrowly escaped entanglement with the red-headed daughter of his commanding officer's cousin, who had hoped that the expense of the trip and her daughter's wardrobe would pay off. Unfortunately for her, Harry's home leave had fallen due before he could be manipulated into a proposal. He had sailed for England a free man, only to be ensnared within a week of his arrival in London by the face and figure and gait of Emily Fanshaw, before he had heard her speak a word.

From Miss Lang's Secretarial College he had

followed her to an address in Streatham, middle-class and shabby-genteel. He had seen her welcomed home by an older lady and guessed a widowed mother, but he learned on tipping the postman that the two Miss Fanshaws were aunt and niece. He sent flowers, which were very properly rejected, and wrote asking permission to call; then found himself, pressed, polished and barbered to parade-ground smartness, standing to attention before the front door. He was in no doubt, and neither was Emily, who could scarcely believe it was true that she was to exchange the expected life of a lady typewriter for that of an Indian Army wife. They were married before Harry's three months' leave was over, in Croft Amberley church by his mother's special wish, where innumerable Norths had been married, christened and buried, and after the briefest of honeymoons in Harrogate and Scarborough, had sailed for India with the Peninsular and Oriental Line.

Once in India, and already pregnant, Emily was an initial success. She knew instinctively whom to flatter, with whom to keep her distance, whom to patronize. Her impoverished years in Streatham since the death of her parents were rapidly forgotten. She began to indulge that taste in dress which had been one of the things about her to catch Harry North's attention until, without his share of the income from Amberley, his pay would have been dangerously overstretched. But he grudged Emily nothing. She was popular with his brother officers, though less so with their wives, and until the scandal earlier this year her life had been as blameless as the strictest husband could have desired. Even the scandal, Major North was certain, had been exaggerated, perhaps by malice. True, Emily had returned home unconventionally late from an expedition with her young brother-in-law in the course of which the accompanying bearers had been mysteriously lost, but there was no need to put the worst construction upon it, as had some of the garrison wives in Cossipore. Major North had been made aware that his wife was not universally popular. In his fashion he had rushed to her defence. When he decided to send Emily home to organize the children's schooling, which could ordinarily have waited till next summer, it was to show his confidence in her. Was he not sending her back to face the very temptation to which gossip said she had succumbed? Not that there was anything in it – his own brother – but a demonstration of trust would do no harm. And he had Jimmy's word of honour, exacted from him before he sailed, that he would not pursue Emily beyond the courtesies of kinship.

The Major bade his wife farewell with a quiet mind.

It never occurred to him that Roddy, aged ten, might succumb to the tender passion, least of all for his cousin Rose. If it had, he would have dismissed it as nonsense, while echoing Nanny Cardew's response to Roddy's avowal of his intentions: 'Yes, dear, but let's wait and see.'

'Perhaps Rose won't want to marry you,' Alice suggested. Why was a woman expected to accept? Why were proposals made by men? When I grow up I am going to Cambridge University, she promised herself. I shan't marry until I'm at least thirty, and then only to a Ph.D. She was not sure what a Ph.D. was, though she thought it meant Doctor of Physic, but she had heard it referred to with awe by her parents and governess, and the title sounded good. Come to that, why shouldn't she be a Ph.D. herself? Dr Alice North, with her own gig and coachman bowling smartly along the country lanes, and with a black Gladstone bag like Dr Paget's in which he brought babies – or so Nanny Cardew claimed. Alice had her doubts about this, but contented herself with the thought that when she was a Doctor of Physic she would know all about it. How lucky Bea was to be going to a real school, instead of having to listen to dull Miss Evans, who made them recite such things as tables, a list of dates in history, and the principal rivers of the British Isles. What use was such information to a future Doctor of Physic? But Mama said higher education for women was unnecessary and Papa said nothing at all except that it was expensive – but he said that about everything. Alice was quietly confident of being able to get round her father. The first step was to go to a real school. Like Bea.

'Is your headmistress an M.A.?' she asked, silencing the others with this non-sequitur.

'Miss Alice, don't interrupt,' said Nanny mechanically. The child was always doing it.

'I'm sorry. Is she?'

Bea felt her face reddening. 'I'm afraid I don't really know. Perhaps Mama . . .'

'Didn't you ask?'

Bea thought of Miss Fortescue saying 'Beatrice is a perfectionist,' and shivered. 'Mama was interviewing her, not me.'

'Didn't your mother ask? How do you know it's a good school? Do they prepare you for examinations?'

Bea shook her head helplessly.

Alice's opinion of Aunt Emily plummeted. She had thought her a woman of the world, a travelled lady fresh from the Indian sub-continent who would know her way around, but she seemed no better in the matter of female education than her own mother would have been. And Alice's attitude to her own mother was one of exasperated affection; indeed, more exasperation than affection whenever the subject of riding came up.

Maud refused to let her daughters learn to ride. She had given it up herself for reasons which George understood all too well, though he did not agree with them, and she was adamant that no daughter of hers was going to sit a horse. But Alice, spirited, active Alice, had set her heart on being able to roam the countryside on horseback, to gallop, to follow the hunt, clearing a hedge as she had enviously watched equestrian ladies do, while standing mutinous and uncomprehending at poor Miss Evans's side. For surely riding could not be unladylike, Mama's usual reason for forbidding anything that looked exciting, when people like Lady St Devereux rode?

Maud, locked in the past, could not bring herself to talk to her daughter. It would be like summoning up tragedy. And George, loyal to his wife but inwardly on his daughter's side and therefore more inept than usual, could only answer Alice's pleas with 'Mama doesn't wish it,' which did nothing to ameliorate the relationship.

Alice would have been astonished to learn

that her mother was in fact afraid of her, and never more so than in this. To Maud, it was like having Lilias come back. Alice held such advanced views, was so instantly the centre of attention even before she opened her mouth. Why couldn't she have been like Rose, whose gentleness and sweetness were apparent even at the age of eight? With Rose one had only to suggest, to voice an opinion, and she complied at once. Twenty years ago Lilias had prided herself on being a New Woman. She had dared to smoke a cigarette. She argued with men as though she were their equal – and the men didn't seem to mind. She read all kinds of books, not just those that were thought suitable. She devoured her father's copy of *The Times*. She argued about the causes of poverty as well as seeking to relieve it. She understood what went on in Parliament.

Alice was going to be the same – Maud could see it coming. She might even – heaven forbid! – become a Suffragette and get her name in the newspapers for unladylike behaviour. Perhaps in due course Madam could be asked to intervene. Her grandmother was one of the few people Alice stood in awe of. Maud wondered if her own awe could be overcome sufficiently to allow her to ask her mother-in-law's help, for George was useless: he would give Lilias – no,

Alice – everything she could possibly want.

For how much longer could he indulge his family, and Alice in particular, George wondered, sitting morosely in his study before his share of the Christmas post, which spelt out ever more bleakly his dire financial straits. If he could hold out till March, when certain dividends fell due, there was a chance of salvation. But if his creditors persisted in demanding immediate settlement, bankruptcy seemed inevitable. Unless Harry and Jimmy . . . He'd written to Harry, of course. Hadn't told Maud – no point in upsetting her – but Harry and his boy were the heirs and Harry had a right to know there might be nothing to inherit, and a right – perhaps? – to do what he could to help. If both his brothers would forgo their income from Amberley over the next few years, George reckoned he might pull through. If only letters to India didn't take six weeks in each direction. He wouldn't get Harry's reply before the New Year, at earliest.

Jimmy, thank God, was easier: he had no commitments. George felt no compunction in asking his youngest brother to stand down. Besides, it wouldn't hurt Jimmy to make a living by his own unaided efforts. He was still articled to a solicitor. Perhaps now he would qualify. The South African War had been no good to Jimmy, tempting him away from his studies just at the vital time and leaving him, like so many others, dangerously unsettled, missing the excitement, disturbed by the experience of his own country's red tape and incompetence, and perhaps imbued with guilt. That was one way of interpreting his decision to stay on in South Africa when the war was over and he had got his discharge. He had worked for a strict but kindly Boer with a farm in Cape Province, 'making the Union of South Africa fact,' as he had written to George, but after five years the irksomeness of the Boer's strictness had outweighed his kindness, and Jimmy had left in a hurry and sailed for India to visit Harry and Emily.

Since his return, George had hardly seen him. It was strange: he had expected Jimmy to come down often if only to give the Mater news of Harry and family, but except for one uncommunicative visit, he had resolutely stayed away. Maud had written inviting him for Christmas, and George, unknown to his wife, had written that there were urgent matters to discuss, but so far no reply had come and it was Christmas Eve tomorrow. It looked as though Jimmy was avoiding Amberley.

George put his head in his hands. He detested family friction, could not see why it should ever exist. Had Jimmy had some row with Harry's wife when he stayed with them in India? Was Emily the reason he didn't come?

In Maud's drawing-room Emily was asking herself the same question on hearing from Maud that Jimmy's arrival was still uncertain.

'Surely he'll come for Christmas?'

'One would think so.'

'Did you – did you tell him the children and I would be here?'

'Of course. Except for Harry, we shall all be under one roof for the first time ever. It will be a shame if he stays away.'

It will also be an announcement of his indifference, Emily thought. Like saying that theirs was no more than, say, a shipboard romance, only whereas she had been perfectly ready to enjoy a mild flirtation with the *Jaipur*'s handsome second officer, her feeling for her younger brother-in-law had been of a different kind. There was something about the good-looking, disillusioned, devil-may-care young fellow that had roused Emily in a way that the polite young solicitor-to-be who had been best man at her wedding never had. When he sailed for home he had promised to write – and hadn't. In London he had failed to look her up. Something must have gone wrong, and Emily was intent on reparation.

She murmured: 'I do hope Jimmy will come.'

In the nursery her sentiments were echoed.

'Is Uncle Jimmy coming for Christmas?' Roddy asked.

'I expect it will depend on his examinations,' Alice said importantly. 'Papa said it was high time he took his law finals. He's going to be a solicitor.'

Could a woman be a solicitor? It was something she must remember to ask.

'I like Uncle Jimmy,' Rose said.

Roddy said warmly, 'So do I.'

What a sensible person Rose was. She knew instinctively the right people to like. Across the tea-table Roddy smiled at her and her answering smile showed dimples in her cheeks. He had not previously noticed the dimples, but that was one of the delights of Rose: each time he looked at her he discovered fresh enchantments.

'When Uncle Jimmy stayed with us in India,' he informed her, 'we went out riding or walking every day.'

'He gave me my best doll,' Rose reciprocated. 'I'll show her to you if you like.'

Roddy was saved from answering by Nanny, who said, 'Not just yet, Miss Rose. After tea Miss Bea and Master Roddy will be unpacking. Their trunks will have arrived. There wasn't room for them in that nasty machine of your father's, so Mr Edwards was bringing them in the carrier's cart. He'll be here by now and I think we'd better see how much needs pressing. Packing never did clothes any good.'

'Why can't clothes be made so that they do pack?' Alice demanded.

'Because they can't,' Nanny said.

Bea was beginning to feel a bit sorry for Alice, whose questions seemed so sensible.

'Uncle Jimmy says packing's easy,' she volunteered.

'That's because he's do so much of it,' Alice responded. 'Papa says he's a rolling stone and it's time he stopped and gathered some moss. But I hope he doesn't. He's much more fun as he is.'

Bea said: 'I do hope he comes for Christmas.'

Three voices echoed her: 'So do I.'

CHAPTER 3

Bea woke early on Christmas Eve, while it was still quite dark, and lay snug in the unfamiliar room, watching the window turn from black to grey. She had slept fitfully in the strange four-poster bed, sunk deep in feathers, with a feather pillow for her head and a plump pink eider-down piled on top. The bed's muslin curtains reminded her a little of the mosquito netting around her small white bed in Cossipore, but these curtains were drawn back as though to ensure that whoever occupied the double bed observed the exhortation above it: 'Be Good.'

A second patch of greyness in the room revealed itself gradually as the oval mirror on the wardrobe door. What fun it had been last night when Mr Edwards had at last delivered the trunks and Rose and Alice had gathered in her bedroom to help her to unpack. Roddy had joined them, and Nanny Cardew had been unable to shoo him out in face of the girls' united protests, even though she pointed out that they would be unpacking underclothes.

'But Beatrix isn't wearing them,' Alice objected.

'Miss Alice, that's enough from you.'

'And besides, Roddy's her brother,' Alice went on, unheeding. 'It's not as if Beatrix were Rose. Or me.'

Alice had developed a habit of using her name in full, Bea noted. She made it sound rather grand, although her cousin had slipped her arm through hers as they went upstairs to begin unpacking and said, 'I think I'll call you Trix when we're alone.' It was as though she were conferring an honour. Bea said, 'Thank you,' and then wondered what she was thanking Alice for. All her life, people would thank Alice for doing what she wanted, but Bea did not know that yet.

What she did know was that she was falling in love with Amberley. For the first time since she came to England she began to feel at home. The comfortable house with its big square hall and shallow-tread staircase, its pillared portico and elegantly proportioned rooms, welcomed her as though she had always lived there. Now that her clothes hung in the wardrobe and her favourite doll (packed protestingly by Ayah in India and unpacked with delight last night by Rose) sat on the bedside cabinet together with candle and matches, the second-best spare room – because Mama, of course, had the best one – had become a small island of repose from which she could gradually flow outwards until she had encompassed the whole house.

Aunt Maud had assumed she would share the best spare room with Mama, but Mama had soon put a stop to that.

'I shouldn't sleep a wink with that child tossing and turning,' she assured her sister-in-law. 'And at her age it's not – well – delicate.'

She did not enlarge on the statement. Beatrix did not ask her to because she did not understand it, and Maud because she thought she did. It was so difficult explaining to girls about becoming a woman. The faces were bad enough. Sometimes she wondered if God had really intended womanhood to be so awful. In cursing Eve, did he have to make her daughters suffer as well? Lilias had asked that long ago, and professed herself unsatisfied with the answers she had been given, but of course that was blasphemy. At the very thought of explaining the matter to Alice, with her questions and her unsettling comments, Maud felt herself cringe.

She would have cringed still more had she known what lay behind Emily's refusal to share a room with her daughter. If Bea shared it, no one else could – and Jimmy was coming down. In India, under Harry's eyes, she had had to be careful, but Harry was now seven thousand miles away. Besides, he had in a sense banished her – she was well aware of the reasons that had prompted him to suggest her absence from Cossipore – so was it really her fault if in his absence she was driven to find a little comfort in this cold and alien country that was her own? Of course Jimmy would have to understand that in granting him her favours she was not breaking up her marriage, but if he sued ardently enough . . .

Aloud she said: 'Besides, I've never shared a room with anyone but Harry,' and smiled because it was the literal truth.

Roddy's first thoughts on waking were of Rose, as Rose's were of Roddy. It was wonderful that he would be here a whole week. She counted: they would have six full days together and part of a seventh and in that time she had all sorts of things to show him – not only the best doll that Uncle Jimmy had given her, but the hollow tree in which you could be invisible, the stair-tread which creaked unless you stood on it a certain way, the place where she had found the hare's form last summer, Papa's watch-chain with all its seals. She would take him down to the kitchen, where Cook presided in genial warmth and a good deal less genial flurry of activity. The kitchen was out of bounds and Mama would be cross if they were found there, but Cookie didn't really mind. 'Miss Rose is no trouble to anyone,' she would say challengingly, looking at Mama, and Mama would say, 'Well, Mrs Roberts, if you're sure . . .' Everyone spoilt Rose, whose greatest charm was that she was unaware of possessing it, coupled with her pretty face.

She got out of bed and began brushing her curls vigorously. In the other bed Alice stirred.

'What are you doing?'

'I'm getting ready so that I can go downstairs to be with Roddy.'

'What on earth for?'

'I want to show him my doll.' The doll stood for everything in Rose's world that was to be hallowed by Roddy's eyes.

Alice said: 'He won't want to see your doll. He'll want to see the estate, meet the tenants. He's going to inherit it some day.'

'But it's Papa's.'

'After Papa's dead, silly.'

'He isn't Papa's son.'

'Neither am I.'

'No, but you're his daughter.'

'Girls don't count. It's because of something called an entail. If I were a boy I could inherit

Amberley. Because I'm a girl, I can't.'

'That's not fair.'

'There's nothing fair about being a woman. That's why I'm going to be a Suffragette when I grow up.'

'Like Miss Bottrall?'

Alice nodded. 'And I'm going to be a Ph.D. as well.'

She had definitely decided to be a doctor and have a black Gladstone bag, though she wouldn't bring babies in it, whatever Nanny said. Instead, she would listen to chests, look at tongues, prod people in selected places, and stop them bleeding to death. You could easily bleed to death – everyone said so. It took a Ph.D. to deal with that.

Rose did not know what a Ph.D. was but she knew something more important. 'I'm going to marry Roddy when I grow up.'

'Bravo! When's the wedding?'

'I haven't asked him yet.'

'A lady doesn't ask. Haven't you heard Mama say so?'

'I shall ask,' Rose said. Why should she not? She had never encountered refusal, and to her the world was without pain. Even Mama and Nanny, who said no to most people, seldom said it to Rose. 'Rose is so reasonable in her requests,' Mama said, looking pointedly at

Alice. 'Miss Rose knows what's what,' Nanny said. And Alice, faced with their uncomprehending opposition, said as she always did, 'I shall ask Papa.'

It was the thought of her father that returned her to the present. Something, she knew, was wrong. Not between them; recently his hand as he ran it over her hair had been unusually gentle, but somewhere within him, deep down. The expression in his eyes had altered; when he looked at her there was always a second before he saw her, before the familiar loving gaze took over from the contemplation of whatever had been there before. Could he be ill? He didn't seem it. Could Mama? More likely. Was she going to have a baby again? (Alice's knowledge of the reproductive process, gleaned from maids' conversation and from observing animals, would have horrified and relieved Maud had she known.) But Alice did not think her father's worries were connected with her mother. He had never before spent so much time alone, driving his motor-car or shut up in his study, where the children were forbidden to go. For the last few weeks he had been closeted in there even before breakfast; she knew his step on the stair – the creaking tread always creaked for Papa, who thought it unnecessary to be silent in his own house. Yes, there it went again.

Alice slipped out of bed, ignoring Rose's 'Where are you going?' and without stopping for her dressing-gown, which would have horrified Mama but no matter, slipped out to the landing like a white wraith. She could hear Nanny busy with Lulu in the nursery; downstairs the maids were at work. The lamp was lit in the hall, and Jarvis the butler, in shirtsleeves, was accepting post at the front door. A blast of cold air came up.

Jarvis said: 'Good morning, sir.'

' 'Morning, Jarvis. Anything for me?'

'I'll sort the post at once, sir. Shall I bring it in?'

'Don't bother. I'll sort it myself.' He was already doing so. 'Never saw so many damn Christmas cards in my life . . . Nothing from my brother, looks as if he isn't coming . . . That seems to be all for me, Jarvis. I'll take these into my study and leave the rest to you.'

Through the banisters Alice watched her father's dressing-gowned back disappear into his study as it had done every morning for weeks. Post used to be put before his place at the breakfast table and was opened with suitable exclamations and comments. Now suddenly he was opening his alone. Was there a letter whose arrival he feared so much he wished to be alone when he received it? Something to be kept from

Mama? Something dreadful affecting them all?

Could Alice have looked over her father's shoulder that Christmas Eve her questions would have been answered. George's principal creditor insisted on full settlement by mid-January at latest, and the bank manager confirmed what he had told Colonel North at their recent meeting: his overdraft could go no higher and must be reduced in the New Year. Solutions – all impossible – buzzed round George's head like flies. Maud's jewellery? She had none to speak of, personal adornment being vulgar in her eyes. His mother's? She had sold it years ago: the diamonds sparkling in her portrait did so only in memory. The pictures? They were all second-rate, hunting scenes and family portraits including the one the Mater had taken to the Dower House; pleasant enough, but hardly saleroom sensations. Furniture? Very little was antique. Cut down staff? The economy would create unemployment, not capital. Friends? Apart from the distastefulness of the thought, none of them disposed of the sum he needed. Only a moneylender did that. No, there was only one hope: the pledge of substantial repayments represented by Harry's and Jimmy's income from the estate. If they were willing . . . Oh God, they had to be willing. He'd go up to London if Jimmy didn't come down. Cable Harry in India, not wait for a letter. And meanwhile he'd sell the car.

At the thought of parting with his treasure, George felt a pang of real pain. The excitement of movement without obvious means of propulsion at twenty-five miles per hour was to him the ultimate in freedom, not a *deus ex machina* but a *machina ex deo.* He still knew a Latin tag or two. He smiled, transported briefly back to boyhood. How he'd chafed at Latin verbs. And here was Alice wanting to learn them. She didn't get that from him! The thought of where she did get it from sobered him. Pity the Rev. Stephen Hunsdon hadn't long survived his elder daughter's death: he could have taught Alice Latin as he'd taught it to Lilias and perhaps found life worth living once again. George could still see the grey, ghostly man who had married him to his younger daughter, a shell in which nothing lived but the voice and eyes; the rest was already in the churchyard, under the white cross with its cascade of marble ivy and its inscription: *Eheu, filia dilectissime.*

He wondered sometimes if the excitement he derived from speed was because it gave him the illusion of escaping from the past. Or from the present: the present as grim enough. And selling the car was no more than a gesture, even if a buyer could be found. He'd have a word with young Dick Sparrow at the blacksmith's, let him think a newer model had caught his eye. It wouldn't do to have anyone think he was in need of ready money. Appearances had to be maintained. And to satisfy himself he unlocked the bottom drawer of his desk where he kept a small leather bag full of sovereigns amassed secretly as the result of visits to a pawnshop in London whenever he went up to town. The shame of it still overwhelmed him. That a gentleman should be reduced to this! But the ready cash was essential, and items like his silver cigarette box, some jewelled dress studs, Maud's best but seldom used cream jug, were unlikely to be quickly missed. By the time they were he'd have an explanation, might even have redeemed them. The bag jingled comfortingly in his hand as he thrust it to the back of the drawer, of whose contents even Maud was ignorant. It also contained his old service revolver and Lilias's photograph.

Maud woke with a headache and knew its source almost before she had registered its existence: Madam was coming today. She would arrive after luncheon in her own carriage and take up residence in the drawing-room. The children, the ostensible reason for the visit, would be interviewed, likewise the servants, while Madam's eyes wandered in search of invisible specks of dust. As if I'm a slut, hygienic Maud thought angrily. And then she'll ring for tea, and Cook will have burnt the tea-cakes or the milk will be spilt on the traycloth or the fire will start to smoke; and she'll endure it all like a Christian martyr while her eyebrows climb into her hair. How could Lilias ever have found Madam amusing? Yet I clearly remember she did. And tomorrow she'll come back with us after church, be here for Christmas dinner, and stay until after tea, and everyone will say, 'Merry Christmas, Madam,' and only afterwards say, 'Merry Christmas, Mrs George.'

After breakfast she would send Emily and the children out to gather greenery and ask them to help decorate the church. That would get them out of the way while she double-checked every surface for dust, inspected the bedrooms, packed one or two parcels, and tried to find out what Jarvis meant about some of the silver being missing – her best cream jug which he alleged he could not find. Such nonsense. All the staff had been with them since Madam's day and were scrupulously honest. The cream jug must have rolled to the back of the drawer.

Maud lay still in the growing day and listened to the sounds of her household. She had heard George leave his dressing-room and go down-stairs and was ashamed of the disappointment that swept over her. Desire was indelicate.

Especially desire for a husband who had never returned it except in a physical, dutiful way, because all the time he was remembering that she was not Lilias, and making her remember it too. Sometimes she hated her dead sister, the cause of all the tension and restraint that ate like acid into her marriage and presumably at times made George so difficult. When she had reminded him about preparing the servants' Christmas boxes he had been positively surly. It wasn't like him – he was always the soul of courtesy. It was out of courtesy he had asked her to marry him, she concluded, but she had realized it too late. After Lilias's death, while still numb with grief, he had proposed in order not to disappoint her parents; the bridesmaid-to-be was elevated to the role of bride, and would not have dared refuse him, even had her heart not gone before her hand.

Maud had loved George since the day he first came calling on her sister, and she had been required to sit decorously by and act as chaperone, or accompany them, unwanted, on their walks together. George wooed one sister and won them both. But on his wedding-night, awakening from a brief, deep sleep to find his bride lying rigid beside him, why had he turned to her and murmured, 'Lilias?' Consenting to the duties of a wife, which had suddenly become those of a concubine, Maud had stifled her tears, and George, apologizing like a gentleman, had taken them as no more than natural to the occasion. Fifteen years of subsequent marriage had not enabled them to bridge the gulf that had opened up that night.

Last night at dinner there had been no discernible difference in his manner to her and Emily. Yet he did not care for Emily, had said once she needed watching, though he did not explain in what way. Faced with her husband's unfailing courtesy, in public as in private, Maud had schooled herself to respond in kind. She had never attempted to tell him what she felt about Madam, and had hidden her grief at the death of her three little boys. True, she had protested briefly at accepting into her home the child who would one day own it, but she had allowed her objections to be overruled. She could not warm to Harry's children, but if it was her duty to house them, then Maud had never shirked a duty to be done.

Aunt Maud made everything sound like a duty, even things which were rather fun, Roddy thought later that morning as he trundled a small wooden handcart along the lanes. His sister and cousins were filling it with ivy and holly while Mama superintended, pointing out any specially good bunch. The lane was ridged and rutted like corrugated cardboard, and iron-hard with frost. White ice crackled in chocolate-brown hollows, unmelted by the morning sun. The bracken climbing the banks was golden-brown and glinted in the sunlight, but on the shady side of the lane each frond was edged with rime.

Roddy drew a deep breath and felt the cold clean air inflate his lungs to bursting. What price India now? A robin sang and rooks cawed from the elms' topmost branches, and to him they were as exotic as peacocks and tanagers. Rose's face looked out from a holly-bush, her golden curls and bright red tam-o'shanter framed by the dark green leaves.

'Aunt Emily,' she called, 'there's a lovely branch here with lots of berries. Can you cut it with the secateurs?'

'I'll do it.' Roddy was across the lane in an instant, leaving the handcart tilting under its load. 'Shall I cut it for you?'

Rose smiled and dimpled. 'It's ever so prickly,' she warned.

Roddy was discovering the prickles for himself. Holly looked less formidable than the thorn trees he knew in India, but it was still an uncomfortable shrub. Yet for Rose he would have fought his way through barbed wire entanglements. There was no Rose without a thorn.

The branch yielded suddenly to the secateurs. With a flourish he laid it at her feet.

Rose clapped her hands in delight. 'It's the best branch of all. Look, Bea. Look, Alice. Look, Aunt Emily. Look what Roddy's done.'

'Yes, dear,' Aunt Emily said. 'See if you can find room for it in the handcart and then we must hurry along. Your mother wants us to help decorate the church, and luncheon is at half past twelve today because afterwards your grandmother is coming.'

'What is our grandmother like?'

Bea's question took Emily by surprise. If it had not been for the restraining presence of Rose and Alice she might well have answered, 'An old bitch,' because when it suited her she liked to think she and her daughter were on an equal footing: it made her feel less old. She herself had been orphaned early, and Aunt Grace who had brought her up had been kindly, remote, ineffectual. Far from being an equal, in her stiff black dresses she had always seemed incredibly old. When she died, Emily was already in India and the solicitor's letter had been a double shock, announcing both her death, which had been sudden, and her age, which was fifty-eight.

Aunt Grace had seemed old, but Madam seemed ageless. Since the day when Emily had first set eyes on her, she had not altered a jot. Her iron grey hair was still worn in a knot on the top of her head, her dresses were still grey, her carriage upright, her back never touching the chair. Worse still, she had the same way of looking at Emily, as if she weren't really there. Fanny North had been a good wife and later a resourceful widow, bringing up her three sons and managing the estate after her husband's death until George could resign his commission, when she had simply extended her duties to managing the estate and George. Only in the last few years had she handed over estate matters and retired to the Dower House. And even from the Dower House she still ruled the village of Croft Amberley. Who would go to Maud so long as Madam was around?

But faced with Bea's direct question, Emily took refuge in saying, 'You'll see what your grandmother's like later on.'

'I like Grandmama,' Alice informed them. 'She thinks women are as good as men.'

In her case it was true, Emily reflected. Madam was the equal of any man. But she had not needed education and the vote to prove it. She would think such props unnecessary.

'I'm sure Grandmama's right,' Emily said, 'but that doesn't mean we have to be unfeminine.'

She surveyed her elder niece with some misgiving as she spoke. Alice's muffler was undone, she had torn a hole in her woollen gloves, her tam-o'-shanter was crammed on at an unbecoming angle; yet no one could say the child was unfeminine. Beside her, the neatly dressed Bea looked prim.

Bea always looked wrong, Emily thought with irritation as she shepherded the children and their load of greenery towards the church. And she had no conversation.

'What are you thinking of?' she asked abruptly, noting her daughter's rapt face.

'I'm thinking I like it here,' Bea answered. 'This is really and truly England, isn't it?'

Yes, this is England, Emily conceded, the good and the bad of it, the land of class distinction and cold draughts, of loyalties unspoken, affections unstated, and the peaceful coexistence of old and new.

'I'm so glad you like your own country,' she said.

'Oh, I do.' Bea turned her shining face towards her. 'This is where we belong.' Her gesture encompassed the land and the hills blue with distance, the village street and the sky arching overhead. It included the tracery of the trees and the smoke from the chimneys of stone-tiled houses. It was all unfamiliar, and yet it was her own. For the first time she understood what it was she had heard in grown-up voices when people in India spoke of Home. How could they ever have left it for that strange, alien land which it was their duty to rule for the King-Emperor?

The crisp clop of hoofs broke into her reverie.

A carriage was coming down the village street, drawn by a high-stepping chestnut. A green-uniformed coachman sat on the box. Alice and Rose were waving and running towards it. The carriage slowed and stopped. A gloved hand reached out of the window and Alice and Rose bobbed a curtsey. Roddy stood open-mouthed. Emily North stepped in front of her daughter as if to protect her.

'It's Madam,' she murmured. 'We shall have to go and give her a good-day.'

If only Bea didn't look so drab. She could imagine Madam's remarks afterwards. 'The poor child looked like a waif.' Thank God Roddy at least was presentable. 'Take your cap off,' she commanded, low-voiced.

Pushing the children before her (and now it was if they were protecting her), Emily approached her mother-in-law's carriage.

'Ah, Emily.' The voice was low and pleasant. Bea allowed herself to look up and met the bluest eyes she had ever encountered, even bluer than her father's and they were blue enough. Amusement made them sparkle and turned up the corners of the chiselled lips.

'So this is your little brood,' the voice continued. 'I was expecting to meet them this afternoon, but we anticipate. Good morning, Beatrix . . . Roderick . . .'

'Good morning, Grandmama,' Roddy managed. Bea was tongue-tied.

Mama said defensively, 'We only arrived last night.'

'So I hear. Mr Edwards, the carrier, told me he had delivered your luggage. How did you enjoy George's motor-car?'

Was there anything Madam didn't know – about them, about their arrival?

'Terrific,' Roddy said.

Emily said, 'It was quite exciting. I've never ridden in one before. George is very enterprising, isn't he?'

'Very,' her mother-in-law agreed. 'But I mustn't delay you any longer. I hear you are to help decorate the church. Mr Woodward, our rector, and some of his more devoted helpers are already hard at work. No doubt they will be glad of all that greenery.' Madam smiled dismissively. (Did she hear everything that went on?) 'We shall meet again this afternoon, children. I just wanted to take this opportunity to greet you, and of course to share the good news.'

'Good news?' Emily queried.

'Ah, I suspected you hadn't heard. There is great excitement at Amberley. A telegram has arrived from James.'

Emily's heart skipped a beat. 'Is he coming for Christmas?'

The blue gaze rested on her lightly, shrewdly. The sharp ear had registered the new note in her voice. 'So we are given to understand.'

Emily compressed her lips to prevent herself asking what Jimmy had said. She would not show eagerness in front of Madam, who was playing with her as a cat does with a mouse.

Madam paused just long enough to make it clear she was aware of Emily's frustration before saying to her coachman, 'Now, Wilkins, drive on,' and accompanying the command with a sharp rap on the carriage panelling. Wilkins flicked the reins. Madam made as if to close the window, appeared to think better of it, and said:

'Dear Jimmy was tantalizingly inexplicit. He just said: "Arriving tonight for Christmas and bringing a big surprise." '

CHAPTER 4

Frances Jackson had been Fanny to her parents and brothers, but to no one else until she married John North in 1863. She did not inspire diminutives. Even as a girl she had been tall, commanding and capable. John North, a bachelor nearing middle age and a landowner in the Cotswolds, had been instantly and indelibly impressed.

He had been visiting friends in Derbyshire. Fanny was the only daughter of the family next door. Her father owned a hosiery mill and had other business interests. His daughter was born, if not to wealth, at least to very comfortable circumstances. Yet to his dismay all she wanted was to become one of Miss Nightingale's young ladies at St. Thomas's Hospital. To nurse. To soil her hands. In her parents' eyes John North was just the man to put an end to such notions. They looked with favour on him from the start.

It was more than Fanny did, but John North was patient and in the end he won. He could hardly help it; the alternative for Fanny was too bleak – to stay at home, the ageing, unmarried daughter, only to become in time the ageing, unmarried sister-in-law, unwelcome in her brothers' homes yet having none of her own. To be mistress of Amberley was, by comparison, good fortune, even if it involved marrying John North. She did not love him, but she had no other attachments. She allowed herself to be led up the aisle.

It was typical of Fanny to turn what might have been disaster into triumph by falling in love, not with John but with Amberley. She managed John, she managed her household, and before long she managed the village as well. She even managed to produce two fine sons to carry on the Norths of Amberley. Just as some people seemed to have the Midas touch, so Fanny seemed to have the touch of success.

Then came disaster. Her third child, a daughter, was stillborn. John North had never seen his wife cry before, for the tears she shed on leaving her Derbyshire home and on her wedding night had been shed in secret; he was as alarmed as though a statue had suddenly wept. He brought Fanny a pearl necklace and made haste to ensure that she had every opportunity of becoming *enceinte* again.

Fanny could not explain how much she

craved a woman's friendship, the feminine influence in her sisterless life which a daughter would provide. Long ago an old woman telling fortunes in tea-leaves had prophesied that she would die when she had a daughter. That prophecy had certainly not come true, except that a whole stillborn side to Fanny's nature was enclosed in the tiny coffin, for she and her mother were not close, and her position as John's wife isolated her from the women of the village while not raising her to the level of the titled St Devereuxs, who owned nearby Mawby Hall. Of course there were the wives of neighbouring landowners, with whom Fanny occasionally socialized, but her forbidding reserve was a barrier, and her intelligence an even greater one.

In general, Fanny preferred men's company and conversation. She envied them many of their pursuits. There were heretical moments when she wondered if nursing was indeed the only role, apart from that of wife and mother, for which women were by nature designed. A daughter would have given her not only companionship, but the chance to try out some of her theories. But it was not to be. Fanny resigned herself and, with innate practicality rather than the Christian fortitude counselled by the rector, produced another son and comforted herself with the distant but delightful prospect of welcoming her daughters-in-law.

In fact, Fanny was to reflect with grim amusement, she had one daughter-in-law whom she disliked and one whom she despised. It was as if Fate were determined to spite her for having welcomed too eagerly the girl whom George brought home. For Lilias Hunsdon was everything Fanny had ever wanted in a daughter-in-law: handsome, spirited, intelligent; well-educated, thanks to her clerical father; well-bred, thanks to her mother's gentle birth. Here was someone to whom Fanny could fitly resign her place as mistress of Amberley and matriarch of the village – a position enhanced by the death of John North from apoplexy some two or three years before. George had promptly, if regretfully, resigned his commission in the army and come home to manage the Amberley estate, and Fanny, who knew far more about the estate than he did, had deferred to her own decisions when he mouthed them, just as she had done with John all the years of her married life. Though she sometimes feared that George was somewhat stupid, if good-hearted, she suppressed the thought as disloyal: George as first-born had inherited Amberley; therefore he was by temperament and inclination the one best suited to the task. And what he lacked Lilias would supply; Fanny was in no doubt of that. What she had never allowed for was Lilias's death three weeks before the wedding. Fate did not do such things to Fanny North.

But worse was to come when George, after the customary year of mourning, brought home Lilias's sallow sister, Maud, a girl who kept her eyes down and mumbled, and all too obviously lacked Lilias's sense of style. After the wedding Fanny had continued to live at Amberley until, in desperation at the absence of an heir which had strained her relationship with Maud to breaking-point, she had had the lodge enlarged into the Dower House. But although she relinquished her interest in running the Amberley estate – not without a qualm, because her confidence in George as a businessman was no greater than her confidence in him as anything else – she continued to direct the village and even the domestic affairs of Amberley when she judged Maud in no fit state to resist. It was Fanny who found and engaged the excellent Nanny Cardew, Fanny who decided that Alice and Rose should be educated at home, Fanny who decided when the dining-room should be redecorated and chose the wallpaper. In doing so she considered she was relieving Maud of responsibilities which might distract her from the primary one of bearing sons, but she remained confounded by the three small tombstones in the churchyard to John, George and Humphrey North. Maud, that pale shadow of Lilias, could not even produce an heir, and Fanny, who had produced three, despised her. George's good-heartedness and stupidity, which she assumed had led him to marry his bride's sister – there was no dodging them on this issue – deserved something better than this.

George could not have explained – least of all to his mother – why he had married Maud. In the welter of grief for Lilias which had flooded his soul and the whole of the Rev. Stephen Hunsdon's vicarage, Maud had seemed the most pathetic figure of all. Not tragic, like her heartbroken father or her proud mother, soon to follow their daughter to the grave; but pathetic because her grief was dismissed as superficial, her efforts to take her sister's place rebuffed. In the parish as in the vicarage, it was made all too clear to her that she was not Lilias.

George, struggling in a world in which he felt inadequate without Lilias by his side, had become aware that here was someone else who struggled, all the more courageously in the face of persistent unsuccess. Courage and a sense of duty were qualities George had been taught to prize, and Maud had both of them. He never asked himself if he loved her, still less if she loved him, but he asked her to marry him in the comfortable certainty that, since he had to marry for the sake of Amberley, he could do a great deal worse.

'Maud is a good girl,' the Rev. Stephen Hunsdon said painfully when George requested her hand. 'She has been overshadowed – as who could not be? – by Lilias, but I am thankful that for her at least "joy cometh in the morning". You have my consent and blessing, George. You will find Maud pliant and undemanding. She will make you a good wife.'

And she had, George supposed. She had indeed been pliant and undemanding. She never attempted to interfere in matters she did not understand, such as mortgages and investments, or the purchase of the motor-car. She refused to ride in the vehicle, but then so did his mother, and Dr Paget openly proclaimed that motoring was unsuitable for ladies, their delicate internal organs being subject to damage if jolted about the countryside at twenty-five miles per hour.

George was not sorry. He preferred to drive alone. In the car he could not be stopped, as he was on his rides round the estate, by tenants who wanted repairs or were in arrears with their rent. Towards the latter George was always tender – who was he to condemn another's financial distress? – but to those who wanted him to spend money, however needfully, he turned the deafest of ears.

In the car, a luxury he ought never to have allowed himself, he could escape from the everlasting anxiety about money, the demands of creditors, the ultimate fear of having to sell Amberley. Not that he would ever leave, George told himself; there were other ways out than that, such as that represented by his old service revolver locked away in the bottom drawer of his desk. Maud and the girls would have enough to exist on; his mother was provided for; if it came to selling the home of his fathers, his bones at least would never leave. Only a few days previously he had visited the family plot in the churchyard and stood beside the graves of his ancestors and his heirs. There was room for him, and his thoughts had been very different from those imagined by the rector, who had come upon him unawares.

Unfortunately the rector chose to speak of the approach of Christmas and the plight of the needy. George's eyebrows shot up as he thrust his hands into empty pockets. 'Surely my mother looks after all that?'

'Mrs North is the soul of charity,' said the rector, who disliked what he thought of as her patronizing ways, 'but there are limits even to her bounty, and at this season . . .' He tailed off hopefully.

'Anyone in particular?' George asked.

The rector mentioned a couple of cases. 'And of course there is the matter of the Bottralls' cottage roof.'

'It's good enough for this winter.'

'Miss Bottrall tells me it leaks.'

'Have you seen the leak?'

'Well, no, but naturally –'

'– naturally a pupil teacher is to be believed.'

'She is an excellent teacher,' the rector said defensively. 'The schoolmistress thinks highly of her and the children like her.'

'She's a radical and a Suffragette.'

'I'm afraid I don't see the connection.'

'It's in her interests to paint me as a black-hearted, cruel landlord.'

'But in the matter of a leaking roof . . .'

'I'm not suggesting she's lying, but you've not seen the position and size of the leak and I have. Of course the roof needs attention – so do others in the village – but it'll see the winter out.'

'Miss Bottrall is concerned for her grandmother.'

'Then let her stay at home of an evening and keep the old lady company, instead of traipsing off to meetings about things that aren't a woman's concern.'

'Surely poverty and injustice are everyone's concern?'

George flushed dangerously. 'Be careful, Rector. Ideas like that have undone the clergy before now.'

The rector stood his ground. 'It is part of my pastoral duty to care about the living conditions of the people I serve.'

'Who include the household at Amberley.'

'I hope I have not implied otherwise, Colonel.'

'You imply that I'm an uncaring landlord. Tell me: do you know what rent Miss Bottrall and her grandmother pay?'

'You can hardly expect me to know . . .'

'If you're making their cause your concern I do expect you to. Do you know that since young Hector Bottrall was killed in South Africa I've let them have that cottage rent-free? Do you think I can afford repairs on top of it, especially repairs that aren't necessary?'

'I'm sorry. I can only apologize.'

'Apology accepted. But don't meddle in matters you don't understand. I look after my tenants in the way that seems best to me, and that's how it's going to be so long as I own the land.'

George strode off, swishing his stick through

the long grass of the churchyard. A leaking roof indeed! There was a leak in one of the attics at Amberley so big that a tin bath was kept beneath it in perpetual readiness for rain. George himself emptied the bath, ladling it out with a dipper into a series of buckets which had then to be carried downstairs, whereas the leak in the Bottralls' cottage was no more than a stain creeping down one wall. The servant was better off than the master, a state of which Mary Bottrall with her radical notions would surely not disapprove.

Old Bottrall, her grandfather, had been gardener at Amberley until arthritis forced him to retire, and the death of his son and daughter-in-law in an influenza epidemic sent him gravewards with unusual alacrity. His widow brought up the two grandchildren, and George could not bring himself to point out that he was having to pay for an additional cottage for the new gardener. Small wonder if a few roofs leaked! And young Hector Bottrall had scarcely begun work as an under-gardener when the South African War broke out and he enlisted, following the example of his adored Master Jimmy, and died storming some inconsiderable kopje in the veldt.

It was Jimmy who had written home to his brother, asking him to tell old Annie Bottrall, who could not read, something more than the contents of the bare War Office telegram which twelve-year-old Mary had opened and read aloud. 'I owe Hector my life,' Jimmy had written. 'He deserves a medal if ever a man did. Details later, but for my sake treat the old woman decently and be kind to the little sister. She'll take Hector's death pretty hard.'

In fact the promised details had never followed, because instead of returning home Jimmy had stayed on to try his hand at farming in the new Union of South Africa. His mother had fretted, though not as much as she had fretted when he had walked in, resplendent in uniform, to tell her he was off to the war because he was sick of studying law in the offices of a London solicitor where life was passing him by. But it was death that passed him by as the bullets from the Boers' long rifles sang out across the scorching veldt, while the red-coated rednecks toiled in parade-ground formation and their enemies on their shaggy ponies made rings round them, sometimes literally. Fanny North had scanned the lengthening casualty lists in *The Times* with outward composure and inner lurking dread, for Jimmy, the scapegrace, the problem, was the favourite of her three sons.

She had hoped that the child which followed

her dead daughter would be another girl, but had then resignedly accepted that she was a breeder of men. She was proud of George and Harry, near in age and from the same mould, but it was Jimmy, the late-born, the unpredictable, who was closest to her heart. Yet the shock of seeing him before her in uniform had been less great than everyone supposed; at his age she could not see him being tied to a desk job in a lawyer's office; she would have felt the same way herself. So Fanny kissed him farewell with unquivering lips and thereafter knelt a little straighter in church and petitioned the Lord to keep a special eye on James Edward North. If in doing so He had to turn a blind one to Hector Bottrall, that at least demonstrated that the Supreme Being had his priorities right. His servants on earth could succour the widow and the orphan; she would personally see to it that they were never in want.

She had even been prepared to take Mary into service at the Dower House if Maud could not find room for her at Amberley, but old Mrs Bottrall displayed unexpected resistance. 'Mary doesn't want to go into service,' she said.

Fanny's mind ranged over the few remaining possibilities. 'What does she want?'

'She wants to be a teacher.'

Fanny said cautiously, 'We'll see.'

There was no question, of course, of sending Mary to a teachers' training college, from which she would emerge certificated, but if the village schoolmistress was willing, she could work as a pupil teacher under her, and – subject to satisfying the inspector on his visits – rise eventually to a village school of her own. The village schoolmistress, when consulted, proved more than willing: Mary, it seemed, excelled at the three Rs. And the school governor – George – could provide her tiny salary instead of her servant's wage.

Fanny would have found it becoming in Mary to show signs of gratitude for such a signal act of grace, but the girl took everything as her right. Did she think her brother's death entitled her to special consideration for ever? When Fanny called at the cottage in the course of her good works, old Mrs Bottrall still struggled to her feet despite arthritis, said 'Good morning, Madam,' and would have overbalanced in the course of a stiff curtsey if Fanny had not urged her to sit down. Mary said, 'Good morning, Mrs North,' and remained upright. For two pins, Fanny thought, I believe she'd shake my hand.

Well, on Boxing Day when she made her Christmas round, she would take the children with her, Alice and Beatrix at least. Beatrix must learn something of a lady's obligations; she doubted if Emily had taught her much. At the thought of her second daughter-in-law Fanny's lips tightened in disapproval. Still, she would not be with them long, and once she had returned to India – and her husband – the children could be trained as they should be. The future was hers – Fanny allowed herself a flicker of anticipation. Meanwhile, the immediate future had its needs. Ringing the small bell which stood on the worktable beside her chair in the morning-room, Fanny summoned her maid, Patterson, and set about making her arrangements for the rest of Christmas Eve.

Roddy and Beatrix had their arrangements made for them.

'This afternoon,' Mama said, 'we're going into town.'

'Town' meant Barford, not the London stores in which she delighted, but it would be better than staying in the house. Had Maud always been such boring company? No wonder George spent so much time on the estate. Or in his study, used as the estate office. Or in his motor-car. Strange that George of all men should have succumbed to the horseless carriage craze. Did Jimmy know how to drive one? What fun if George would let him take her out!

Roddy interrupted her thoughts. 'Is Rose coming with us?'

'Yes, of course. And Alice. I'm taking you all.'

'What's in Barford?'

'There are shops and a market. I thought you'd enjoy looking round.'

'Can I buy Rose a present?'

'We've already bought her one. It's packed up in my bag.'

'I mean a present from me. With my own money.'

'If you've any pocket money left you can spend it on what you choose. But I'm not giving you any more. Tell Nanny that I want you all in the hall, ready dressed, at half past two. And make sure you wrap up warmly. It's turning very cold.'

'Will it snow? Is it cold enough?' Bea demanded over lunch.

Nanny Cardew looked at the heavy sky. 'I shouldn't be surprised, dear. Now finish your rice pudding. A bit of fuel inside you is better than an extra coat.'

Bea also looked at the sky. It was so different in England: never the magical clarity of Simla, nor the steaming grey dampness of Cossipore before the monsoon broke. The rain when it came was soft and gentle, not leaden lines that struck the ground like spears and thudded on every hollow surface as if trying to pierce a shield. English weather was cool and dank, like the inside of a cistern. The mists were chill and gathered at the ends of streets like enemy troops massing. There was no comfort in the Earl's Court flat, where fires smoked and draughts snaked under doors and the curtains shivered in a perpetual draught. Only at Amberley had she encountered comfort. There the fires were glowing caves of heat. Last night there had been a stone hot-water bottle in her bed, and she had snuggled deep in the feather bed (there were none in the London flat) and pulled the plump eiderdown up to her chin. Opposite her was her reflection in the oval wardrobe mirror: a pale face becomingly flushed, long fair hair well brushed (a hundred strokes, Nanny had counted), her best nightgown, its collar edged with crochet lace.

'I am here in England,' Bea whispered to convince herself, 'staying in Papa's old home which is owned by Papa's elder brother, and tomorrow I shall meet Papa's mother, my grandmama.'

But now that she had met Grandmama, albeit briefly, she could see nothing to be afraid of – and yet Mama was afraid. Bea knew it without knowing how she knew it: Mama did not like Grandmama. So perhaps Grandmama did not like Mama either. Bea was well aware how mutual such feelings could be. Nor did Mama like Aunt Maud. So did Aunt Maud also dislike Mama? Now that she considered the matter, Bea recognized that there were ladies in India who had not liked Mama, as well as one or two on the boat. Yet Mama was always very polite to them and did everything she had taught Bea a lady should. Perhaps she just didn't enjoy their company. She never laughed, as she did with gentlemen, a little trilling laugh, often accompanied by a tap on the forearm with a well-gloved hand or a fan. And the gentlemen would pay some outrageous compliment, or murmur something very low that only Mama could hear. Then she would laugh some more, and turn away to speak to one of the ladies who had gathered watchfully about her. And after a while the ladies would draw away. And soon there would be other gentlemen and other watchful ladies. And Papa smiling proudly to see Mama the centre of attention, but with something watchful about him too.

Dear Papa! If only he were with them. The servants' way of calling Mama 'Mrs Harry' was a perpetual reminder of him as well as a perpetual explanation of their presence at Amberley. How wonderful if people could fly, all the way from the Indian sub-continent to England and its Cotswold heart. There would be no need for those long sea voyages of separation: they would travel faster than Uncle George's motor-car, faster even than the express train from London, which was so much more comfortable than the night mail from Cossipore to Bombay. It would be like a magic carpet, a step towards making every wish come true.

Compared to their exciting arrival yesterday, the journey this afternoon into Barford was slow, even though the pair of greys who pulled the carriage kept up a steady trot. Roddy clutched in his hand the two pennies saved from his pocket money and tried yet again to get used to the feel of these large coins, so different from India's annas and pice. Under his breath he repeated to himself that twelve pennies made a shilling, and twenty shillings, ten florins, or eight half-crowns made a sovereign. Sovereigns and half-sovereigns were gold, the other coins silver, like rupees, and then there were confusing oddments like sixpences and threepenny bits, not to mention halfpence and farthings. However many farthings was a sovereign worth?

'Why are you frowning?' Rose asked.

'I'm thinking.'

'Is it so painful?' Alice laughed.

'I'm not used to it.'

Alice laughed again. 'Lots of people aren't.

When I'm a doctor I shall have headache pills specially for people who think.'

'Are you really going to be a lady doctor?'

'Yes.' Alice was quite certain on this point.

Mama said: 'I expect some gentleman will change your mind.'

'No, Aunt Emily, I don't think I want to get married.'

'I do,' Bea said.

'So do I,' echoed Rose, slipping her hand into Roddy's.

Emily smiled at them all. 'We shall see.'

Because of course they would marry, and be thankful to, just as she had been. All this talk of careers for women was a fad, a fashion. Given the choice, any woman would opt for the married state, which assured her of a certain social standing, if also of a certain monotony. Decorating the church this morning, she had been reminded vividly of her wedding, for she and Harry had sailed for India soon after their honeymoon and she had scarcely set foot in the church since. She had been married at St Peter's, Croft Amberley, because Madam had decreed it and because she had no close links elsewhere. Besides, the church was so much prettier than the new suburban one in Streatham to which she made token visits with Aunt Grace. George had given her away, Jimmy had been best man, and she had worn ruched white satin with leg-of-mutton sleeves. The church was packed with locals, though Lord and Lady St Devereux had been unable to attend, leaving Emily unsure if she had been slighted. Would they have come had she been the Honourable Emily? Harry in his uniform had been a blaze of colour at the altar. A breeze of heads turned as she came up the aisle, for the bridegroom's supporters filled the pews on both sides and many had not previously glimpsed the bride. 'Dearly beloved, we are gathered here together . . .' She scarcely heard the rector's voice. With eyes modestly lowered, she concentrated on the gleaming toecaps of her about-to-be-husband's boots. 'Henry Arthur, wilt thou take this woman . . . ?' She heard Harry say, 'I will,' and then it was her turn – '. . . forsaking all other, keep ye only unto him as long as ye both shall live?' Forsaking all other . . . There had been none before marriage and it had seemed easy. Afterwards . . . Well, Harry's brother officers had too much respect for their careers to get entangled in a liaison that would result in their having to resign their commissions, and there had been no one else. Only the monotony of Harry. Holy matrimony – they should call it holy monotony. Twice a week for the next – what? – thirty years? And every little ritual faithfully followed as if military precision still held sway behind the bedroom door. A place for every article of apparel and every article in its place. Even on their honeymoon – all that bracing Yorkshire air and open windows! – Harry had been meticulous, only then the long-drawn-out ritual had been part of the preparation for the moment when he climbed into bed beside her, looked down on her with that blend of wonder and desire which was his unfailing response to her presence, and reached to put out the light.

Had he changed, or was the change in her? Since Jimmy, she could hardly bear the predictability of it all. But then with Jimmy everything had been so unpredictable, beginning with the affair itself. She had not found Jimmy North particularly attractive when, during her brief engagement, she had met Harry's brothers for the first time. The prospect of his visit to them in India had been more a bore than anything else. Yet within a week of his arrival she wanted desperately to share his body. Within three weeks she had.

It had happened in Simla during the siesta hour, in the swinging wickerwork seat on the verandah where she was reclining after the midday meal. There were only the two of them. Harry had had to go up country and would not be back until after dark. The children had been dispatched to take their rest in charge of the ayah. The servants had cleared away and vanished to wherever Indian servants vanished to. They had taken coffee and Jimmy had smoked two cigarettes. She had said then, 'I must go in,' and made no move to do so. They talked in fits and starts.

'It's so pleasant here,' Jimmy said, looking across to the opposite side of the valley and the bungalows dotted about the wooded slopes. They had names like Balmoral Cottage, Laurel Villa, Sunset Ridge, and Helenscot. 'It's like being in another life, another dimension. I can't believe it's real.'

She held out her hand. 'I'm real enough.'

He came and sat beside her. 'I know, but even that I can't believe. I've hardly seen you since I was best man at your wedding, and here you are, the Major's wife, mistress of an establishment, mother of a splendid little chap like Roddy, and all this time I've thought of you as a young girl.'

This was not the turn of conversation Emily had envisaged. She said quickly: 'And what about you?'

'What about me? You've heard all my adventures.'

'Not the adventures of the heart.'

'Oh, those.'

'Yes, those. Are they too numerous to chronicle?'

'They didn't mean a thing.'

This was better.

'Except one. And that was nothing. It wasn't even an affair.'

'Tell me about her.'

He got up and went to stand at the edge of the verandah, his back towards her as he lit another cigarette. The wicker swing creaked as she composed herself to listen, hoping the recital would not be long.

'It was in South Africa –' he began.

Of course. Where else had he been?

'– in the Cape when I was working for Piet Botha. His orphaned niece came to stay. She was young. I thought her a nice kid, not really pretty, but pleasant to have around. And around was the word. She was always there – quiet, unobtrusive, but *there.* I used to tease her – she liked that. So did the Bothas. The old man would slap his thigh and say it was good that Briton and Boer should tease each other, for you only tease your friends. And we must be friends now that the war was over, so that the new Union would last a thousand years. Not all the Boers felt like that; most were very bitter –'

'And the girl, the niece – what of her?'

'She said nothing. The women keep quiet

when the men talk politics. But she followed me around like a dog.'

A bitch.

'And then somehow – I don't know – I began to notice her: the way she walked, her white teeth when she smiled. I knew her so well I wanted to know her better. How can I explain?'

'I understand.' It was how she felt about him.

'I knew you would.' He returned to sit beside her and went on: 'One day, almost without meaning to, I kissed her.'

'What happened?'

Was it going to be a blow-by-blow account?

'She clapped a hand to her face and ran to tell her aunt. She was hysterical. She was so ignorant, so strictly brought up, she thought it amounted to rape.'

'Difficult for you.'

'It was – very. To this day I don't know what old Piet believed. But of course I told him I wanted to marry Jacoba. That was when all hell broke loose.'

'Why?'

'Because I was English. It seemed that Briton could not marry Boer.'

'But I thought you said –'

'That was on the surface. No, it went deeper than that. He'd been very good to me. I think he liked me. But when it came to one of his women, he'd rather have seen Jacoba dead.'

'So you left?'

'Yes.' He laughed. 'I left the Union of South Africa which was never going to unite.'

'And Jacoba?'

'I had one glimpse of her, face all swollen with crying, before they sent her away. It was my fault. I should have realized.'

'Have you learnt better since then?'

'I don't know. I've avoided that kind of situation.'

'Or haven't recognized it.'

'Maybe not. But it's been marvellous being able to tell someone. You are marvellous, you know. Harry's a very lucky man.'

She turned her face away. 'It's all very well for Harry . . .'

'Hey, what d'you mean? Is something wrong?'

'Oh, Jimmy, Jimmy . . .' Her eyes had flooded with tears, which they did easily.

He mopped them away. 'What is it? Can't you trust me with your secrets as I trusted you with mine?'

She was in his arms.

'I am so lonely. I share Harry's bed but not his life. Nor his heart.'

'Do you mean he's rotten enough to –'

'No! I am not sure of it. A wife can never be sure.'

That was true, at least, though she had never suspected upright Harry.

'Do you want me to tackle him about it?'

'No!'

He looked down at her, reading her expression.

'Do you want me to –'

'Yes!'

The shadows on the verandah roof moved to and fro very swiftly. She was aware of the creaking of the swing, its rhythm quickening, changing. He smelt of sweat and cigarette smoke and cologne. She heard herself laugh – not the little trilling laugh she gave at parties, but throatier, more like a snarl. And when she re-emerged into an afternoon on the verandah it was late, the siesta hour was almost over, and it was time to go in and change.

'I must go in,' she said. This time she meant it.

He rose also. 'Please come back again.'

She had. Many times.

And now it was his turn to come back, back to Amberley, back to her, back to where they had left off. He was coming, and whatever had kept him from her in London would not be operative here. As she hurried the children through the streets of Barford she was too preoccupied to notice the man who emerged from a doorway, started as though he had seen a ghost, and turned hastily down a side street. But Alice noticed him.

She had been about to cry out in glad recognition when she realized he did not want to be recognized. Papa, her own Papa, did not want her to know him, had turned away so that they should not meet. What was he doing in Barford? He had not mentioned that he was coming in. The motor-car had been parked as usual in a disused stable. There had been no sign of it on the road. So he must have ridden in, keeping well behind them. And he did not want them to know he was here.

She rejected the idea that he was Christmas shopping. She had caught only a glimpse of his face, but enough to see that it was set and troubled. Besides, he had not come out of a shop, there were no packages in his hands, no bulges in his pocket. No one was ill – one could not count Mama's perpetual ill-health as illness – and in any case the doctor lived in another part of town. He had not emerged from a bank, or from any place in which he did business. The name Dunstan Street meant nothing to her. She had never noticed it before: a street of small terrace houses, apart from the buildings on the corner where Dunstan Street joined a more bustling thoroughfare. It was from the side door of one of these buildings that he had emerged, seen them, dodged back and turned down Dunstan Street. But there was no brass plate on the door, no sign above it, nothing to indicate what lay within.

'Come along, Alice.'

Aunt Emily's voice, impatient. Alice had not been aware of standing still. The others were some way ahead of her. Already Rose was turning to run back.

'Alice, we're waiting.'

She hurried after them. 'I'm sorry, Aunt Emily.'

'What on earth did you see, dear, in that uninteresting little street?'

'Oh –' Alice's mind scrabbled for footholds – 'just a – just a rather handsome tabby cat.'

She had not seen the young woman a few paces behind them on the other side of the road, who had also stopped, ducked into a doorway, and followed George North's movements with her eyes. They were blue eyes, sharp and shrewd, accustomed to assessing. They belonged to Mary Bottrall, pupil teacher at Croft Amberley village school, who like many others shopped late on Christmas Eve in Barford because then all the best bargains were to be had. She had walked in, thereby scuffing the three coats of varnish with which she waterproofed the soles of her boots, but her thoughts had been a thousand miles from Barford – her mind could travel even though she never could. Now, having finished her shopping, she was on her way to the Public Lending Library to borrow the two books at a time that were allowed her and which would enable her to endure Christmas with her grandmother and Gran's interminable monologues.

She had not been thinking of Colonel North, but the sight of him emerging from that particular doorway had stopped her in her tracks. After he had disappeared down Dunstan Street, she crossed the road to take a closer look at it: a plain dark brown door with an oblong light above it and a small round bellpush at the side. 'Press' said the white enamel button in its unpolished brass surround, but Mary did no such thing. She had heard too many stories of those who fell into the clutches of J. Reuben – the name in smudged ink on the card pinned above the bell. Reuben the moneylender, one of the evils of capitalism, a shadow which the New Socialist Dawn would sweep away. And on Christmas Eve Colonel North had visited him. Mary went thoughtfully on her way to join the general exodus from Barford by assorted private conveyances or, in her case, Mr Edwards the carrier's cart, which after a long cold wait departed about the time the various members of the North family reassembled at Amberley.

Tea in the drawing-room was almost over, Madam having declined to stay for it, much to Maud's relief. For once the children had been allowed to take tea with their elders, delighting in the tall Christmas tree which in their absence had mysteriously been erected in the hall. Its scent reminded Bea of the pines in Simla, though resin under gaslight was not like resin under sun. But they never spent Christmas in the hills and there were no pine trees in Cossipore to bring indoors and decorate with the piles of glass balls and candles and strings of tinsel which Aunt Maud had unearthed that afternoon.

'We hang them on the branches,' Rose explained to Roddy, 'and the fairy doll goes at the top. We only ever use her at Christmas. The rest of the year she's packed away.'

Roddy thought Rose, all pink and gold and warm and glowing, a great improvement on the waxen-featured doll. If only she could be packed away in layers of tissue paper in a lace-edged cardboard box, her fairy beauty preserved for ever in the bottom of a schoolboy's trunk. Except that there was something rather frightening about being a schoolboy, especially at Bradwell House, where he suspected he would not have been allowed to take a miniature Rose even if one had been available, for before they left India his father had come in one evening to survey his packing and had picked up his teddy-bear.

'Not taking this, are you, old man?'

Roddy looked at him reproachfully. 'Bear goes everywhere with me.' Surely his father knew that?

'Of course,' Major North said, not looking at Roddy. 'Small chaps like to have a toy along. All right too – for the *babalog*.' He used the Hindustani word for children advisedly. 'But you're not a small chap any more.'

Roddy stood straight. Small or not, he was defending a loved one. 'Bear wouldn't like to be left behind.'

'I dare say he wouldn't,' said the Major, 'any more than you and Mama and Bea like being left behind when I have to go on manoeuvres or up country. But you put up with it for my sake, and Bear will put up with it for yours. Fact is,' he went on, 'teddy-bears – that sort of thing – aren't a good idea when a chap goes to boarding-school. The other fellows might rag you a bit.'

'Don't they have toys?'

'Not that sort.'

Roddy digested this.

'Then I think I'm going to be different.'

'Not a good idea, old man. When you become part of an outfit – a school or a college, say – you give up something of yourself for the privilege of being part of something bigger. When I wear the King-Emperor's uniform, as I hope you will some day, I'm a serving officer with duties and responsibilities. I can't spend time being Roddy and Bea's papa. That's for when I'm on leave or off duty. It'll be the same for you. Keep Bear for the holidays. Better still, leave him here. He'll be waiting for you when you return.'

He did not add that return was several years away, by which time Bear, mildewed and forgotten, would long since have been destroyed, but Roddy, in the midst of fireside tea in the drawing-room at Amberley, suddenly remembered his toy. His eyes filled with tears of recollection, and apprehension at the new and unfamiliar existence that lay ahead.

At once a soft hand slid into his, a fair head leaned towards him. 'What are you crying for?' asked Rose.

'I'm not crying.' Roddy glared at her. 'I – I just had something in my eye.' He sought desperately to divert her, and his quick ear saved the day. Faintly he had heard the crunch of gravel, the sound of horses' hoofs.

'Someone's coming,' he sang out. 'There's a carriage.'

Uncle George, nearest the window, moved back the curtain. 'By Jove, it's the station fly.'

'Jimmy!' Emily had said his name before she even realized it.

Maud glanced at the clock. 'He must have caught the early train.'

The children were on their feet. 'Uncle Jimmy!'

Alice said: 'I wonder what he's brought us as a surprise.'

The bell pealed. The parlourmaid hurried to answer it. Maud's pugs yapped excitedly into the hall. She herself rose, hostess-like, to greet her brother-in-law, but Emily was not far behind and the children poured past both of them as George shouted for Jarvis to come and help with the bags.

And then the front door was open and, on a waft of cold air, Uncle Jimmy was in their midst, lean and laughing and just as they remembered him, and Roddy was first into his arms.

Emily was conscious of a quick peck for Maud and another – even quicker? – for her, and then Jimmy was turning away from them, back to the station fly. He was helping down a young woman – brown, dancing eyes, shabby coat, an unfashionable hat – was leading her forward as though she were made of spun glass, his white teeth gleaming, his feet almost dancing, as he said in a ghastly parody of Harry when she herself had first set foot in Amberley:

'Maud – Emily – may I present Miss Poppy Richards, who has done me the honour of consenting to become my wife.'

CHAPTER 5

Jimmy North, hands thrust deep in pockets, stood looking out of the drawing-room windows at the snow. It had come in the night, several inches of the damn stuff, wet and white and slippery. Cold icing on a sad Christmas cake.

It had been a mistake to bring Poppy to Amberley. He should have had more sense. But their private whirl of happiness had seemed such that nothing could withstand it. Wherever they went – stores, theatres, tea-shops – people had smiled on them. Park-keepers had looked indulgently at their clasped, gloved hands as they huddled together on a bench; crossing-sweepers touched dirty forelocks. Even the porter at Paddington had held open the compartment door as if for royalty while they hurried down the platform, and the guard waved his green flag with a flourish as his whistle crescendoed to undreamt-of heights.

It had seemed too good to be true that they had been in time for the early train, that Mr

Edelstein, owner of the art gallery where Poppy worked as a lady typewriter, had decided in a fit of benevolence to close early on Christmas Eve. It was only in the station fly on the way from Barford that Jimmy had begun to doubt the wisdom of this visit, unannounced. Poppy's vibrancy seemed stilled; her vitality shrunken; her hand lay unaccustomedly passive in his.

'Don't worry,' he said. 'They'll love you.' And felt her fingers move.

Immediately he reproached himself. He should have said, 'You'll love them.'

But would she? He could not see Poppy as one of the Norths of Amberley, any more than he could see himself. That was part of her attraction: she offered a way of escape. But escape from what? To what? Now that he had passed his law finals, thanks to the stimulus of her presence in his life, what exactly lay ahead? Marriage and a small house – his income from Amberley would ensure that. His principals had hinted at a junior partnership if he could raise the capital – he would have to have a talk with George. In any case, George had written that there were important matters to discuss, so it would be appropriate. George was a good sort: he'd welcome Poppy kindly. And Maud wasn't greedy. Not like Emily.

His thoughts shied away from Emily, but he

forced himself to rein them in. Emily had to be faced, both in person and in all that she represented. He did not know which was worse. Last night, watching her slow, demolishing survey of Poppy before she extended her hand, he could have struck her. Instead he had kissed her briefly, saying (and meaning), 'You two have much in common. I hope you're going to be friends.' Friends at least for Christmas, until Emily sailed for India and finally out of his life, so that he could blot out the folly and betrayal of those brief, heady, dangerous days. He had avoided Harry's wife in London, hoping that the discourtesy would make plain that what had been had never been, that they were brother- and sister-in-law, no more. His fiancée's existence would confirm that, and loyalty to her would cancel out his disloyalty to his brother. If only there were nothing to cancel out.

Behind him the drawing-room door opened.

Poppy said, 'Everyone's getting ready for church.'

He turned. There was appeal in her face as she said in a small voice, 'Do we really have to go?'

'Oh, I think so,' he said. 'It's expected. We're the Family.'

'I don't think I want to be that.'

'We'll have a new family,' he promised.

She came and stood beside him. 'Somewhere else?'

'Yes. There's nothing for me at Amberley.'

She snuggled against him. 'I'm so glad.'

And I? he wondered, surveying the room, familiar despite Maud's Art Nouveau décor. In this house I grew up. I know every corner, every cupboard, every creak of the stairs. All my life it has been home, except once, briefly, when I envisaged home as an African farm. Am I ready to leave it and all it represents for some raw brick villa in the suburbs? He looked at Poppy and his heart said incontestably, Yes.

Maud came sheepdogging in. 'We shall be leaving in five minutes. We can't walk fast in this snow.' and to Poppy: 'May I lend you a prayer book?'

'Thank you, I –'

Poppy had been going to say she wasn't coming, but something held her back. Jimmy was one of this alien race of Norths, the rituals and assumptions of their imposing residence posed like a bulwark against time and chance and change. She found them awesome and also ridiculous – their paintings alone ensured that: stilted equestrian portraits of gentlemen, and provincial ladies painted by provincial hacks. The worst were in the dining-room, lowering over every meal, but the hall was bad enough with its foxes' masks and stags' heads interspersed as if they ranked with the ancestors. Only in the drawing-room was there any awareness that taste, like all else, moved on.

'– I was admiring your drawing-room,' she said to Maud on impulse.

Maud's drab face flushed. 'Thank you. I chose the decorations for this room myself.'

Poppy caught the personal emphasis.

'It must have been fun.'

'Yes. Yes, it was, rather.'

For once I came into my own. I wasn't George's wife or Madam's shadow or Lilias's sister. I was me, Maud Hunsdon North. But no one before had ever commented. George just said, 'Well, so long as it's what you want;' and added: 'Hope you realize we can't afford to re-do everything on this scale.' Madam said nothing at all; and Emily's interest in things around her was reserved exclusively for clothes. She had certainly missed no detail of Poppy's. 'Cotton gloves . . . Did you see her hem was turned? . . . I did not know that style of hat was still in fashion . . .' until at last Maud had burst out: 'Perhaps the girl hasn't any money.'

Emily met her sister-in-law's eye. 'Then she knows where to come for it, doesn't she?'

You're wrong, Maud thought. She's in love. Anyone can see it – anyone who's ever been in love, which probably doesn't include you. For what do we know of you, Emily Fanshaw, except that Harry fell for your pretty face? You have no birth, no breeding, and no connections – but it is your son who will inherit Amberley.

The old bitterness had made her cast a glance towards the hall where the children, aided by Jimmy and Poppy, were decorating the Christmas tree. What would become of Alice, Rose and Lulu if anything happened to George? Lately he had been looking strained and worried. He spent hours shut in his study, brooding over accounts. Yet when she asked him if there was anything wrong, he smiled and said there was no need for her to be troubled. As if she were a simpleton. Sometimes Maud felt she understood all too clearly why women like Mrs Pankhurst wanted the vote. It wasn't the election of MPs that mattered, though no doubt the MPs thought it did; it was the admission wrung from men that women were more than playthings to be picked up and put down at will. Lilias had always maintained that they were something more, but then no one would have mistaken Lilias for a plaything: her beauty and personality saw to that. Whereas she herself was neither plaything nor partner. She simply ran George's home, received his conjugal attentions, bore his children, endured his mother, and did whatever lay to hand in house or church or village, without payment (which did not matter) and without thanks (which did).

On occasion she even sympathized with Alice's rebelliousness, though she wished it would take a different form. Why did the child always look as if her clothes didn't belong to her? Why couldn't she dress neatly even for church?

'Your tammy is askew, dear,' she chided her eldest daughter, who had joined them in the hall. 'And put on your gloves – a muff is not sufficient.'

As Alice turned she saw that the hem of her coat was coming down. There wasn't time to mend it – and Madam would be in church. Madam would be sure to notice, and comment on it later. At least Rose and Roddy, standing side by side, were presentable.

George was fuming at the front door. 'Are we all here? Where's Emily? Late again, I suppose.'

As if on cue, Emily made her entrance. She had dressed with special care. Even Maud admitted to herself that Emily looked good. Her make-up too, though discreet (no lady *painted!*), concealed the fact that she had not slept. Compared to the plainly dressed figure who had appeared briefly at the breakfast table to exclaim over the children's gifts, sip a little China tea without milk or sugar, which had had to be specially prepared, and break a triangle of toast into pieces, not one of which, Bea noticed, she ate, Emily was transformed into an exciting, desirable woman. By Gad, George thought, she's a looker, all right.

He held the door open and Emily sailed through in the wake of the rest of the party, giving him a dazzling smile. Harry was certainly lucky in his wife's appearance; lucky even in the timing of his Christmas mail which had arrived so opportunely last night. When the evening post had come and Jarvis had brought the letters to the drawing-room, arranged fanwise on a silver tray, the exotic stamps had stood out among the green halfpennies of late Christmas cards. The letter had been comfortably plump, but Emily had not opened it, no doubt wishing to be alone to savour to the full her husband's greetings which chance rather than forethought or organization in faraway India had delivered on time. Indeed, she had slipped the letter, which had been forwarded from Earl's Court, so swiftly into her handbag that the children had not realized it had come. Perhaps it contained letters for them – that would explain its plumpness – and Emily was keeping them back.

Harry's letter had indeed contained an enclosure, but it was not for Roddy or Bea. It still lay in Emily's handbag, which swung beside her as she walked. The village church of St. Peter lay too near the gates of Amberley to make it worth while to drive, so the Norths, in overshoes, boots, galoshes, picked their way through the snow, the men leading, beating a path, the women following with little shrieks and squeals, and the children darting off in all directions, heedless of warnings of wet feet.

They passed the lodge – Madam did not join them, so she must have gone on ahead – just as the single bell began to give forth short hurrying notes designed to speed the laggards, while the rector waited at the door. He and George shook hands in manly fashion, as though there were nothing amiss. Goodwill to all men, George thought grimly. Did it include women too? He could see old Mrs. Bottrall's black bonnet and Mary's plain hat an inch or two higher to her left. They always sat in the same place, immediately below the brass on a right-hand pillar recording those who had died in the South African war. Private Hector Bottrall, MM, was first both alphabetically and by virtue of his decoration – the Bottrall women derived a certain distinction from this which George at least did not grudge them, any more than he grudged them their cottage. What he grudged was their lack of gratitude. There had been that business of his ricks last summer. Two of them had burned down. Damp straw, spontaneous combustion, maybe; but George was convinced they had been fired. And who but Suffragettes in the person of Mary Bottrall would have set out to destroy his ricks, leaving him to find money for animal fodder and bedding in winter when pieces were higher and when he could least afford the extra expense. Of course he could prove nothing. He had complained to the police, but they said there was no evidence. His friends on the Bench had been sympathetic but there was nothing they could do. And now, thanks to Mary Bottrall and a score of other reasons, he was in the moneylender's hands. At the shaming thought of it George sank to his knees in the front pew with unusual heaviness, thankful that for once his ever-punctual mother was late.

Mr Reuben had been polite – oh, so polite – and sympathetic. How sad that the Colonel was in difficulties, though it happened to so many these days; but with a fine property like Amberley as security, the difficulties must be temporary to say the least. A loan until the next harvest? No problem. Though of course the interest would not be low. How could it be, with agriculture so rewarding but so chancy; and

English weather not always kind. Business now, that was more predictable. Still, land values tended to keep up, and a gentleman's residence seldom lacked for buyers. Yes, the security was good. Of course the Colonel must understand that the formalities would take a day or two. Even one in his business, while not observing the festive season in any religious sense, would be closing his office. But immediately he reopened he would have the necessary documents prepared, and if Colonel North could see his way to call on – should they say the 27th? – everything would be ready for signature, and the money, in cash if the Colonel preferred it, would be at his disposal at once. So now they had only to shake hands on it, a gentleman's agreement, and he could be relied upon to do his part. He existed only to provide a service; he was sure the Colonel realized that.

He existed to feed on other men's misfortunes, George reflected grimly, scavenging amid family collapse. He had heard unsavoury stories about Mr Reuben, but at least he would provide immediate cash over and above the dwindling hoard of sovereigns hidden in the drawer of his desk. And cash was needed for wages, for food and clothes and fuel, for essential repairs (which did not include the roof of the Bottralls' cottage), cash above all to buy time – time until he could talk to Jimmy, hear from Harry . . . In a haze he heard the rector announce the opening hymn.

George inflated his lungs and squared his shoulders. He was still squire of Amberley. His baritone bellow lacked nothing in volume and assurance. Behind him, the congregation struggled not to be outdone.

Bea, gazing in wonder at St Peter's ivy-swagged Norman pillars, with which the Victorian gothic ironwork of St Mark's, Cossipore, could not contend, eyed with particular contentment the window-ledge for whose untidy heap of holly and winter jasmine she alone was responsible, and raised her clear young voice in the familiar hymns.

She liked it at Amberley. A congenital love for house and grounds and village was stealing through her veins. It was good that she would come here with Roddy in the holidays. It had a feel of home. She had not even minded when the unexpected arrival last night of Uncle Jimmy's fiancée, Miss Richards, meant that she had had to give up her room and share Roddy's more spartan quarters. It was still Amberley. And when she had wakened in the dark to an unfamiliar whiteness that had nothing to do with dawn, and had run to the window to view the snowbound wonderland of the garden, it was as if God had answered all her prayers.

The snow had come first, a few flakes, last evening while the carol-singers gathered at the door, with a shuffle of feet on gravel, some coughing, a little giggling, and the hoarse command of 'Now!' The strains of 'Good King Wenceslas' rose heartily on the night air. Uncle George and Aunt Maud exchanged glances; then, with good-humoured resignation, rose.

'It's village people,' Alice said in explanation. 'They come carol-singing every year and they come to us last because Papa is always so generous.' She hurried after her parents to the front door.

Everyone else, including the servants, was gathering in the hall. The outer doors were flung back despite the rush of cold air and the excited exit of the pugs and Rastus, who provided occasional staccato accompaniment. The carol ended, there was a spatter of applause. Bea had time to notice that most of the singers were shabbily dressed, and to catch the blue gaze of a tall young woman with a good voice who stood a little to one side and seemed intent on gazing in.

'Who's that?' she whispered to Alice, under cover of 'The First Nowell.'

'Miss Bottrall. She teaches at the village

school. Papa doesn't like her. He says she's a Suffragette.'

Bea was about to ask what a Suffragette was when her curiosity was deflected by a white speck floating downwards before her eyes, then another and another, settling on the hats and coats of the singers, giving them a speckled effect.

'It's snowing!' Alice exclaimed.

Bea echoed her silently: it's snowing. She could not believe it was true. Was this what lay all year round on the mountains above Simla and sugar-iced their tops? She went to the edge of the porch and made a slight footprint, holding out her hand to the snow's white, stinging kiss. Umbrellas were going up. Jarvis came forward with a tray of steaming glasses.

'Papa gives everyone mulled wine,' Alice said.

'Us too?'

'No. It's alcoholic. Come on, we always choose the last carol. What shall it be? You can choose because you're the visitor.'

' "See amid the winter snow",' Bea said.

The singing was slightly off key. Aunt Maud and Mama, growing chilly, had retreated to the drawing-room. Uncle Jimmy and Miss Richards, matched unconsciously by Rose and Roddy, were standing hand in hand. God came down to earth each Christmas and this year he was bringing snow. Please, Bea had prayed, as Uncle George distributed money and there was a chorus of 'Merry Christmas', let there be lots and lots and let it be here by morning. And behold, that strange brilliant whiteness that crowned the high Karakorams were here, balanced on ledges and branches, awaiting her on Christmas Day.

She had crept back to bed and huddled under the blankets, unwilling to think of sleep, uninterested even in her stocking: this was a moment that would not come again. In the bed next to her Roddy stirred and muttered; though she could not know it, this moment also would not come again. For the last time the two of them were sharing a bedroom, and behind them a door of childhood closed.

Behind them now the congregation resumed their seats in church with much bustle. Many of them were speculating on the connection between the presence beside Mr Jimmy of an unfamiliar young woman and the absence of Madam from the front pew. Jimmy, accustomed to such false connections, was aware of it and hoped that Poppy was not. Whatever kept his mother away – and he could not remember an occasion when she had not been present for the Christmas morning service – could have no connection with Poppy: she did not know

Poppy was here. Last night, as the station fly passed the lodge, he had wondered whether to stop and introduce her, but had decided against this double shock. They were early, the Mater would not be expecting him, let alone his fiancée; Poppy might find Maud and Emily more than enough. He had said nothing, and the fly had trundled past without stopping. Poppy's hand tightened in his.

'We're almost there,' he said. 'That was the lodge. We renamed it the Dower House. It's where my mother lives. You'll like the Mater –' he was not sure of this but it needed saying – 'and she'll be thrilled I am at last settling down.'

Poppy said nothing. It might be settling down for Jimmy, but it was all upheaval for her. Since the day he had walked into the Edelstein Gallery her world had stood on its head. It was the most delicious sensation, but she was still struggling to reorientate. She had looked up from her typewriter in a dark corner of the gallery because the doorbell pinged. Mr Edelstein was with a client in his office. She rose to greet a young man.

'Good morning. Can I help you?'

'You have a picture in the window,' the young man said. 'A watercolour. Very small. Some farm buildings –'

'Oh,' she said, 'you mean "The African Farm".'

'It's certainly African.'

That was what had brought him into the gallery. It might have been Piet Botha's house, though Boer farms were all alike, long and low and whitewashed, with a woman sitting on the stoep, hands busy with knitting, mending. It could have been Jacoba who sat there, as once he had thought she might sit on the stoep of his farm in Africa. But Briton could not marry Boer . . .

'Would you like to see it?' the gallery girl was asking. She had a pleasant voice.

'If you please.'

And a good figure, he noticed, as she turned to the window.

'Who is the artist?' he asked, hoping to sound knowledgeable.

The name meant nothing to him.

It meant nothing to Poppy either, Mr Edelstein having accepted the picture simply as part of a lot.

'How much is it?' the young man asked.

Poppy told him. It was the cheapest picture on sale.

She watched disappointment shade his face. He was a change from most of the clients, to whom the sum would have been trivial.

She said boldly: 'If it would help, we could keep it for you till next month.'

What bright, friendly eyes she had. If they kept the picture, he could come and look at it again, could come and look at her . . .

'Are you over from South Africa?' she was asking.

Jimmy said: 'I served in the South African war.'

'Oh, did you?'

'And lived there afterwards.'

'You must know it very well.'

'Yes. I thought of settling there.'

'But you preferred England?'

'Yes.'

'I hope you've no regrets.'

'None at all,' Jimmy said positively. And all at once it was true. Jacoba's blue eyes were obscured by a pair of brown ones. Emily's never entered his head at all.

The gallery girl was still holding the picture. She had strong, capable hands.

'It's no good keeping it for me,' Jimmy blurted, 'I can't afford it. I haven't yet qualified, you see . . . I'm a solicitor. At least, I'm going to be.'

'That must mean a lot of exams.'

Behind them the inner door opened. Mr Edelstein was ushering his client out.

'May I see you again?' Jimmy said, not knowing why he said it.

The girl smiled. 'I work here every day. Until six,' she added.

'So perhaps I might see you home?'

She inclined her head – her neck was graceful – but it could have been at the client going out. Mr Edelstein was looking in their direction.

'Good morning,' Jimmy said. And fled.

'A waste of time, Miss Richards,' said Mr Edelstein. 'That young man, one could see he would not buy.' And returned to his office never noticing that his efficient lady typewriter had entered another world.

Since last night Emily too had been living in a different world, a world of bitterness and darkness, shot through with the sharp light of revenge. Harry's letter in her handbag glowed like a hot coal against her. Never had she expected to have such power over the Norths, over Madam, Jimmy . . . Her neat pink tongue peeped out to caress her lips.

Harry had written frankly of George's financial difficulties. Emily did not understand the technicalities, but the picture was clear enough. He had concluded:

And so, dearest, George has asked if we

would forgo our income from Amberley. It is not for me to apportion blame in this letter, but I want you to know the facts, since you more than anyone will be affected. And the facts, dear Emily, are these. I can hardly expect further promotion in the immediate future, so my pay will remain the same. Like most officers, I rely on private income to provide the luxuries of life – the servants, your dress allowance, a little hunting, not to mention our travels in India. And these would have been in any case curtailed by our decision to send Roddy and Bea home to school. The fees, even the modest establishments (and I am sure you will choose wisely for Bea), are still a considerable drain, particularly in the case of Roddy, for whom we must eventually envisage Sandhurst or perhaps university. When I endowed you with all my worldly goods at our wedding, I truly thought I was offering you a life of ease. Now, while we shall not be exactly penurious, our way of life must change.

I say must, but in fact it depends on you, dearest. I know how much it means to you to be the fashionable Mrs North, to have an elegant carriage, a home which other women admire. Can you bring yourself to live without these things for a few years? I feel it is for you to decide and to write to me as openly about your feelings as I have written about mine.

I should like to save Amberley – for George, for myself, for Roddy, but I value my wife even more. If you say no to my suggestion, you will hear no word of reproach from me. But if you say yes, as I hope and believe you will in your generosity, will you forward the enclosed letter to George? It contains my written consent to forgoing the Amberley income, and should help to relieve his mind.

Relieve his mind indeed! Emily eyed her brother-in-law's broad back in the pew in front of her with loathing. His mismanagement was bringing her down. Because of him she was being asked to become one of those wives she had so often pitied, reduced to living on their husbands' pay. She knew exactly what that entailed: pathetic alterations to last season's dresses, refusing hospitality one could not hope to return, a social life dominated by occasional tea-parties and the Ladies' Sewing Circle – none of it was Emily North, who could cut a dash with any wife in the regiment and was known as 'the belle of Cossipore'. It was like

Harry to be accommodating to George's impossible request. Without her to stiffen him, he would always be over-generous. His attitude to the children showed that. He showered them with treats and presents – nothing but the best would do – although she had often pointed out that children, having no discrimination, could be cheaply provided for; whereas she herself . . . Emily choked discreetly into her prayerfully folded, gloved hands. Harry was asking her to live quietly, to look shabby. No wonder her shoulders shook.

She became aware that Maud had half-turned, was offering her something. A wintergreen lozenge! Emily shook her head. She was racked by rage, not by the English climate, with all its winter horrors of rain and fog and snow. Next year Maud wouldn't be so smugly patronizing, the Squire's lady in her pew. Where would they live? Perhaps in just such an anonymous suburb as she herself had come from. That would be justice if you like!

And Jimmy – Harry said that George was also asking Jimmy. If Jimmy said yes – and he would, because he was just as soft as Harry – he could kiss goodbye to that common little trollop who thought him the catch of the year. A lady typewriter – whatever next? A lady engine-driver? Emily conveniently forgot that she herself had been attending a course designed to fit her for the commercial market at the time she had met Harry North. Miss Richards – did she expect them to call her Poppy? – could be counted on to disappear swiftly from a moneyless scene, leaving Jimmy in even more need of consolation than that South African bitch had done. And she, Emily, would be on hand to provide it. She need not sail before February, perhaps March. And the children would be away at school. The pleasures of London were before her, with Jimmy once more at her side. In saving him from an obvious misalliance she could almost be said to be doing her duty. Emily smiled to herself as the congregation rose for the last hymn.

Roddy, seeing the bright colour in her cheeks, her erect bearing, straightened likewise. He was proud of his beautiful mother. Only Rose was more beautiful in his eyes. After church, Rose had explained, they went back to Christmas dinner; after dinner they had the presents from the tree, which were from people like Mama and Papa, whereas it was Father Christmas who had filled their stockings. Perhaps he had, though Roddy was doubtful about this and intended asking Uncle Jimmy. He did not see how Father Christmas, who delivered in India, could also deliver in England, especially with so much snow. Suppose they were snowed up at Amberley? It would mean extra days with Rose. Mama too would enjoy being snowed up with Uncle Jimmy. Was it because of him that her cheeks glowed? He had seen them glow like that in Simla, especially after siesta-time, when they gathered for tea on the verandah and the cushions on the swing were still warm. His mother and Uncle Jimmy often spent the siesta in the swing – he had glimpsed them occasionally on his way to the bathroom, alerted by the swing's wicker creak. They did not lie resting as he had been told to – wrestling was more like, but the ways of grown-up people were unfathomable (and looked uncomfortable). Roddy dismissed them from his mind. Nevertheless, the game might be fun to try . . . Only there were no wicker swings at Amberley. And other things to do with Rose.

He could not get out of his mind that image of her sleeping when Bea had led him on tiptoe to the room she shared with Alice, stockings and candles in hand. Alice was awake, expectant, but she put a finger to her lips, gesturing to Rose.

At that moment Rose woke up.

The first thing she saw was Roddy. It was the best of beginnings to Christmas Day or any other. She smiled widely and held out her arms.

The vision was to stay with Roddy all his life. It lasted long after they had turned to their stockings and dug down to the sugar mice in the toes (Rose ate the white one but not the pink one, which was put carefully on one side). Even now, in church, gazing at the back of her hat and the blonde curls tumbling over her shoulders, Roddy felt his heart bound. Sudden knowledge of his mother's feelings for Uncle Jimmy illumed him. He put his hand protectively on her coat. Emily, glancing down in the middle of 'Hark, the herald angels sing', looked into Harry's eyes. George's eyes too. And Jimmy's. Madam's eyes, come to that. Those eyes that had rested on her so assessingly when Harry first brought her to Amberley. But where *was* Madam this Christmas morning? Why was she not in her pew? There was something ominous about her absence. She sensed George and Maud and Jimmy felt it too.

George in particular was uneasy. The Mater had never not joined them before. Maud's whispered suggestion of early service did not reassure him. She could have let them know. Besides, his mother detested early service. And if she'd gone, she'd still have joined them now. The snow? No, it wasn't deep enough to deter her. If she'd been ill, Patterson her maid would have sent word. He'd have to call in at the

Dower House, risk her displeasure (she hated being what she called 'run after') just to assure himself that all was well. Unless Maud was right and she really had gone to early service. Woodward, the rector, would know.

The congregation waited respectfully for the Family to leave their pews. In any case, half of them wanted to catch a glimpse of the unknown girl beside Mr Jimmy, and Mr Harry's family. George, bowing right and left, to Mrs Bottrall but not to Mary, a somewhat difficult feat, was aware that his own family was no longer the centre of interest. Did they realize Roddy was the heir? And what did it matter, since next year the Family pews might be empty, or occupied by a different family. What was it Reuben had said – a gentleman's residence seldom lacked for buyers? Would he really have to sell Amberley?

Beyond the door he glimpsed the rector waiting, trying not to shiver in the cold. A cassock was no substitute for an overcoat. Even buttoned in an ulster, George could feel the keenness of the air.

'Merry Christmas, Rector.'

'Merry Christmas, Colonel, Mrs George. And a cold one. We shall have skating on the lake at Mawby Hall if this keeps up.'

'You think so? I was hoping for a thaw. The

hunt meets tomorrow.'

'So it does. I'd forgotten, not being a Nimrod. Mrs North all right?'

So his mother hadn't been to early service.

'Thank you,' George said. 'She's very well.'

He made himself believe it.

'So glad.' The rector was clearly puzzled, but had no time for more.

'Merry Christmas . . . Merry Christmas . . .'

The greetings fell on them like snow. As impersonal, George thought, and almost as chilling. Next year, would they be for someone else?

He responded to other enquiries.

'Thank you, yes. My mother is very well.'

CHAPTER 6

About the time the North family were emerging from church Fanny North settled herself a little more uprightly than usual in her favourite chair in the drawing-room at Amberley.

She had spent the night wrestling with intolerable pain, a pain so sudden that it seemed like a visitation from on high, yet so deep-seated that it was as though it had slumbered in her for ever and was only now waking to stretch itself. The first twinge had come as she was preparing for bed and had been dismissed as indigestion. An hour later she knew it was no such thing. It was no use crying out – it would arouse her maid, but what could Patterson do? Even if she went on foot through the falling snow to Amberley, she could only summon George and Maud, and they could do as little as she. It was impossible to fetch the doctor from Barford before first light, and then only if the roads were passable. Besides, some things were better borne alone.

She braced herself against the next wave that was gathering – her nerve-ends prickled before they sensed the actual pain – and lay with teeth clenched to ensure silence, letting it wash over her. But unlike a wave, it never receded; it simply went on and on, until, just as familiarity began to diminish the agony, a fresh wave gathered and broke. No position offered ease; her continued tossings merely loosened the bedclothes, which lay around her in a heap. She could feel her pillow damp with sweat, her fingers slimy. It could be no worse to get up.

Slowly she stood, struggled into her dressing-gown, and crept the few steps to the fire. There was still a glow; with a little coal from the bucket, the grate became a living heart of warmth. Outside the snow fell soft and steady, wrapping the cold stiff earth in a winding sheet. Such a deathly image. She shook her head against it, and twisted wretchedly in her chair.

A draught set the candle-flame a-tremble, its thin smoke trailing aloft. Darkness lurked in the corners of the room as pain lurked in her body. Both would conquer if she did not fight. If only there had been a daughter, like the dark-eyed girl in her favourite portrait, the one picture she had insisted – with George's consent – on bringing from Amberley. This eighteenth-century girl, some unknown ancestress of her husband's, was Fanny's secret vision of what her own daughter might have been like. There was a warmth, a glow about her, which the other portraits lacked. Almost, Fanny could have imagined her speaking, leaning out from her frame as from a window in the picture-crowded sitting-room. In these painracked hours the girl in the portrait would have been warm and loving, comforting by her very presence, bone of her bone, flesh of her aching flesh. For this pain was different – worse – than any pangs of childbirth, even the birth of that daughter-no-daughter which had been the most difficult of all. This pain had no known cause, no end and no beginning, only degrees of intensity.

She recognized now that some occasional twinges which she had been easily able to dismiss were harbingers, black imps with pincers, before the onset of the devils of hell. Should she have told Dr Paget? No, Paget was at best a fool and at worst an undertaker's lackey. She had no use for him – never had. Somewhere in the world there were good doctors, perhaps at hospitals like St Thomas's where nursing was now an established profession, where she herself had wanted long ago to train. For a moment she imagined cool whiteness, quiet voices, competent, caring hands, then dismissed the thought. What could they do in this private battle – herself versus the pain?

I've always been a fighter, Fanny thought. If I'm going to die, I'll die fighting. As I've lived. She had never before thought of life as a battle, but then she had never thought of her own life as something terminable by death. Around her people died – her parents, daughter, husband; young Hector Bottrall killed in South Africa; Lilias – but she herself, unbowed by these calamities, head that much higher, back that much straighter, faced death down and dared him to do his worst.

And now, it seemed, he was taking up the challenge. She gripped the arms of her chair against the next onslaught of pain. She was to be reduced by siege unless she could summon up reinforcements in the shape of her iron constitution, her steely will. 'The days of a man's life are threescore years and ten.' She had heard the words so often. But she still had five years to go, five years in which to watch over the upbringing of Harry's children as she already watched over George's girls. Roddy who would inherit Amberley – he was a precious charge, Harry's son in build and bearing, but Emily's in features and good looks. What sort of a squire would he make? And how far distant? George was only forty-two, but lately he had aged, looked worried, claimed he was not, the air between them stiff with silences. Should she have relinquished control of the estate? She had never trusted George as a businessman – too unmethodical, too easy-going – but he had to take over sometime. Suppose he was in financial difficulties?

And Jimmy – it was time he settled down. He couldn't for ever blame himself for that incident in South Africa. It was not his fault that Hector Bottrall had been killed. No one asked the under-gardener to volunteer just because his beloved Master Jimmy appeared in uniform. No one had asked him to commit virtual suicide. 'It was my fault, Mater –' she could hear Jimmy's voice, the voice of a schoolboy, telling her the whole sorry tale. 'It was meant to be a surprise dawn attack and I botched it. The Boers were waiting for us, and they potted us on that hillside where we lay. Hector and I were lucky: a few boulders gave us cover, but every time a rifle cracked, one of my men died. We were there to create a diversion, and I knew the rest of the company would be working their way round under cover of darkness to storm the kopje from the other side, but that wouldn't be time enough for us. The moon had risen and the whole landscape was grey and silver. You've no idea how bright night can be in the veldt. And the stars! I wish you could have seen them, Mater. South Africa's diamonds aren't only underground.

'The damn thing was –' he was too upset to apologize for swearing in her presence – 'we knew the kopje was held by only a handful of men. We could have overrun them if they hadn't had us pinned down.' He laughed bitterly. 'Then Hector said he had an idea. He thought he could see how to distract them, though he wouldn't say what he was going to do. Just told me to watch and set off wriggling from one bit of cover to another, making diagonally for the top. Once there was a shot fired in his direction and I thought they'd got him, but after a bit I saw him moving on again. He'd isolated himself by now and the Boers weren't looking for trouble from that quarter. Then all at once I heard two grenades explode. There was shouting, firing, another explosion. I saw Hector black against the moon. I heard him shout – it sounded like "Boer bastards!" – then they got him. But by that time all those of us who could move had slithered down to the cover at the bottom of the kopje, leaving only Hector and the other casualties. That's how he got his MM.'

An hour later the main body of troops had swept over the kopje from the far side. There were no prisoners, but he did not tell his mother that. Any more, Fanny thought, than he has ever told me what it is he is not telling me about the incident, and why he chose to stay on in South Africa when all the rest of the volunteers came home.

Her small fire had died. She dragged herself to the window and parted the curtains. Surely the blackness had given place to grey? Or was that the deceptive snowlight? *You've no idea how bright night can be in the veldt.* Nor how dark it can be in Croft Amberley when no living creature is astir. But she could distinguish the garden wall and, beyond it, the tower of St Peter's Church. It was dawn, she had survived the night, the pain was easing, and Christmas Day was ineluctably here.

Christmas Day. Alice said the words over to herself on first waking, though of course it had been Christmas Day for hours now. Nearly one-third of it was over – and for her it hadn't even begun. Like so much else in childhood, it was unfair. She had heard the grown-ups wishing one another 'Merry Christmas' last night when they came up to bed, and had envied Rose the slumber that possessed her even on this most magical of nights.

In the dimness that was no longer darkness she could see the stockings at the foot of their beds. Long black ones, hers because Rose's weren't big enough, now bulging interestingly. These were the presents from Father Christmas, or so the grown-ups claimed, and Rose believed them – 'They aren't *from* anybody, Alice!' – but she herself knew differently. Last night she had lain awake long after the chorus of goodnights on the landing and watched her father come in on slippered feet, carrying the filled stockings which he substituted for the empty ones hanging at the foot of the bed. At least he wasn't wearing a cottonwool beard and whiskers and a garment like a red dressing-gown with a hood such as he had worn to distribute gifts at the village school's Christmas party, when he had looked, Alice thought, a fool. She and Rose attended by special invitation and had seats in the front row, but Alice would gladly have exchanged hers for a crack in the floorboards when in answer to a knock at the door Mary Bottrall opened it to let him in, announcing 'Here's Father Christmas, children,' with an unmistakable giggle in her voice. Thereafter Papa, sounding just like Papa, which frightened some of the children, had gone from bad to worse: 'Here you are, m'dear . . . well, don't stand there like a johnny, come and take it' – as bashful recipients were called forth. Papa, who was the kindest and gentlest of men, so often sounded terrifying, especially when he roared. It was hard to believe he was the same person who had leaned over her to stroke her hair last night.

Alice had pretended to be asleep when he came in with the stockings because that was part of the game, and Papa thought she was. Mama wouldn't have been deceived, but Papa was different, and Alice didn't want him to discover his mistake. So she lay quietly and breathed very deeply and Papa came and stood by her bed, gazing down at her, until he lifted a long lock of her hair in his fingers and carried it to his lips. He did this several times, and his big hands were so humble that she longed to sit up and say, 'I love you,' fling her arms around him, and kiss all his worries away. But she didn't, and after a while he retreated – she heard the floorboards creak. And now another creaking floorboard roused her, and Bea's head came round the partly opened door.

'Are you awake?'

'Yes.'

'Merry Christmas. It's been snowing.'

'Merry Christmas.' Alice saw no need to comment on commonplace snow.

'Can I come in?' Bea whispered. 'Roddy's still asleep.'

'So's Rose. You'd better come into my bed. Have you got your stocking?'

'Yes, but I haven't opened it.'

'We'll open them all together later. What did you ask Father Christmas for?'

'I don't believe in him.'

'Nor I. He's all right for Rose and Roddy.'

'I don't think Roddy believes.'

'Papa brought our stockings. I saw him.'

'Why do grown-ups think it's fun?'

'They don't. They think we do.'

Bea considered this. 'So if we said we didn't . . .'

'They wouldn't like it. They decide when the game stops.'

'But that's silly.'

'They *are* silly.'

It was a curious relief to say it to someone who might understand, but Bea did not respond. Instead she said: 'What do you want to find in your stocking?'

'A riding crop.'

'But you don't ride.'

'They might be going to let me.'

But they weren't. She could see already her stocking lacked the desired rigidity. The blank refusal which was all her impassioned pleas extracted from her mother extended to Father Christmas too. She had even written 'a riding crop' on her Christmas list and posted it to him up the chimney. She didn't believe in him but you never knew . . . It had gone straight up too, whereas Rose's list had subsided into ragged ashes and she had had to be comforted.

'There, my lamb,' Nanny Cardew soothed her. 'You'll get what you want, never fear. A Dutch doll and a trumpet, wasn't it? They'll be there come Christmas Day.'

'What about my riding crop?' Alice had demanded.

'Now, Miss Alice, you know your mama doesn't want you to learn to ride.'

'Why?'

'I'm sure she has her reasons.'

'But what are they?'

'That's not for me to say.'

To the other servants Nanny was more forthcoming. 'It's unjust, that's what it is, making those children suffer for what happened before they were born or thought of. But it's not my place to say.'

'Pity,' opined Jepson, the groom. 'Miss Alice is a natural. She'd be queen of the Hunt, she would. Miss Rose, she'd look pretty on a pony, but Miss Alice is a horsewoman.'

'Mrs George doesn't want another tragedy,'

someone murmured.

'There's tragedies and tragedies,' Nanny said, 'and not letting a child grow as she was meant to is just as big a one, if you ask me.'

Only from her father did Alice gain some satisfaction in answer to her insistent why.

'Mama's sister was killed by a fall out riding. She doesn't want the same to happen to you.'

'Mama's sister – do you mean Aunt Lilias? But she died years ago.'

I know that, George thought, but she's standing here before us. He said: 'You must try to understand how Mama feels.'

And how I feel. Not that I would deny you your riding lessons, but there are times when I cannot restrain myself from kissing those long dark silky locks that spread so enticingly over your pillow, and believing it is Lilias again.

Why doesn't anyone try to understand how *I* feel, Alice wondered. Sometimes I hate Aunt Lilias. It's all her fault. I don't believe Aunt Emily would have made such a fuss if it had been *her* sister . . .

She said to Bea: 'Does your mother ride?'

'Yes, but not very often. She hates the flies and the dust.'

The flies round her face and the dust on her habit. I can picture it, Alice thought.

'When I'm grown up I'm going to ride,' she

announced, 'and I shan't ride side-saddle. I shall ride astride like a man.'

'But your skirt . . .'

'I shall wear breeches. Some ladies already do.'

Bea shivered. Cousin Alice was nice but rather frightening. A bit like Grandmama. If she said she was going to do a thing you somehow knew she'd do it. If she said you were, you knew you'd do it too. Whereas most people said things that did not matter, Alice's pronouncements were of a different order, uttered in that unexpectedly musical voice. It was not a child's voice; it did not voice childish sentiments. Those other than children listened when Alice spoke.

'What do you think of Miss Richards?' the voice now demanded.

Bea said: 'I think she's nice.'

'Yes, but is she a suitable wife for Uncle Jimmy?'

'If he loves her, of course she is.'

'Not quite the opinion of our mothers. When he introduced her, mine looked furious and yours looked sick.'

'Why should they care? They don't want to marry Uncle Jimmy – they're married already.'

'Mama says Miss Richards is Not Our Class.'

Bea pondered the phrase. She had heard it

used in India of gentlemen a little too eager to be on good terms with other gentlemen, of ladies a bit too bright, a bit too loud, and of one lady in particular, immaculately turned out in quietest pearl grey, who for unknown reasons had been snubbed by a visiting dignitary. There had been tears in the woman's eyes as she turned away. But in India, within the white communities of Cossipore and Simla, it was easy: everyone knew – or knew of – everyone else, and even the woman in pearl grey ranked far above titled natives by virtue of being white. In England, where all skins were white, the gradations were more subtle. It was not easy to understand why women like Miss Richards and Mary Bottrall who worked for their living were in some way inferior to those like Mama who did nothing but enjoy themselves, especially when one was taught that idleness was an invitation to Satan. Why was charitable work, like sewing garments for the poor which they did not always appreciate, superior to nursing them or teaching them, which they did?

'Why does Class matter?' she asked her cousin. 'When you're a doctor, won't you treat the poor?'

'I expect so. Why?'

'Will that make you Lower Class?'

'Why should it?'

There was no answer to that.

'I like Miss Richards,' Alice announced. 'I'm going to call her Aunt Poppy without waiting till they're married.'

'Won't your mother object?'

'Yes, of course she will, but she can't stop me. So long as you're prepared to put up with being punished, grown-ups can't *make* you do a thing. They can only stop you doing what *you* want to.'

This doctrine was too revolutionary for Bea.

'When I'm grown up,' Alice went on, 'I shall ride and smoke cigarettes and wear short skirts and drive a motor-car like Papa's. I might even have my hair cut short.'

Before this glimpse of the future Bea recoiled in horror. 'It isn't ladylike.'

'Who says? You sound like Mama. Come on, let's open our stockings. It's daylight, sort of. I'll wake Rose and you go and fetch Roddy. And I'm going to sit next to Aunt Poppy at breakfast.'

Alice's independence was infectious.

Bea said: 'I'm going to call her Aunt Poppy too.'

This mode of address had warmed Poppy Richards's heart, still chilled by the cold eyes of Maud and Emily, her prospective sisters-in-law. George was all right: a bit of an old buffer but discernibly Jimmy's brother. It was the women who were formidable.

She had been wrong to let Jimmy bring her to his people for Christmas. They should have stayed with her own folks in the terrace house in Battersea which had always been her home. She'd been proud of Dad when he'd welcomed Jimmy into the family: 'If you're going to marry our girl, you're one of us. But you treat her right, mind. To us she's someone special. Only the best is good enough.'

'She's a good girl,' Mum had offered. 'You won't find a better.'

'I know that, Mrs Richards,' Jimmy said.

'Well, you see as she stays that way, and respect her.'

Embarrassed, Poppy had said: 'Oh, Mum.'

'You know what I mean right enough. No taking advantage.'

Poppy was as red as the flower she was named for. 'Jimmy's a gentleman, Mum.'

'So I see, but he's still a man, isn't he?'

'And man enough to take a jar of beer.' Her father busied himself with hospitality. 'And what for you, Mother – a drop of stout?'

'Yes, I'll have my usual.'

It was forthcoming, and so was Poppy's: a half-pint of light ale.

Jimmy grinned at her. 'I can see I'm going to feel at home in this house.'

And suddenly her eyes were dancing again.

They were not dancing now as she walked back from church on Christmas morning, her arm through Jimmy's because she was his wife-to-be and wore his engagement ring. She wouldn't have chosen it, but a fiancée had no say in the selection. Besides, it was too big and slipped on her cold finger so that its diamond half-hoop lay against her palm, making it look like a wedding band already. The future Mrs James North tightened her grasp on her husband's arm. She needed his support, not in the snow, which was half melting in what had become weak sunlight, but in all the ordeals that lay ahead. Christmas dinner, with an array of cutlery even worse than that at breakfast, where, despite a hearty appetite, she had intended to limit herself to the safety of a slice of toast, until Alice, the dark intelligent child who stood out from the others, had sat down beside her and announced: 'I'm going to have bacon and sausage and mushrooms, Aunt Poppy. Are you going to have the same?'

'Yes, please,' she said, copying Alice's assurance among the knives and forks. Perhaps she could do the same at dinner. She mustn't let Jimmy down.

His arm pressed against hers as if in reassurance. Under his hat-brim his eyes were bright with love. If only someone other than the children would warm towards her. And there was still his mother to face. The old lady had not been in church, and Poppy had been conscious of an element of consternation when the service started and it was clear that the Mater, as George and Jimmy called her, was not going to take her place in the front pew. George had gone on ahead now to the lodge to make sure all was well with her, but already he was coming back. The look of relief on his face reassured them all.

'It's all right,' he announced. 'Patterson says she's gone on up to the house and she'll be waiting for us. I've never known her miss church before, but I suppose there's always a first time. After all, she's getting on a bit.'

As I suppose I am, Fanny North thought, adjusting her position in the high-backed chair which was her favourite in the drawing-room at Amberley. But I'm good for a few years yet. She was feeling better by the minute, the warmth of the fire suffusing her, flushing her cheeks.

'Are you all right, Madam?' Jarvis had asked on admitting her, as startled by her grey looks as by her unheralded, solitary arrival.

'Perfectly all right, Jarvis,' she had assured

him and herself. 'It's just the snow and the cold.'

The butler had brought her a glass of sherry while she waited, and that too had set warmth flowing through her veins.

'A real family Christmas, isn't it, Madam?' he observed. 'Mrs Harry and the children here for the first time, and now Mr Jimmy bringing a young lady . . .'

'Indeed, yes,' Fanny North said.

Mr Jimmy bringing a young lady? So that was the 'big surprise' promised in his telegram. Her Jimmy bringing home a girl – the girl he wished to marry, for there could be no other explanation of this momentous step. Of course he should have married years ago – somewhere she suspected an ill-starred love-affair, though he had never mentioned any such – but now at last there was a girl, a prospective daughter-in-law to rank with Maud and Emily. To compensate, perhaps.

No trace of these thoughts appeared in Fanny's face or voice as she acknowledged Jarvis's information. One did not reveal to servants, or even to kindred, that there were family matters one did not know about, any more than one admitted to pain or weakness. Or to mortality.

The butler had withdrawn, leaving her alone with the bright fire, the brightening sky, the winter landscape, the drawing-room with its paper chains made by Rose and Alice with cold water paste and much application, just as they had done last year. And would do next year, and the year after, with baby Lulu joining in. And I shan't be here to see it, Fanny thought suddenly. Next Christmas I shan't be here.

Death had his scouts, his outriders, and this thought was one of them. She tensed, not now with pain, but as at the approach of an enemy with whom one must join battle however much disadvantaged, however much destined to lose. Not that that was any reason for not fighting; the greater the odds, the fiercer the desire to win. Hector Bottrall must have felt it as he scaled that kopje, Lilias as she fought to control that bolting horse. They had been defeated, but they were young, they hadn't her experience. I have years ahead of me yet, Fanny thought, willing it to be so, bracing herself for the arrival of the churchgoers as she heard feet stamping in the hall. The children's voices were high with excitement. Then George came bursting in.

'Merry Christmas, Mater. We were worried you weren't in church.'

'I thought you'd manage very well without me,' she said, refusing to wonder if they might have to in the future. 'A happy Christmas, Maud.' Not that Maud, crowding in behind

George, ever looked happy. 'You too, Emily.' Why was Harry's wife so overdressed? 'Children, has Father Christmas been? Did you get your stockings? Jimmy, my dear, dear boy . . .'

She allowed herself to reach up and rest a hand lightly on his shoulder. They had not met since October and already her maternal eye was taking in that air of glossy well-being which surrounded him as protectively as had once the walls of her womb. Jimmy was happy. Her beloved son was radiant with happiness. Hovering behind him was its cause. And now he was bringing her forward, introducing her . . . Poppy . . . Poppy Richards. A stumbling 'How do you do?' A struggle to remove her glove. A warm, strong hand extended, vibrant with vitality . . .

Poppy saw an old woman, eyes shrewd but sunken, face flushed – was it rouge or fire? – stately, full-figured; a Presence dressed in severe grey softened by lace.

Fanny saw a pair of bright eyes sparkling, cheeks fresh with the icy winter air, dark curls like those of the girl in her favourite portrait clustering about a head poised every bit as proudly as her own.

This wasn't Lilias – she wasn't beautiful enough. This was Poppy. This was Jimmy's future wife. This was the daughter so long withheld and now given back to her – she would not think in the closing months of her life.

Fanny rose, proud that she could still do so without touching the arms of her chair, and took a step forward to embrace the young face raised, hesitant, expectant.

'Welcome, daughter,' she said.

Christmas dinner had been a success. Maud allowed the thought to surface and remain in her consciousness. The meal had been excellent, thanks to Mrs Roberts the cook and a bevy of sweating, red-faced helpers in the kitchen. The children had been well behaved; Emily less so; Madam had not eaten as heartily as usual, but had more than made up for it with the lavishness of her praise. George had seemed more relaxed than he had for weeks. Doubtless Jimmy's news, which had delighted him, had something to do with it. George was a great believer in the virtue of settling down.

'Fellow can't keep sowing his wild oats,' he had said last night in the bedroom as they were preparing for bed. 'All right for a youngster, but Jimmy's thirty. I was married by the time I was his age.'

And already we had buried our first son, Maud remembered. Aloud she said: 'I expect he wanted to be sure. Better safe than sorry.'

George laughed. 'Marry in haste, and all that.'

Had he repented at leisure, Maud wondered. Their wedding had certainly been hasty, a bare twelve months after Lilias's death. But there was no point in waiting, with Mother dying and dear Papa already retreating into that limbo in which he had spent his last years. He seemed such an old man, eyes vacant, hands shaking, trailing a few inconsequential remarks as he shambled from one room of the vicarage to another, yet he was younger than Madam was now. But then age and Madam were incompatible. She looked the same when I first saw her, Maud thought. Only she didn't call me daughter and make me sit beside her and ply me with questions about what I did and where I worked. As if there were something meritorious about having to earn one's living. Truly, Madam was making a virtue of Poppy's necessity.

'Girl seems all right,' George said.

Maud didn't answer.

'Better than Emily, anyway. Not such a looker, of course.'

As if looks mattered when one had borne a son, was mother to the heir of Amberley . . .

Very tentatively, Maud said: 'George . . .'

'Yes?' He was tunnelling his way out of a

shirt and his voice was muffled. When he emerged she was sitting up in bed, hands clasped about her knees.

'George, do you . . . are you going to sleep in your dressingroom?"

'Yes, of course,' George said on a reflex. From any other woman he might have construed the question as an invitation; but not from Maud. Not from his own wife. Yet she looked strained, and her query was unusual, prompting an anxious 'Are you all right, m'dear?'

'Perfectly. I just thought . . . well, it's Christmas . . .'

'So it is,' George said over-heartily, stifling nascent desire. 'All those damn stockings to hang up. What's the betting the children are still awake and I'll be up half the night waiting for them?'

'You could go later.'

'I may have to. If so, I'll try not to disturb you. Let you get your sleep.'

'Oh, I'm all right.'

You're the one who isn't sleeping. I've heard you tossing and turning in there, but you won't confide in me, won't come to me. The wife of your bosom sleeps in a separate bed. And I don't know how to say to you, 'I desire you. My flesh cries out for you and hungers for us to be one.' I don't how how to open myself to you, my arms, my legs, my body, unless you first come to me seeking. Unless you give me another chance to bear your son.

'Good night, m'dear.' A snowflake kiss as kind as a brother's. And as passionless. Oh, for the bruising lips, the urgent hands, the straining body . . .

'Good night,' Maud said. 'Will you put out the light?'

Afterwards she lay awake in the dark and heard him tiptoe into the children's rooms. He stayed a long time with the girls. Then she heard him return and settle with a creak of bedsprings, while her taut flesh cried silently, 'I am here.' Towards morning she slept, and woke heavy-eyed with headache to the domestic exigencies of Christmas Day. Only now, with the worst of them behind her, could she begin to think – to dream – of Christmas night.

For her second daughter Christmas night was something she wished could be postponed for ever. Rose did not want this day to end. From the moment she had roused to Alice's shaking and held out her arms to Roddy, it was the best and most wonderful Christmas yet.

First of all there was her stocking, which did indeed contain a trumpet and a jointed wooden Dutch doll, just as she had laboriously spelled out on her list. Even though it had burned instead of flying up the chimney, Father Christmas had still known what to bring. How could Alice pretend it was Papa when parents' presents came later, under the Christmas tree? Or most of them did, for Mama had given her a new petticoat and matching drawers which she was to wear on Christmas Day. They had scalloped hems and were threaded with two rows of pink ribbon, much too pretty to hide.

'Couldn't I wear them down to breakfast?' she had pleaded.

'No, dear,' Nanny said. 'Underclothes go under other clothes. Now let's be getting you dressed.'

But it wasn't the same, wearing them under your best alpaca with the tucks in the skirt to allow for growth. She had lifted the hem to show Uncle Jimmy the petticoat at least.

'Look. Pink ribbon. Two rows.'

'I say!' Uncle Jimmy goggled. 'Poppy, come and have a look at this. Have you got pink ribbon on your underclothes?' he added, lower.

Aunt Poppy laughed. 'You'll have to wait and see.'

Alice had said it was all right to call Miss Richards Aunt Poppy, but Mama and Aunt Emily had been quite vexed.

'It will be time enough to call her aunt when your uncle marries her,' Mama remonstrated.

'*If* he marries her,' Aunt Emily said.

'But we've already started calling her Aunt Poppy,' Alice pointed out, all sweet reason. 'Wouldn't it be rude to go back to calling her Miss Richards now?'

'Perhaps,' Mama said helplessly. 'What do you think, Emily?'

'Oh, for heaven's sake don't make such a fuss, Maud. They'll probably never see the woman again.'

So Miss Richards remained Aunt Poppy and Christmas Day was wonderful once more. Specially wonderful this year because of Roddy. There had never been a boy at Amberley before. Never someone near her own age who looked at her as he did, wanted to do whatever she wished, and begged so hard to sit next to her at Christmas dinner that the seating was rearranged.

'Are you glad to have your little beau beside you?' Aunt Emily asked her.

'Yes, thank you,' Rose said, not understanding the word but striving for politeness. 'Are you glad to have yours?'

Aunt Emily immediately turned to Alice, who was next to her, and began telling her for the second time how they celebrated Christmas in Cossipore, while Uncle Jimmy, who was on her other side, glanced anxiously across the table at Aunt Poppy, who was talking to Papa and hadn't heard.

Roddy whispered: 'When do we pull the crackers?'

'At the end of dinner. When we can't eat any more,' Rose said.

'And when do we have the big presents?'

'In the drawing-room after dinner. Jarvis brings them in one at a time.'

'At home,' Roddy said, 'my father gives out the presents.'

'Do you wish you were back in Cossipore?'

'I wish I hadn't got to go away to school. I'd much rather stay here at Amberley.'

Rose squeezed his hand. 'I wish you could stay too. I'm going to ask Papa to let you.'

'No, don't. He'll think I'm scared.'

'Well, aren't you?'

Roddy bit into a mince pie. 'Yes, but a boy can't say so. It's different for a girl.'

Rose was accustomed to hear Alice railing at the misfortune of being born a girl, but it struck her now that the misfortune of being born a boy was greater. What was the point of being allowed to drive a steam engine or lead troops into battle if you could not admit to fear and pain and grief? Except to girls, since Roddy had just done so. She began to have an inkling of the complexity of human relationships.

It was more than had been vouchsafed to her father. George had always thought in straight lines. Which is why he is so confoundedly difficult to deal with, Jimmy thought, facing his brother in the room he called his study in the interval after tea on Christmas night. The children had not yet retired, extra grace being allowed because of the occasion. His mother had already returned to the Dower House, accepting with fewer protests than usual that Jepson would drive her. Before she left she had invited Poppy to visit her.

'Come by yourself,' she said. 'I should like to get to know my new daughter better.'

Poppy smiled radiantly. 'I'd like to get to know you too.'

'Then that is settled. When do you return to London? The twenty-eighth? How enlightened of your Mr Edelstein to allow an extra day. In that case, call on me the day after tomorrow. You will find me at home in the afternoon.' Madam moved on to the next item on her agenda. 'Maud, tomorrow I must visit in the village. I should like Alice and Beatrix to accompany me. They are old enough now to take a share in the duties of their position, and it will do them good to see how the less fortunate live. We must not forget in the midst of plenty that there are those among us who are in want.'

Too right, Jimmy thought. Trust the Mater to hit the nail on the head. Trouble is, she doesn't realize that 'those among us' can include those at Amberley. There was no way he and Poppy could manage comfortably on his present income. He had to have a partnership. And that meant drawing on his share of the capital his father had left, which was invested in Amberley. Which in turn meant an interview with George, and though Christmas night was not a time for business, it seemed the ideal opportunity.

So he stretched with pretended nonchalance in the armchair in George's study while his brother sat behind his desk, looking inappropriately magisterial and at the same time hesitant.

'I want to talk about money,' Jimmy said. He remembered that George's invitation for Christmas had contained a reference to the need for important discussions, but George's face remained impassive; so it could hardly be anything financial he had in mind.

Quickly Jimmy outlined his plans.

'. . . So if you could release my share of the capital, I could buy into the partnership and still have something over for a house.'

'There are plenty of good houses to rent,' George offered.

'True, but you've always said property's the best investment. After land, of course.'

'The best investments can be . . . unreliable.'

'That's why I'm investing in myself. I've got youth, strength, brains, qualifications now, thanks largely to Poppy, and I'm going to make my own way.'

'I'm glad to hear it. You've left it late enough.'

'An added reason why I can't afford to wait. I don't want to press you unreasonably, George, but how long would it take to make my share of the capital available? If I can give my principals a definite date, I'm sure they'll be willing to hold the offer open.'

'I don't know,' George said.

'But you can find out, see the bank and so on.'

'It wouldn't do any good.'

'What do you mean?'

'I mean the money isn't there. If I can't meet current liabilities in the next three months I shall be declared bankrupt. Amberley will have to be sold.'

'It can't be. It's our home, our children's . . .'

His and Poppy's, unborn, as surely as George's and Harry's. It was unthinkable they should not know Amberley. 'We'll be a new family,' he had promised Poppy, but the new still had links with the old.

He said: 'Have you told Harry?'

'I wrote three months ago.'

Four weeks by boat to Bombay, then the night mail to Cossipore, and another four weeks back. In the New Year he should have Harry's answer . . .

'I wrote to ask,' George said, 'what I'm asking you now. If you could forgo the income from Amberley for a year or two and leave the capital intact, I believe I could pull through. The estate's basically in good order. It's just that I've . . . overspent.'

He looked bleakly round the study which he used as an estate office. Disorder was everywhere. If he endeavoured to tackle one aspect of it, a thousand counter-demands crowded in, each one more urgent than the last. He could not bring himself to tell Jimmy of the shaming visit to Reuben, that Amberley was already as good as pledged. If Jimmy wouldn't play, if Harry wouldn't, the estate could be considered gone. What would Reuben do with the place? Sell it? Move in himself? He was rumoured to aspire to gentility . . . The thought of Reuben in his home made George feel physically sick. Of course he hadn't yet signed, but he was going to. What other course was open to him? Unless . . . He glanced across at his brother.

Jimmy glared angrily back. 'Damn it, George, you can't sit there and say you've overspent. What on, man? Considering that it's in part my money that you've been so free with, I think I've a right to know.'

What on? How to explain to Jimmy, who for years had been a rolling stone, that the demands were all too often human. The village looked to him. It was not just Maud's and Madam's charities, the rector's intercessions on behalf of this cottager or that, a tenant farmer in difficulties, a wall in bad repair; there were the demands of Amberley itself – that leaking roof, the hungry paintwork – and the demands of its inmates: wife, daughters, servants, there were even, George reflected, his own.

The motor-car. His guilt and his extravagance. His toy and his escape. He should never have bought it, but a man needed some indulgence to offset the nights of self-denial since Maud's last stillbirth. Soon, perhaps . . . He had almost thought last night that she . . . But no, he must remember Dr Paget's strictures. The motor-car was better for Maud, could she but know it. Would she have him take to drink or women, as Eddie St Devereux was rumoured to do?

Sure enough, Jimmy was on the motor-car. '. . . Can't think what you want it for. Chugging in and out of Barford, surely you could use the carriage? Or are you trying to cut a dash, keep up with the St Devereuxs?'

This was hitting below the belt. Maud might aspire to keeping up with their titled neighbours, might hanker after a telephone, that extraordinary invention, as yet limited to a few businesses and fewer private houses, that condemned you to endure the conversation of those who bored you even when they were not physically there, but George was never anything but himself. He had no need to be: the Norths had been at Amberley for longer than the St Devereuxs had been at Mawby Hall. Had been. In future it would be the past tense. It was a shaming thought.

'I'm sorry, Jimmy,' George said awkwardly. 'If I had the cash, you'd have it like a shot.'

'Much use that is when you've frittered it away. Good God, man, it wasn't all yours in the first place. Do you realize Harry and I could sue?'

'Be like flogging a dead horse, wouldn't it, if there's nothing with which to settle the claim. Cost you, too – the lawyers win, whoever loses.' Too late George remembered his brother was now a lawyer. 'Of course I don't mean you.'

In the face of personal crisis Jimmy too had forgotten his profession.

'How can I expect Poppy to marry me,' he burst out, 'when I tell her I'm just as penniless as she is? What will her parents say? They think I'm the catch of the season, God help them. Fraud of the season's more like. How can I ask her to wait until I'm in a position to offer her what I've promised? She'd do better to marry a tradesman than me.'

'At least she's still free to do so,' George retorted, 'whereas Maud is tied to me, and I must tell her that far from providing for her and her daughters, I am selling the roof over their heads. Oh, they won't starve – they'll exist in some wretched villa – but it won't be what they're accustomed to. Alice has always wanted to earn her own living. Well, that's one wish that's certainly going to come true.'

But she wouldn't be one of those blue-stocking Cambridge graduates. She'd be a lady type-writer – like Jimmy's girl.

'. . . Can I see the estate accounts?' Jimmy was asking.

George gestured to the disorder around him. 'Help yourself.'

'Have you thought of selling one of the farms?'

'And turn the tenant out? At least, if the whole lot goes, they'll keep their tenancies.'

'What else is there you can sell?'

'The car. What's left of the silver – I've pawned a bit here and there. Couple of horses.

Get rid of Jepson, one of the maids – it's a drop in the bucket. Not worth the distress it will cause.'

'The Mater –'

'The Mater has only the income from what Father invested for her. I can't touch her capital. And we both know she's as fit as a flea. If we ever inherit, it won't be yet awhile.'

Jimmy's trained eye was meanwhile taking in the chaos.

'It can't be as bad as it looks.'

'It's worse,' George assured him. He pulled open a drawer of his desk and papers, released, bubbled over like boiling milk. He had always hated paperwork, writing letters. They were unnecessary when a gentleman's word was his bond. But the paperwork had accumulated despite him, and by now only the locked bottom drawer was empty, except for the bag of sovereigns, his service revolver, and Lilias's photograph.

'Of all the goddamned messes! Did you have to ruin us all?' Jimmy's anger was getting the better of him.

'I'm the one who's ruined,' George reminded him. 'You and Harry are merely inconvenienced. And since you'll be that in any case if Amberley goes under the hammer, I'm asking you to accept that inconvenience for what I hope is a limited period and help me try to save it. For you. For Roddy. For us all.'

'No!'

Jimmy's fist crashed down on the desk, making the inkpots rattle, and a stick of sealing wax flew up and broke.

'No, I'm damned if I'll help you save Amberley in order to preserve your way of life. Why should you lord it over the village because you're rich enough to give trade and employment? Why should your kind lord it over blacks and Boers wherever the map shows red? What right have you to privilege and patronage except by the accident of birth?'

George was on his feet now. 'The accident of birth, as you call it, involves responsibilities, though you could hardly be expected to know that: you've always ducked out of yours. You've been ready enough to take your income from Amberley while you swanned off to foreign parts, where I've no doubt you did your share of lording it over blacks and Boers –'

'That's a lie! I worked for a Boer farmer.'

'Learning estate management, no doubt.'

'Learning to love and understand the very people I'd gone out to South Africa to kill.'

'An exercise which can hardly be termed successful, since I understand the farmer threw you out.'

Not for anything I did but for something I wanted to do. For wanting to marry Jacoba. Briton and Boer could work together, but Briton could not marry Boer.

'You know nothing about it.'

'True,' George conceded, 'but I know something about you.' I know you're unmarried, free to play the field, unhampered by consideration of a wife, by a doctor's self-denying ordinance, by your own damned concept of decency. 'I'll bet the enemies you loved were of the fair sex,' he said aloud.

Jimmy's hand came up in a reflex and the flat of it connected with his brother's cheek. Seconds later the sound of the slap was echoed by a muffled scream from across the hall.

George was nearer the door, but Jimmy was first through it. He had recognized Poppy's voice. As he reached her she turned to him, half crying, half laughing, and pointed towards the dining-room.

Roddy, prime cause of her scream and first to be affected by it, looked up from the window-seat in astonishment. In the somnolence following an afternoon tea which no one really wanted, for him boredom had set in. Aunt Maud was sitting by the fire with a book open and her feet up, pretending to be awake; Grandmama ditto, though her feet remained firmly on the floor; Uncle George and Uncle Jimmy had disappeared into the study; and Mama and Aunt Poppy were playing card games with Alice and Bea. Presents newly opened and abandoned lay scattered in glorious disarray; even the Basset-Lowke engine and coaches from his parents had temporarily palled, chiefly because Rose did not care for them, any more than he cared for the golliwog from Uncle Jimmy which she continued to clutch even when offered the chance to uncouple the locomotive – an honour which everyone with sense knew could not be performed with one hand.

'Let's go and play by ourselves,' Roddy suggested.

'In the nursery?'

'No . . .' It was too far away, too much under the eye of Nanny Cardew, who had descended to reclaim Lulu from doing the round of female laps. The unheated bedrooms were dark and chilly, and so was the morning-room. 'George is very economical with coal,' Mama had noted. 'At this rate he'll die a millionaire.' And it was true that even today, Christmas Day, only the drawing-room and dining-room were warm and cosy, and the kitchen below stairs, of course. Warmth and laughter floated up into the hall from these regions.

Rose said: 'Let's go and see Cook.'

'No,' Roddy said again. He did not want to share Rose. All day he had craved to be with her alone – on a raft in the ocean, on a desert island, lost in the unending steppes or the jungle's immensity. Every place he had ever read of would be enhanced by Rose's presence. In the absence of such exotic locales there remained the dining-room. He had seen the parlourmaid come out and close the door behind her, leaving the table laid and the fire banked high. It would be hours before anyone thought of a cold supper. Meanwhile . . .

He seized Rose's hand. 'In there.'

She allowed herself to be propelled, but once the door closed behind them, her high spirits, repressed all day in the name of good behaviour, bubbled over and she broke away from him. 'Catch me if you can.'

Roddy laughed, and they were off, round and round the table, sometimes under it, panting and laughing, shrieking at every near-miss. Rose was nimble and knew her terrain, but Roddy was faster and heavier. A final burst bore her backwards to the window-seat. Adult games, half glimpsed, half remembered, in the swing on the verandah, were surely nothing to this, for Rose proved to be deliciously ticklish and as supple as an eel. The two rows of pink ribbon on her new underclothes were much in evidence, but she had forgotten them as Roddy knelt over her, flushed with exertion and the excitement of the conqueror, hands seeking her ribs while her legs thrashed wildly . . .

A horrified cry put an end to the romping as effectively as a bucket of cold water.

Roddy looked up to see Aunt Poppy in the doorway. Other doors were opening, footsteps hurrying across the hall, other faces crowding behind her: Aunt Maud, looking equally stricken; Mama with her hand to her mouth; Uncle Jimmy with his arm round Aunt Poppy; Uncle George, his face as red as a Turkey carpet, demanding in a parade-ground voice:

'What are you doing, sir?'

Roddy stood up. Behind him Rose dissolved in tears at the prospect of trouble.

'I wasn't doing anything, Uncle.'

'Don't lie to me, sir!'

'I'm not!'

Defiance and incomprehension fought in Roddy as he faced his commanding officer, to whom explanation seemed due.

'We weren't doing anything, honest, Uncle. Rose and I were only playing – playing at being Mama and Uncle Jimmy in the swing.'

CHAPTER 7

'It would be best if you caught the early train,' Maud said stiffly.

'If you will be good enough to arrange for the carriage to take me to the station, I shall be ready,' Emily replied with equal stiffness.

Maud noted the singular pronoun.

'There is no reason why the children should leave . . .'

Emily corrected her error at once.

'Naturally Roderick and Beatrix will accompany me. They will not wish to stay where their mother is not welcome.'

Are you going to tell them why? Maud wondered. They're innocent, whatever you are. They're beginning to enjoy it here, Beatrix especially. Why should they not stay?

'I thought in the circumstances,' she said, choosing her words, 'you might find it – convenient – to be without them for a few days.'

'What circumstances?'

'No doubt you will wish to return to India somewhat earlier than you had planned.' Maud was astonished at her own guile. 'There is always so much to do when one is preparing for a voyage –' at least, everyone said there was – 'that I should have thought you might find it preferable to be free.'

I should certainly find it preferable to be free, Emily admitted to herself. Free of you and George, free of Amberley; above all, free of Harry. And as Jimmy also will presumably be returning post-haste to London, it is more than ever desirable that I should be free in the next few days.

Since that moment of deathly silence in the hall, she had not seen him. He had turned at once to the Richards girl, who predictably shrank from him as if he had the plague. That and the ridiculous scene on the stairs said everything necessary about her background, the rigid morality of the lower middle class. Aunt Grace would have reacted similarly and had brought her niece up to do the same, but Emily had learned first by observation and then by experience that rules were made to be bent, though never broken, and the only one that mattered was: Never be found out.

And now she herself had broken it and the North clan were sitting in judgement upon her. Not on Jimmy, they would never admit to doing that, but on Jimmy's temptress, on Harry's faithless wife. The eyes of Maud and George were upon her, appraising, as if they had always known, as if Madam's first assessment of her, that she was weighed and found wanting, was accurate to a hair. In that second Emily vowed vengeance, the more impassioned for being inchoate: they would pay for this condemnation, though she did not yet know how.

She flashed her sweetest smile at Maud. 'It is true I shall be very busy and unable to give the children much attention.'

'Then why not let them finish the week here? If you can find some reason for your return –' Maud hesitated – 'George and I would never contradict.'

Children, your mother is an adulteress. She is leaving Amberley in disgrace. She will return to India and your wronged father, and should he ever learn the truth it will be for him to decide whether to forgive her. I can just hear them, Emily thought. Things can be said without ever being spoken, and Roddy and Bea will know that their mother is for ever unwelcome in their father's family home.

For ever?

'I am sure I can rely on your discretion,' she

said, raising downcast eyes. 'Particularly since Roddy is the heir.'

Maud's flush was as soothing as a poultice.

'So it is settled you are to return alone?' Maud said, hating the hot colour staining her cheeks. 'I will ask Roddy and Bea to come to you so that you can tell them. I expect you would prefer to take supper here in your room.'

Like a child sent to bed. A delinquent.

Emily inclined her head. 'Something light. A poached egg on toast would be delicious. And a little wine to help me sleep.'

It was a very little wine, she reflected later. Trust the vicar's daughter to make sure of that. But no amount would have made her sleep that night. She burned with humiliation as though she tossed and turned on hot coals. Would they write to Harry? She did not think so, but one never knew. What ought she to tell him about this Christmas visit to counteract reports of her early return? Because the children would write, and from boarding-school it would be impossible to censor their letters. What a cursed nuisance letters were. And suddenly she remembered with the force of a thunderbolt Harry's last letter to her. What had he said? 'It depends on you . . . if you say yes, will you forward the enclosed letter to George? It contains my written consent to forgoing the

Amberley income and should help to relieve his mind.'

It depends on you. On me, Emily, who must not linger under their roof. In her handbag lay Amberley's salvation. Destruction rather, since *it all depends on you.* Why deny herself the small pleasures of Cossipore society, the glances of admiration directed at the fashionable Mrs North, in order to maintain George and Maud in their straitjacket of virtue, especially when from Harry there would be no word of reproach? True, she was depriving Roddy of his birthright, but it was a birthright he did not want. He wanted to be a soldier, not a squire – he had said so, and somehow she never doubted it. Besides, he would never know of her decision . . .

In an instant the envelope, left unsealed though she had never bothered to read the contents, lay stiff and angular in her hands. But only for a moment. The next, it was in the grate. The heat charred a corner but went no further. She blew on it, making the embers glow. Slowly the charring spread, the ink standing out with desperate clarity against the encroaching brown: '. . . my dear wife . . . it is through Emily's generosity . . . we both feel . . . we wish . . . we are as one . . .' In every line she was being associated with Harry's decision, but it was not a decision she had made. Hers lay smouldering obscenely, writhing as if in pain. All at once, with a plop, the letter was transmuted into a noisy flicker and the shadows on the walls danced in glee. Then the fire sank back into apathy, leaving only a drift of carbonized flakes, like black snow.

Emily returned to bed and lay wakeful, but no longer seeking sleep. Her mind raced. Jimmy in London. In need of consolation. Even more so than after that South African bitch. Too bad the Mary Queen of Scots costume would not be worn tomorrow at the St Devereuxs' fancy dress ball, but there she could at best have dazzled him, whereas now she would comfort as before. Comfort him so that there was no question of reconciliation with that – that shopgirl. She could withdraw her greedy little claws. Had she not seen that a tigress in India had already marked the prey as her own? Such a surge of power swept through Emily that she started up in bed as though she too had burst into flame, but – like the letter's – her brilliance subsided into blackness and on stealthy feet, sleep came.

Unknown to Emily, her daughter had also lain wakeful, haunted by the sound of sobbing from the second-best spare room. Never had she heard such desolate weeping. She longed to go to Aunt Poppy and comfort her, to chase away that stricken look that had shadowed her face as she shied away from Uncle Jimmy's hand, entreating, and darted up the stairs.

'Poppy!'

He started after her, but she turned on the half-landing.

'No! Don't touch me. I don't want you to. Ever again.'

'At least let me explain –'

'You can't. Oh yes, you'll talk and keep on talking. Lawyers can always talk. But you can't make black white. You're an adulterer. And with your own brother's wife too.'

'It wasn't like that.'

'Oh, wasn't it? Spare me a description.'

'Poppy, I swear to you –'

'I don't want to hear. I feel sullied. And I thought you were a gentleman!'

'No, just a man. A man who loves you.'

'And half a dozen others besides.'

'You don't understand –'

'Don't I? Perhaps I don't want to. Oh, why did you ever come into Edelstein's?'

And with a loud sob, Aunt Poppy gathered her skirts about her, rushed up the stairs and slammed her bedroom door.

The group in the hall came to life.

Uncle George said: 'Maud! The children!'

And to Uncle Jimmy: 'You will leave this house tomorrow.'

Aunt Maud said: 'Off with you, children, shoo! Nanny is waiting in the nursery.' And to Mama: 'I expect you would like to go to your room.'

Mama said: 'I note you all assume I'm to blame.'

Uncle Jimmy said: 'Oh God, Emily, not self-righteousness.'

Rose, still weeping, said: 'Why is Aunt Poppy crying?'

Aunt Maud said: 'Don't call her that.'

Roddy repeated: 'We were only playing.'

Mama said: 'You should know better than to play games like that.'

And Alice said: 'What a lot of fuss about nothing. I thought Aunt Poppy and Uncle Jimmy were supposed to be in love.'

It didn't seem much like it, Bea reflected. Was Uncle Jimmy crying too? Oh no, men didn't cry, though she wondered. Uncle Jimmy's eyes had been so very bright . . .

'Here's a fine how-d'ye-do,' George said later to Maud as he closed the door of their bedroom.

Maud, exhausted with domestic complexities – trays in rooms and no one wanting the excellent cold supper set out on the dining table – did not at first reply;.

'A fine how-d'ye-do,' George repeated. 'What time's the first fast train?'

'Ten o'clock,' Maud said; and then, coming to the nub of what was really troubling her, 'George, we can't send Jimmy back on the same train with her.'

She did not specify whether she meant Emily or Poppy, though it was of her sister-in-law she thought. It would be like putting temptation in Jimmy's way. All at once she knew what George had meant when he said that Emily needed watching and understood her own distrust of her. It was nothing to do with Emily's dashing way of dressing; she would have been a dangerous woman in rags.

George, whose thoughts had run on other lines, said hopefully: 'They might make it up on the way.'

'George!'

'Well, why not? I'm not saying he should have done it, mind, but once they get over it . . . She's a nice girl. She'd be good for him.'

'His own brother's wife!'

'What? No, I meant the other. Don't tell me she's staying on?'

'They can't all travel together in the carriage.'

'Send Jepson in to fetch the station fly. She came in it; it won't hurt her to leave in it.'

'Couldn't you take her in your motor-car?'

'The state she's in, she'd get hysterical. No, I'll run Jimmy in.'

'You don't think your mother . . .'

'Leave the Mater out of this.' George spoke with unusual firmness. 'Thank God she'd gone home before it all blew up. She looked tired, I thought, and I noticed she left quite early. She must be feeling her age.'

'She'll have to know sometime. She's invited the Richards girl to call on her.'

'She needn't know the reasons,' George said. 'Lovers' tiff. Incompatibility. Let's leave it at that.' Pity, all the same – he had liked Poppy. 'I suppose the girl's crying her eyes out,' he said. 'Ought you to go to her?'

'I have,' Maud assured him. 'She says she only wants to be left alone.'

The hot milk had been cold and skinned over, the biscuits uneaten, when she had gone to fetch Poppy's supper tray.

Maud seated herself on the chair by the bedside. 'My dear, is there anything I can do?'

'No, thank you. I've packed. I'll leave you in the morning. Never mind a conveyance – I can walk.'

'You certainly can't,' Maud insisted, even though the little valise looked light.

'I'm perfectly used to walking.'

I'm sure you are, Maud thought. She said: 'We can easily get you to the station. You will need to leave at nine.'

Nearly another twelve hours. Poppy glanced at the bedroom clock in desperation. How could she hold out that long? And then the drive into Barford, the two hours' journey to London, the omnibus from Paddington to Battersea – there wouldn't be many on Boxing Day, but she'd walk if she had to in order to get home to Jubilee Terrace, every step of the way.

Mrs North was saying: 'Are you warm enough? Let me get you another hot-water bottle. The one you have must be stone cold.'

As if anything could ever again warm her. It was her heart, not the bottle, that was stone cold.

'No, thank you,' she said again. How kind Mrs North's eyes were. This must be spoiling Christmas for them all. 'I'm sorry –' she began, and then the tears overcame her.

Maud patted her icy hand. 'Try to get some sleep,' she said, wishing there was some such possibility. 'If you're sure there's nothing I can do . . .'

'N-no.' The monosyllable was strangled. 'Except to draw the curtains back.'

Maud complied, while observing that it would make the room cold.

'I don't mind. So long as I can see out.'

The girl was in no state for argument. Maud hesitated whether to kiss her, decided against it, and said an awkward goodnight.

Left alone, Poppy fixed her eyes on the square of window. The moon was shining in, white and high and round as a pebble. The same moon was shining on them at home. They wouldn't have gone to bed yet, they stayed up late at Christmas. Dad would be slicing the cold beef. There'd be plenty of mince pies. And Mum's pickles. The ladies would all be sipping port. Fred and Daisy, her brother-in-law and sister, would have come round as usual. Aunt Elsie would be there. Uncle Ben if he wasn't on the late shift. Her brother Denis, with or without a girl. They'd be missing her, asking after her. Mum would say: 'She's gone to her young man's. Big place in the country. Ever so grand, but he wanted her to go.' Aunt Elsie would wipe her eyes. 'Wedding bells, eh? That's another one flown the nest. So long as she knows what she's in for –' with a glance at Daisy, whose first pregnancy was beginning to show. Dad would say: 'He's all right, our Poppy's fi-ancy. He'll take care of our little girl.' At the contrast between reality and her father's imagination, Poppy's tears flowed afresh.

How could he? Especially with that woman, dressed to kill and with such a disdainful smile. She was cheap even if she was a lady. And Jimmy had sullied himself with *her*. She could never again bear him to touch her. Every time she'd be reminded of what he'd done. They said it was different for men, but it wasn't. Suppose she'd . . . How would he feel if she had done the same?

Could I feel worse, Jimmy wondered, surveying that same high white moon from the dormer window of the room that had been his since boyhood. He had not gone to bed. What was the use? He wouldn't sleep. Instead he stood huddled in his overcoat, watching frost flowers form on the pane. Coming some years after his brothers, he had remained at home when they had gone to Bradwell House, and had appropriated this attic room in a fit of bravado and independence to demonstrate that he was not a baby any more. It was full of angles and shadows, stifling under the slates in summer and in winter one of the coldest rooms in the house, but he had resisted all attempts to move him to something more comfortable and convenient, and even though the Mater no longer presided over Amberley, the room remained untouched and was known as Jimmy's room.

The narrow iron bed was uninviting – never more so than now. It reminded him of army camps and barracks and a thousand things he had tried fervently to forget. It also reminded him of the narrow bed in his room in the bungalow in Simla, and the wide double bed occupied by Harry and Emily in the room next door, whose nocturnal creaking often paralleled in rhythm the creakings of the verandah swing. And that little bastard Roddy must have spied on them, no doubt with the prurient curiosity of small boys, only to re-enact his version of their coupling with George's precious Rose. And Poppy – Poppy of all people – had come upon them; Poppy who thought he was Galahad. He hadn't meant to deceive her with any such pretensions, had merely been waiting his opportunity to acquaint her with some measure of the truth. Not all of it; not Emily – of that he was too ashamed – but sufficient to bring home to her that, as her mother had so cannily put it, a gentleman was still a man.

And now? He could not banish her stricken face from his mind, her hysterical 'Don't touch me. I don't want you to. Ever again.' Would she still mean it in the morning? His knowledge of her told him yes. To her the world was black and white and he was now one of its villains.

Would she ever learn to see it in shades of grey? The second-best spare room where she slept was below this. Was she sleeping? The thought of her distress wrenched his heart, and the knowledge that he was the cause of it set him pacing back and forth between the window and the bed. If only he could break through the boards, lath and plaster that divided them and gather her into his arms. But: 'Don't touch me. I don't want you to.' Oh God, was it for ever? Did she really mean, 'Never again'?

When he came downstairs next morning the first person he saw was Roddy, standing palely in the hall. The dining-room looked like a station buffet, with the breakfast dishes on the sideboard in all stages of disarray.

'Had your breakfast?' Jimmy asked curtly.

'Yes, thank you, Uncle.' Roddy took in the overcoat, the suitcase. *You will leave this house tomorrow.* He asked: 'Are you going away?'

'Yes. Back to London.'

'With Mama and Aunt Poppy?'

'We shall have to travel on the same train.'

In separate compartments. Ladies Only. No Smoking. And it might not be a corridor train.

'Why?' Roddy said. 'What's happened? Is it because of Rose and me?'

Except for Mama's 'You should know better

than to play games like that,' no one had reproached him, yet he felt a heavy burden of guilt.

'You could say so.'

'But we were only playing. Like you and –'

'That's enough of that.'

'Why are you angry?'

Jimmy set down his suitcase. 'Because in Simla you came prying and spying on things that were no business of yours.'

'What things?'

Jimmy ignored him. 'And as if that wasn't bad enough, you had to sneak. You know what a sneak is, don't you?'

'A sneak is someone who tells tales.'

'That's right. They had an unpleasant way with them at Bradwell House, as I remember. Perhaps you'll find that out.'

The child gazed at his hero with tormented eyes, but Jimmy was in no mood to notice.

A vibrating roar and rattle announced George's arrival in the car.

'Uncle George is running me to the station,' Jimmy explained.

The carriage was already waiting for Emily. He wanted desperately to be away before she appeared.

Maud emerged from the desecrated dining-room.

'Goodbye, Maud. And thank you.'

Of Poppy and the station fly there was no sign.

But there was a clatter of hoofs as Jepson rode in. He had been sent to order the fly.

'What's up?' George called with forced jocularity. 'The old horse given up the ghost at last?'

'No, sir.' Jepson dismounted. 'There weren't no point in bringing the fly. They've had heavy snow in the West Country and the line's blocked. There won't be no trains to London today.'

Alice and Bea sat side by side opposite their grandmother as she made her rounds of Croft Amberley. Wilkins was on the box, and Jepson, borrowed for the occasion, on the footplate. On the floor, and on the seat beside Madam, were the good things they had to distribute: bowls of jellied stock and egg custards for invalids; packets of tea and biscuits for the old; two half hams for needy families with many children; barley-sugar twists and striped peppermint sticks for handing out at will.

When the carriage stopped Jepson hurried to open the door and Madam descended, followed by her grand-daughters. The requisite offerings were put into the basket which Jepson carried, and covered over with a white cloth. Then, selecting one small item from another basket which she bore in person, Madam approached the cottage door, with her grand-daughters behind her like train-bearers and Jepson bringing up the rear. She seldom needed to knock; everyone could see her coming; it would not have been Boxing Day if they had not. Men touched their forelocks, small girls curtsied; even women with babes in arms essayed an awkward bob.

Madam was gracious to everyone, remembering names and ages and performance at the village school; enquiring after absent relatives, admiring new babies, and in closeknit families condoling over the inevitable gaps. Bea and Alice had little to do but stand behind her while all this was going on, taking in, in Bea's case with the interest of the unfamiliar, in Alice's with boredom, something of how the poor lived.

They crowded in the one low living-room, which was airless, with small windows, stone-flagged, not always clean, perceptibly smelly, and they all gathered round the fireplace where the fire was sometimes very small. In others it would be crackling and blazing and Madam would nod her head.

'Plenty of wood around for those not too lazy to fetch it,' she observed to her grand-daughters. 'It gives out a good heat, as I expect you noticed, and the wood ash is so good for strawberries.'

Bea wondered how many poor cottagers grew strawberries, but did not like to enquire.

Alice asked: 'Why can they take wood from our land but not hare or pheasant?'

'We have no need of the wood.'

'We don't need the hares and the pheasants. We've always got plenty to eat.'

'That is not the point. The pheasants have been reared specially at considerable expense and have probably escaped from the St Devereux coverts.'

'They need them even less than we do.'

'It is not a question of need. Need does not justify dishonesty, and poaching is a form of theft.'

'What about hunting?'

'There is no question of theft. We don't eat vermin and foxes are vermin.'

'I think foxes are beautiful,' Bea said.

'When did you ever see one, dear?'

'This morning, early.'

She had breathed on the frosted pane and its transparency had revealed a line of tracks in the snow. Following them with her eyes, she had seen a large dog-fox, driven by cold to within the confines of the garden, standing with forefoot upraised and gazing up at her. His legs were black (or wet?) but his russet coat gleamed flamelike against a patch of whiteness; his brush seemed tipped with snow. He was wary but quite unhurried as he turned and trotted on. His movements were quick and economical; he was more like a cat than a dog. For an instant his eyes met hers again in contempt or challenge. With a sudden sideways twist of his body he was gone.

Later that morning, outside the Fox and Hounds public house near Barford, she had scarcely known how to endure the laughter, banter, barking, drinking, that accompanied the Boxing Day Meet. It had been George's idea to take the children to see it. 'It'll get them out of the house,' he said to Maud. He was not hunting himself this season, it was too expensive, but of course he knew everyone there.

' 'Morning, Colonel. Sorry you're not with us. There's a fine dog-fox been seen in Weston Wood. Should give us a good run if we can start him. Probably be crossing your land.'

The Master handed back the stirrup-cup to the innkeeper.

George said: 'I hope you make a kill.'

I don't, Bea thought, I hope the fox outwits

you. I hope he lives and laughs at you.

'Ah, North.' A new voice broke in upon them.

Uncle George almost clicked his heels.

'Good morning, my lord. Lucky the snow's cleared. You'll have a good run, I think. Is her ladyship out?'

Lord St Devereux gestured with his crop to where a top-hatted woman sat slim as a willow wand.

'Can't stop her. Never saw such energy. She was dancing last night till two. We've a houseful – all ages – and the fancy dress ball tomorrow. You're coming, of course? Tell me, shall I recognize you?'

George hoped he wouldn't. He considered his pirate's costume undignified, but Maud had hired it at considerable expense and he was no odder a pirate than she was incongruous as a gipsy. He wished very much that the ball wasn't fancy dress.

The top-hatted lady had joined them. George's heels almost clicked again.

'Good morning, my lady. May I present my niece Beatrix, my nephew Roderick. My daughters you already know.'

Lady St Devereux smiled down at them kindly.

'You must bring all four children tomorrow,

Colonel. We've two staying and they need company.' She turned to Bea and Roddy. 'Come as you are: twentieth-century children. Isn't it fun to be twentieth-century?'

'You're most kind, my lady.' Alice wondered if her father was going to start bowing. 'My wife will be delighted. And I know the children are thrilled.' A warning glance set them nodding agreement.

Rose said: 'We've got fairy dresses.'

Lady St Devereux eyed her golden curls. 'How appropriate. We'll have to put you on the Christmas tree. Yes, Eddie, I'm coming –' this to her husband as the hunt moved off. 'We'll see you tomorrow.' She raised her riding crop in salute and a moment later was gone.

George was quite pink with pleasure. 'So generous. So thoughtful.'

'So convenient,' Alice said.

'What do you mean?'

'She only wants us to keep the other children company – you heard her.'

'Alice, dear, I think that's a little hard.'

Alice shrugged. It was envy that had made her say it – envy of Lady St Devereux and her mount. There she went, sitting as trim as if she and her elegant habit were fused to her horse like the troopers among the lead soldiers that had awaited Roddy under the Christmas tree. Why wouldn't Mama let her learn to ride? She had tried again, quite recently, and Maud, seeing the question coming, had steeled herself to answer this disturbing, challenging daughter as obstinately as she always did.

'Mama, can I learn to ride?'

And be like Lilias – Lilias who had despised her.

'No,' she answered her sister's niece. 'You can't.'

You can't sit proud and high on Farmer Lewis's black hunter that he so loved you to exercise. You can't look down on me with the corners of your mouth turned up in your special smile and say, 'Poor Maud. You're such a rabbit.' You can't.

'You can't.'

You can't hand over to me your portion so that I become Mrs George North of Amberley. This was to be your home. Your children should inherit. I and mine are here only by your favour – the last, unreturnable favour of the dead.

'I was only asking.'

'Yes, dear,' Maud said more gently. 'But you heard Mama say no.'

It was strange, Aunt Maud's prohibition against riding, Bea reflected. She and Roddy had ridden almost as soon as they could walk.

It gave her no particular pleasure, though she loved the horses, but whether in Cossipore or Simla, it was essential exercise. They rode round the maidan in Cossipore, which in the early morning or cool evening was like a local Rotten Row, and in Simla ponies were the only means of locomotion up and down the steep hillsides, apart from rickshaws, and very much more fun. To be unable to ride was a strange gap in Alice and Rose's unbringing, for they lived in the country and there were horses in the stables at Amberley. Seeing her cousin's rebellious face as the hunt moved off, she slipped her arm through Alice's and said:

'Perhaps you should go to the fancy dress ball as a huntswoman instead of a fairy.'

'That's not funny!'

'I'm sorry, I –'

'Come along, come along.' Uncle George was beckoning impatiently. They had seen the Meet, he had done his duty, he was anxious to get home. He shepherded them into the trap (the motor-car would have frightened the horses), gave the reins a shake, and they were off.

Their progress home was much swifter than their slow afternoon progress round the village; Croft Amberley was compact and the distance from one end of its little High Street to the other was barely a quarter of a mile.

'There's only the Bottralls now,' Alice whispered as they emerged from yet another cottage. 'Grandmama always leaves them till the end.'

Bea nodded, uncomprehending, and looked with interest at their last charitable call.

It was a stone cottage like all the others, but standing somewhat apart. Geraniums glowed in the windows. The front garden had an air of neatness despite the straggle of snow. But no one was watching from the window, ready to open the door. When Grandmama knocked there was a slight scuffling, before an old voice called quaveringly, 'Come in.' At the same moment the door was opened – wrenched open – and Grandmama sailed in, not noticing – perhaps ignoring? – the young woman who held herself rigid behind the door.

'Good afternoon, Annie.'

'Oh, Madam.' The old woman sitting by the fireside struggled to rise, sending the comfortable cat sliding from her knees with miauling protest. 'Oh, Madam, I'm so glad you've come. We've been that worried, Mary and me, ever since you weren't in church on Christmas morning. I said to Mary, Madam must be ill. Nothing else would keep her away. Not with Mr Jimmy bringing home his young lady – such a sweet face we thought she had. Depend upon it, I said, there's something the matter with Madam. Oh, I am glad to see I was wrong.'

'Quite wrong, Annie.'

It wasn't really a lie, Fanny thought, she had never felt better. Yesterday's agony was no more than a bad dream.

'I have brought my grand-daughters to see you,' she went on. 'Alice you know, and this is Beatrix, Mr Harry's daughter, home from India.'

Clinging to the arm of her chair, the old woman sketched a curtsey.

Fanny expected but did not enjoy feudality. 'Do sit down again, Annie.' There was no need to be obsequious. She turned to the young woman standing behind them. 'I hope you had a pleasant Christmas, Mary. Girls, this is Miss Bottrall.'

Shrewd blue eyes assessed them.

'Good afternoon, Alice . . . Beatrix.'

Not Miss Alice, Miss Beatrix. She was holding out her hand. Were they to take it? Bea glanced at her grandmother, but Alice had already stepped forward.

'We had a lovely Christmas,' she said, taking the hand. 'Did you?'

Mary Bottrall eyed her with approval. 'I wouldn't call ours lovely,' she said, 'but I got a small joint cheap in Barford and Gran still makes a good Christmas pudding, so we did better than some.'

'Christmas in England is beautiful,' Bea assured her, shaking hands in her turn. 'I've never seen snow before.'

'And wouldn't want to again if you lived here,' Mary said pointedly. 'Not if you've a roof that leaks.'

'Our roof does leak,' Alice said. 'I've seen Papa emptying the buckets.'

'Well, he's only got to have it repaired. But of course if he's not interested in repairing his own property, it's a poor lookout for his tenants.'

Bea had been surveying the living-room. The stone-flagged floor was scrubbed white. There was a skin rug before the range, which had recently been blackleaded. The fire was warm and bright. A kettle simmered on the hob and something sizzled in the oven. Slices of bread for toast lay on a plate, and the toasting-fork by Mary's chair suggested her occupation, as did the face downwards open book.

'What are you reading?' she asked politely.

'Nothing that would interest you.' It sounded ruder than Mary had intended. 'I read aloud to Gran,' she hastened to explain.

Fanny picked up the book without a by-your-leave and put it down quickly. The works of John Stuart Mill. *The Subjection of Women* hardly sounded suitable for old Annie. Or for her grand-daughter, come to that.

'Are you enjoying it?' she asked Mrs Bottrall.

'Oh, Mary reads aloud a treat. She can read as well as the rector, though she don't read the Bible as much as I should like. There's nothing like the Good Book, I tell her.'

Mary said boldly: 'You can have too much even of a good thing.'

'I hope you don't teach your pupils that,' Fanny said; and to Beatrix by way of explanation: 'Mary is a pupil teacher at the village school.'

'I'll be satisfied if I can teach them to read, Mrs North. They can choose their own subject matter. The Public Lending Library in Barford has books galore.'

Fanny noted another of the evils of mass education, as well as the egalitarian 'Mrs North'.

'You mustn't mind Mary, Madam,' Annie Bottrall quavered. 'She knows she owes it all to you, getting her took on the way you did after our poor Hector perished in South Africa.'

Her eyes went to the sepia photograph of the young soldier on the mantelpiece, above the calendar of Queen Alexandra in Court dress. Next to it, in its case, a medal glittered. There was an answering glitter in her eyes.

Fanny laid a hand on her shoulder. 'You can be proud of him, you know. He died for Queen and Country. And it was his own wish to go.'

'It was the Lord's will, I tell Mary. The Lord giveth and the Lord taketh away. But I don't see why he had to take our Hector – not when he'd had his mum and dad as well.'

'Perhaps he wanted Hector to join them,' Fanny said uncomfortably. Why had he taken her daughter? And Lilias? And George's sons? No good came of questioning these matters. Particularly not in front of the young.

'I've brought you a little Christmas cheer,' she said, reverting to practicalities. 'Just one or two things I thought you might like. This –' she indicated the bowl she had set down on the table – 'this is some good beef stock. With a few vegetables it should make you soup for several evenings – Jepson will put the vegetables in the scullery. And here is a quarter of tea and a few of Cook's mince pies –' she was taking the things from Jepson's basket. 'And the girls have each a little offering.'

She pushed her grand-daughters forward and Beatrix presented two pears. Alice held out a tin of mint humbugs. Old Mrs Bottrall beamed.

'It's so good of you, Madam. You don't know how we appreciate it. I said to Mary, Madam's sure to come. That's if she's not ill, I said, and who can wonder with this bitter weather, but I'm thankful to see I was wrong. We shall enjoy it all, shan't we, Mary? God bless you, Madam and young ladies. Yes, dears, you can put the sweeties and the pears down there.'

'No, you can't. You can take them away again.'

Mary Bottrall's voice was harsh.

Alice and Beatrix paused in mid-movement, their gifts poised above the chenille tablecloth. Even Alice, normally so self-possessed, looked to her grandmother for guidance.

'Mary, whatever do you mean?' old Mrs Bottrall said anxiously, struggling to get to her feet.

'Sit down again, Gran, do. How can you bear to take charity?'

'A little kindness never did anyone any harm. Don't listen to her, Madam. She's not quite herself today.'

'No need to distress yourself, Annie. I can see that Mary is a little overwrought.'

'Can you really, Mrs North? How observant of you.' Mary had positioned herself against the cottage door and stood as if barring the way. 'Can you also see that I despise you, you and your charity?'

'I do not propose to argue with you, Mary.'

'Because you've nothing to say.'

'Nothing that can be said in front of my grand-daughters. Come, girls, we must be going home.'

'Yes, young ladies, thank you for calling . . . Miss Alice . . . Miss Beatrix.' Mary swept a mocking curtsey. 'Don't forget your gifts.'

'Don't you like them?' Bea asked, bewildered.

'I don't like charity. And I'm sick of kowtowing – "Madam" this and "Madam" that and "Madam" the other. What's so special about being Mrs North?'

'Take no notice of her, Madam. She's gone clean out of her mind. But I know you're too good to hold it against her. I was saying to her only the other day, if it wasn't for Madam and the Colonel, I said – didn't I, Mary? – we'd not have a roof over our heads.'

'Yes, Annie, I know you're grateful.'

'Oh, I am, Madam, I am. And for the sweeties – my favourites – and all the other things you've brought.'

'Just to make herself feel comfortable,' Mary said fiercely. 'What's charity but the conscience-money of the rich? And she's only rich because she was born so. She's never earned a penny for herself.'

'You wicked girl, where do you get such notions? Not from me. If you read the Good Book more –'

'I'd know how much use God has for riches, wouldn't I, Gran? What is it – "easier for a camel to pass through the eye of a needle than for a rich man to enter the kingdom of Heaven"?'

'Then don't you think rich people need your prayers?'

Bea's remark silenced everyone, but only for the moment.

'They're welcome to them,' Mary retorted, 'for all the good prayers do.'

'That I should live to hear such blasphemy!'

'Oh, be quiet, Gran. We prayed that Hector would come home safe and sound, didn't we, and a lot of notice God took.'

Regret to inform you Private Hector Bottrall killed in action. Mary was twelve again and holding the War Office telegram in her hand, repeating its meaningless words: in action . . . what action? . . . killed in action . . . killed in action . . . killed . . . killed as a hog was slaughtered or a chicken's neck was wrung, as a pheasant was shot, or a rabbit . . . Private Hector Bottrall. Killed.

'Alice . . . Beatrix . . . don't listen,' Fanny commanded. And to Mary: 'How dare you defile children's ears with such wickedness! You are not fit to be a teacher, and I shall so inform my son.'

'If it wasn't for your son my brother would be alive. Oh, I don't mean the Colonel. I mean the other one – your precious Jimmy.'

White-lipped, Fanny turned on her. 'Be good enough to tell me what you mean.'

'In front of Alice and Beatrix?'

'They have heard the slander. Now let them hear the truth.'

'Your Jimmy,' Mary said very distinctly, 'bungled the action in which our Hector was killed. He was supposed to lead a small feint attack of a kopje while all the rest of them went round the other side. But he started out too late. The moon rose, and there it was as bright as day. The Boers could see them crawling up the hillside and they picked them off where they lay.'

Had Jimmy been late in starting? *You've no idea how bright night can be in the veldt . . . Every time a rifle cracked, one of my men died* . . . The two accounts were so close except for that one vital difference.

Fanny said: 'Where did you hear this?'

'One of Hector's friends wrote to Gran, but of course I had to read her the letter.'

'It isn't true.'

‘How do you know?’

‘Jimmy talked to me, told me what happened.’

‘What makes you think he was telling you the truth?’

‘My son does not lie.’

‘Why should my brother’s friend be any different?’

‘The word of an officer and a gentleman –’

‘– is more to be believed than that of a ranker? Pardon me if I disagree.’

‘You impertinent hussy! The sooner you go, the better. I shall speak to Colonel North at once. He will be deeply grieved after all he’s done for you, and letting you have this cottage rent free.’

‘We’re very grateful to you and the Colonel, Madam. There are some as would’ve turned us out.’

‘Conscience-money, Gran, and you know it. What is there to be grateful for?’

‘To think how you’ve always been so good to us, Madam. I don’t know what’s got into the girl.’

‘I do,’ Fanny said. ‘It’s all those books, this reading. A woman’s head’s not meant for it.’

Not a woman’s of a certain class, that is. Above that, it was different. She turned magnificently on her heel.

'Please stand aside,' she commanded Mary, who was still positioned near the door. 'And do not trouble to return to the school after Christmas. There will be no place for you.'

Mary stepped back, making a mocking obeisance. 'Just as you wish, Mrs North. But until your son turns us out, don't you dare set foot in this cottage. And take your charity where it belongs.'

She had gathered up the tea, the mince pies, the humbugs ('My favourites!' 'Hush, Gran, I'll buy you some more') and bundled them back into the basket of the astonished Jepson, who was still standing patiently by the door.

'As for your good beef stock, you can take it with you.'

She had the basin in her hands, and suddenly she sent its contents flying, dowsing Fanny and spattering the girls.

'Perhaps that'll teach you – my last lesson as a pupil teacher.' Her voice was high and unsteady, but she went determinedly on: 'Next time you want to condescend, pick those below you. If you can find anything lower, that is.'

CHAPTER 8

'What is it?'

George's voice betrayed his irritation. It was well known in the household that in his study he was not to be disturbed. This morning of all mornings, after his meeting with Reuben, he was in no mood for interruption, not even interruption by Alice, for whom, as always, exception could be made.

But it was not Alice at the door, it was Jarvis.

'Beg, pardon, sir –' the butler was deferential but determined – 'Miss Bottrall is asking to see you.'

'Miss Bottrall? What does she want?'

'She wouldn't say, sir, but she's very insistent.'

I'll bet she is, George thought. She has always assumed everything to do with the Bottralls to be of paramount importance. But I'll not see her now. I cannot face further argument about that cottage roof. Let her learn for herself that she must make representation to a new landlord. It will soon be nothing to do with me.

'Tell her to go away,' he said to Jarvis.

'I have, sir, but she won't budge.'

'Warn her that if she stays, she's trespassing.'

'I doubt if it'll make much difference, sir. She says she'll wait until you see her.'

'Where is she?'

Jarvis glanced over his shoulder. 'In the hall.'

None of your friendly morning calls at the back door for Miss Mary Bottrall. No cup of tea in the kitchen with Cook and the maids for the likes of her. No, she rang at the front door as if she was gentry, causing Jarvis, who was cleaning silver (Mrs George would entrust it to no one else since the business of the missing cream jug), to wipe his hands, don his jacket, and hurry to open the door.

'I'd like to see Colonel North, please,' Mary told him. She sounded bold but her face looked pinched.

'The Colonel doesn't see tenants without an appointment,' Jarvis replied with satisfaction.

'I know, but this is important, Mr Jarvis. Please!'

Mr Jarvis, eh? It must be important for the little madam to address him like that. And *please*, when it was a plea, not an order. In spite of himself, the butler was intrigued.

Like the other servants, he had heard from Jepson what had happened at the Bottralls' cottage yesterday afternoon. Wilkins, Madam's coachman, lived out, as did Cook and the kitchen maids and the gardener, but Jepson, being young and unmarried, lived in. When he had come down to the kitchen for his tea after returning with Madam and the young ladies, he had been bursting with the news he had to impart. And news of such a startling nature had caused even Jarvis to listen, though he usually considered below-stairs gossip beneath his dignity.

'So what did Madam do?' someone asked in the pause following the climax.

'Stood like a statue,' Jepson said, 'with her face as white as flour and soup dripping off her fur pelisse and running down her skirt in rivers, and she looked at Mary and she never said a word. Old Mrs B. was twittering in the background – "Oh, Madam, what a dreadful accident . . . Mary didn't mean . . . Your hand slipped, didn't it, Mary?" And Mary, she says, "Gran, just sit down and shut up." Well, the old 'un did the first all right – reckon her legs wouldn't hold her – but she kept it up in the background: "I'm so ashamed . . . To think a grand-daughter of mine . . . Oh, Madam, I'm so thankful our Hector isn't here to see it, it would break his heart, it would." And all the time Madam just stood there till I wondered if she'd had some sort of seizure. Then she turned on her heel and swept out.'

'And the young ladies?'

'Miss Bea looked fair frightened, but Miss Alice, she was enjoying it. Her eyes were gleaming, and as for the soup splashes on her coat, I don't think she even noticed them. You know how she is about clothes.'

'It sounds to me,' Cook remarked meaningly, 'as if Annie Bottrall will soon be needing a new home.'

There were murmurs of agreement.

'That foolish girl,' Cook said, 'she should have thought of that before she lost her temper. They'll never keep her at the school.'

'And no one's going to want her in service,' one of the maids put in, smooth as cream but with a hint of sourness, 'when she gets in a paddy like that.'

There was a pause while they contemplated Mary's fate with pity and satisfaction.

And now here she was on the doorstep, and it was *Mr* Jarvis, and *Please*.

'If you'll wait there," the butler told her, indicating the least comfortable chair, 'I'll enquire if the Master will see you.'

Nevertheless, he hesitated before knocking on the study door. The Master had come back with a face like thunder from Barford (and what could have taken him there on the day after Boxing Day?) Even Rastus had been thrust aside, though the labrador's greeting was usually returned with affection. There was obviously something wrong. And Mary Bottrall's visit wasn't likely to improve things. Jarvis knew what the Master thought of her. But he also knew Mary's formidable determination. If she meant to see the Master, she'd stay. And they couldn't leave her sitting on a chair in the hall for ever. He cleared his throat.

'I think, sir, to see her might be the quickest way of getting rid of her. If you can spare the time, that is.'

'Oh, all right, show her in,' George said with weariness. What did it matter now? He could refuse her demands with firmness. They would soon be no concern of his.

He had presented himself punctually at Reuben's office – George prided himself on punctuality – and had been kept waiting half an hour in an ante-room, he supposed to humiliate him. When Reuben emerged to invite him in, the moneylender was even more polite, if that were possible. He hoped the Colonel had had a pleasant Christmas – a family party, of course? He himself was not a family man, not yet, the more the pity, but there was nothing like one's own flesh and blood. It gave a man immortality – he hoped the remark was not offensive – something to fight for, an inheritance to preserve. The Colonel could have no idea how he sympathized with him in his battle to keep Amberley; it was as though he personally was involved. Unfortunately there were difficulties (opportunities) which he had not appreciated when last they met. In his desire to help (himself, of course) he had been perhaps over-generous. He much regretted that the interest rate would have to be raised.

'But that's outrageous!' George protested.

The moneylender spreads his hands. The Colonel could be sure no one regretted it more (less) than he did, but business was business, after all.

'And our gentleman's agreement?'

The Colonel must understand that it was only when he came to look at it during the peace and quiet of Christmas (and to recognize what a desirable property Amberley was, and that it was one he wanted for himself as a first step towards his gentrification) that he became aware of the miscalculation he had made. He was borrowing money to help the Colonel, and interest rates were high. (Conversely, the price of a forced sale would be low, and he had already borrowed the ready money.) The Colonel would surely not expect him to abide by an impulsive undertaking that put his own business at risk. Though if the Colonel preferred, instead of higher interest, they could shorten the term of the loan. (And shorten the time before he had the opportunity to acquire Amberley . . .)

The Colonel did not prefer. In his anger George marched out and slammed the door, stamping down the linoleum-covered stairs with their tarnished brass treads that for too long had never seen polish, and banging the outer door. The oblong light above it rattled, echoing down Dunstan Street still sunk in post-Christmas torpor. He'd be damned, George repeated to himself (he had already told Reuben), if he'd sign an agreement like that. He might as well make Amberley over to him straightaway – the moneylender smiled thinly – and if there was one thing certain in this life, it was that he'd never do that. The moneylender's smile became very thin indeed at this point, but George did not notice. The immediate relief of telling the man what he thought of him had set the adrenalin coursing through his blood, but by the time he reached home reaction had set in: it was all very well quarrelling with Reuben, but he had been the last hope of saving Amberley.

Alone in his study, George fought to accept that an era was coming to an end, not only for the family but for the village. There would be no more Norths at Amberley. The old caring relationship between landlord and tenant, tenant and landlord, had run its course at last.

And now one of the most importunate of his tenants was here waiting at the door, asking – no, demanding – admittance in pursuance of her rights. Well, she would learn that when a relationship broke down, rights had no meaning; they became an empty formula.

When she came in he did not even say good morning, though inbred courtesy forced him to rise. For an instant they stood staring at one another, each startled by the change read in the other's eyes.

Mary said, a little breathless: 'Yesterday afternoon I was very rude to Mrs North – to Madam. I lost my temper and I'm afraid I threw something and ruined her dress. I tried to see her today, but her maid said she isn't seeing anyone. So I came to you. To apologize.'

George was thunderstruck. He knew nothing of the incident, for though he had realized the servants were agog about something, servants often were, and no one would have dreamed of asking the cause of the excitement: it would have been undignified. Alice and Bea had been well and truly scolded for the splashes of soup on their coats, and Bea had got as far as saying,

'It wasn't our fault, it was Miss B . . .' when Alice trod heavily on her toe.

'It was my fault, Mama. I spilt it.'

This was all too easy to believe, and Alice accepted her punishment with unaccustomed meekness: pocket-money to be stopped until both coats had been cleaned.

Afterwards Bea asked: 'Why did you say it was your fault?'

'Because I think she was right.'

'Right to throw the soup?'

'No. Right in what she said about us. Who are we to go round patting people on the head and giving them soup and custard? Why should they curtsey just because we've got more money than they have?'

'She didn't curtsey,' protested observant Bea.

'No, and for that I respect her. At least she doesn't pretend.'

'But it isn't wrong to be rich.'

'Nor to be poor. We're equals.'

'You mean the servants as well?'

'Why not? They're paid to look after us, that's their job, but it doesn't mean we're better than they are.'

This was an alarming doctrine. 'What about native servants?' Bea asked.

Fifty years ago there had been something in India called the Mutiny, still spoken of with horror in Cossipore, where a memorial on the maidan recorded names of officers, their wives and children, slaughtered by servants who did not accept their own inferiority. She and Roddy used the stone obelisk as a marker. 'Race you to the memorial,' they'd say. Suppose the servants once again thought themselves equals? Would there be another bloodbath some day?

'Native servants are different,' Alice pronounced. Were they not heathens? She was always being made to give pocketmoney to church missions. Empire did not seem to have a very civilizing effect.

But Miss Bottrall was neither native nor heathen. She was almost one of them. And she'd be in enough trouble when Papa found out the truth, as he would, because Grandmama would tell him. Anything that served to delay or deflect his anger was a good thing, even if it involved a lie.

'When I grow up I shan't have servants,' she informed her cousin. 'I shall have –' she sought for a word – 'staff.'

It sounded impressive, and Bea nodded. She could imagine Alice with staff. But however hard she tried, she could not imagine what had happened in the Bottralls' cottage after her grandmother had swept out.

She had trailed out behind Grandmama,

wishing she were not there, stepping round the spilt soup as though it were a pool of vomit. Alice, on the other hand, had held her head high, glancing about as though anxious to remember for ever the erect, defiant figure of Mary Bottrall and the old woman whining and fawning in her chair, making repeated attempts to rise and watched with equal contempt by her granddaughter and the black cat who had retreated to the windowsill, where he observed everything through slitted amber eyes. Jepson, bringing up the rear, had closed the cottage door behind them and signalled with a nod to Wilkins on the box, who needed no further bidding but straightaway headed for home.

Within the cottage there was silence for a moment before the old woman burst out: 'You wicked girl! You'll have us both in the workhouse. What devil's got into you?'

When Mary didn't answer: 'Madam'll never forgive you, never as long as she lives. You shouldn't have said that about Master Jimmy. He's the apple of her eye.'

'As Hector was of ours.'

'Yes, but he's dead –' Annie Bottrall glanced at the photograph – 'and wishing won't bring him back alive.'

'I know that, Gran. How do you think it feels to know that if it hadn't been for her precious

Master Jimmy, our Hector need never have been killed?'

Killed in action. Potted like a pheasant, a rabbit. Jimmy North might as well have fired the gun. Master Jimmy out shooting, as he had been so often, with Hector admiringly looking on.

'I don't know about that . . .'

'I do.'

'. . . but I know you've destroyed the roof over our heads. Oh, your wicked tongue. The Colonel will never let us stay here, any more than they'll keep you at the school.'

'I'll get lodgings.'

'And how will you pay for them when there's no wage coming in?'

'I'll get a job. I'll go away. To London.'

'And what's to become of me?'

'They'll not turn you out.' Mary's voice was less confident.

'Oh, it's the workhouse for me. You might as well have cast me out and barred the door against me. To think that I should come to this, when I've always lived respectable and worked hard. You're a wicked girl . . . Here, what are you doing?'

Mary had seized the big black kettle from the hob.

'The Lord above will record your wickedness.'

'Oh, spare me your pious cant. And sit still until I've scrubbed the floor, that soup is greasy.'

'Better I broke my neck than finish my days on the parish. And a pauper's funeral to end it all.'

'It won't come to that,' Mary vowed. She took down a sacking apron. 'I'll go and apologize.'

'Much good that'll do. And Madam so kind to you, getting you taken on as a pupil teacher. I said to her then, Mary'll make you proud. You'll not regret it, I said. And look what's happened. I'll never be able to hold up my head again.'

Mary went on scrubbing. Action was the one solace left her. She scrubbed the whole living-room floor, heedless of her grandmother's protests that her rheumatism wouldn't stand the damp. Only then did she permit herself to think of the vision of the future so luridly presented and to allow that it might become fact.

She had not expected that Madam would see her when she called to apologize, so it came as no surprise to be turned away at the Dower House; but to continue on to Amberley and to insist on seeing George had taken all her courage. As she sat in the hall her heart was beating so wildly she was afraid she would not control her voice, and indeed, when she was shown in after a shorter wait than she had expected and the Colonel rose, unsmiling, unspeaking, the words of apology had come out in a breathless rush.

But the breathlessness was in part due to shock, for the eyes that regarded her held an abyss of misery far greater than her own. She watched his lips move stiffly. 'Thank you, Miss Bottrall. I will convey your sentiments to my mother. Meanwhile I appreciate them.'

She said, without volition: 'What's the matter?'

There was a perceptible pause while George North seemed to be gathering his wits. Or his words. Then he said: 'I have to sell Amberley.'

The words lay like a corpse between them.

'Sell it! You mean – go away?'

'Yes.'

'But the Norths have always lived here.'

The man shook his head as though trying to clear clouded vision. 'That is true, but it won't be any more.'

She sat down, unbidden. Her legs would no longer support her. 'What has happened?'

George looked down at her. Why was he telling this schoolgirl schoolmistress before even his wife, his daughters, except that she happened to be there?

'I am heavily in debt,' he said. The words still meant nothing to him but at least they were uttered, and hung like hot breath on cold air.

'I know,' Mary said unexpectedly, remembering Christmas Eve in Barford. 'You went to Reuben the moneylender. I saw you coming out.'

George bowed his head in shame and assent. Probably the whole village knew by now. Except that the Bottrall girl had always kept herself aloof. 'Stuck up' was the general verdict. But no matter. The whole world would soon know.

'Wouldn't Reuben advance you the money?' she was asking.

'He was only too eager to, but in the last few days he's upped his terms.'

'He's always doing that. Then he buys cheap at forced sales. Did you sign anything?'

'No, I told him to go to hell.'

Mary clapped her hands in approbation. 'If only a few more victims would do the same.'

'That doesn't help Amberley.'

'But it helped you,' she said perceptively. It must have been like letting fly at Madam.

'For the moment,' he agreed. How well she understood. Maud wouldn't have done so, though she'd have to understand the consequences. He tried to imagine telling Maud.

'Where will you go?'

Mary's matter-of-factness made departure seem almost normal.

'Somewhere a long way away.'

'Amberley won't be the same.'

It was true. For the first time Mary realized how completely she and the whole village revolved around the Norths. Her brother, father and grandfather had worked for them, and there were other families who could say the same. Everyone knew the comings and goings at the big house – they saw the carriages pass and Mr Edwards the carrier reported on any unusual consignments. The Norths' births, marriages, deaths, were a part of the village's life. And it was a two-way traffic, for there was little that went on in the village that was not known at Amberley. Mary could tell from the way people looked at her as she walked down the street that yesterday's events within her cottage walls were common knowledge. They would be known at Amberley as well. Indeed, Jarvis's expression as he opened the front door confirmed it. Desperately she had heard herself pleading: 'This is important, Mr Jarvis. Please!'

But she had come to Amberley seeking mercy, which was an attribute of power. Now suddenly that power was broken and there was no mercy to be had, not from this sad-eyed man who stood gazing down at her. This was not the formidable Colonel North. Colonel North drove a yellow motor-car, gave out Christmas presents at the village school (and frightened the children), strode round his estate, gave orders, sent messages, commended, criticized, was never less than confident. This man stood in his own study looking lost and lonely and helpless, like a five-year-old in school on his first day.

'I'm sorry,' she said. She was sorry for both of them.

'Thank you.'

She was even sorrier than he knew, for she had helped to bring about this disaster which was sweeping them both away.

She said, because she wanted to acknowledge it: 'I fired your ricks, you know.'

'Yes.' He had always known it and now she had confessed it. She could go to prison for that. But what would be the point? He was long past thoughts of vengeance or even justice. Instead he asked simply: 'Why?'

Mary found she could not answer. Had it been protest against what he stood for, or an act of petty spite? At the time it had seemed a heroic gesture; now the heroism had gone. In her insistence that she was as good as she was, she had denied that he was every bit as human as she. If she was vulnerable, he was also. This traffic, too, was two-way.

The eyes she raised to his had a new softness. 'It was foolish. I see that now.' When he said nothing, she added: 'Please forgive me.'

He gestured wearily, but still he said no word. Her presence was relief, neither upbraiding nor condemning. If he spoke, the illusion might be destroyed. If he moved, the spell of the present would be broken and past and future would come rushing in.

She put out a hand towards his monumental isolation. He did not notice it until he felt its warmth and looked down wonderingly to see her shoulders shaking. Head bowed, Mary Bottrall wept.

Like most men, George detested tears. He said automatically: 'Don't cry.'

She wept the harder, words tumbling out, incoherent. 'I didn't mean . . . it wasn't you I was attacking . . . unfair of me . . . you've always been so kind . . .'

'Stop it!' He pulled her to her feet with something of the old overlord still in him. 'What's done is done.' He shook her. 'It's my affair. No need for you to cry.'

Through her thin coat he felt the bones of her shoulders. The shoulders too were thin. Her hair was freshly washed and he caught the scent of cheap soap. Without any conscious intention on his part, his arms opened and took her in.

He had just time to think that this was madness before he was submerged in a desire whose existence he only now acknowledged as it surged over its banks and carried him away. All the bitterness of failure, the frustrations of his marriage, found outlet in a long, hungry kiss. And she responded. Her lips were moist and eager. Perhaps it was she who had moved into his arms. All he knew was that she was there, warm yielding woman, her breath quickening in unison with his, the tides of her body rising to meet him, her back arching and straining against his hands.

Seconds, minutes, hours had no meaning. Time lost in the suspension of time. Until some sound he had not registered caused her eyes to open and to gaze past him, widening in recognition and alarm.

His back was to the door, but even as he turned he knew it must have opened.

'Am I intruding?' asked Emily's silken voice.

The girl would have to go. Fanny North was in no doubt of that. She had known it last night when she came in, marching past the astonished Patterson and straight upstairs to her room, and this morning it was no different.

Mary Bottrall would have to go.

Where, she did not know, but away from the village school before her subversive ideas could corrupt the children. And away from Croft Amberley before she could spread her lies and slanders about Jimmy. Responsible for Hector's death indeed! It was like Mary to insist that, whatever happened, the Bottralls were not to blame. It was like her to make the Norths the scapegoats, the people responsible for all her ills. Her nonsense about votes for women was harmless: the impossible could not happen; but this was something else, this was an attack on the Family and on the member of it closest to Fanny's heart.

Yet she was not without a certain sympathy for Mary. The girl had courage; she was no one's fool. A tithe of that character in Maud or Emily would have been welcome. Thank God Jimmy at least appeared to have chosen well. A little polishing would not come amiss there, but that was easily managed. Poppy would be quick to recognize what was needed, and quick to learn. Her visit – the first of many – would be a pleasure, and Fanny looked forward to it.

Meanwhile the matter of Mary demanded consideration, for she had been in no condition to do so last night. In her room she had thrown off the congealed pelisse, the grease-stained dress, and commanded Patterson: 'Burn them!' The maid looked at her in horror so Fanny repeated her order, though the woman was no doubt thinking that the fur would not burn. Well, if she could clean it she could have it, but Fanny never wanted to see either garment again. As Patterson scuttled out with the clothes she found she was trembling. Never in her life had she encountered anything like that. Like the pain, it was an attack, and like the pain too, it was entirely unexpected, whatever warning signs she might with hindsight have perceived. There had been such venom in Mary's voice, the blue eyes had blazed with such hatred. Yet what have we done to her? Fanny thought. George has given them a home; I have found her the kind of job she wanted; even our visit today was prompted by kindness, as old Annie recognized. Why should she hate us so? *If you can find anything lower* . . . What does she think we are? We have never claimed to be gods, but we are certainly not vermin. We've as much right to live as anyone else. Ah, but it's not the right to live that's being challenged, it is the right to live as we do, to accept by custom, income and inheritance the fiefdom of Croft Amberley as our due. Well, Mary Bottrall might challenge it but she would have to live with it. The Norths' line would carry on, through Harry and Roddy if not through George. A pity it couldn't have been through Jimmy. She would have liked to see Poppy's son.

Would have liked? She checked herself sharply. It was defeatist to think like that. In a year or two the child might be among them. And she would still be here, of course she would. That agonized night she had spent was beginning to recede like a nightmare. She had conquered; she would conquer again. Fanny changed her dress and went downstairs proudly. She was still Madam, still a queen, and a queen had one duty: to reign.

By the time she went to bed – and she went early – she was less certain. The exhaustion that overwhelmed her was complete and her confidence was fraying at the edges. When she knelt (stiffly now), as she had done every night since childhood to repeat the Lord's Prayer followed by her own petitions, the usual careful order was gone. God bless us all, especially Jimmy . . . Don't let Mary Bottrall's lies be true, because I have never been sure what happened in South Africa, though I know that something did . . . Send Mary Bottrall away . . . George is looking worried . . . Can Maud be pregnant again? If so, let there be a son to inherit, though of course we have Roddy . . .

Somehow I can never picture him as squire . . . But Jimmy's son, Poppy's son, regardless of whether he ever inherits, I long to hold in my arms. This will be my favourite grandchild. Lord, let me live that long . . .

However long she lived, it did not seem as though Fanny's prayer would be granted. It was after lunch before Jimmy managed to see Poppy alone, or even see her at all, for once again she had stayed in her room all morning and Maud, with a sigh, had had a luncheon tray sent up. It was a depleted family around the table, for the children were taking theirs in the nursery, so Jimmy lunched with George, Maud and Emily in an uncomfortable silence of which only Emily seemed unaware. She really is thick-skinned, Jimmy thought. Instead of embarrassment, humiliation, her face was smugly complacent, especially when she looked at George. George kept his head down, ate little, and excused himself as soon as he decently could. Maud, having exhausted every one of her conversational gambits, looked after him with troubled eyes.

'George is going out shooting,' she said to no one in particular. 'The fresh air will do him good. He spends far too much time shut up in that study.'

Emily purred: 'It's not good for a man

to be so much alone.'

Was there a slight emphasis on the 'alone'? Jimmy eyed her, but her gaze was bland as a doll's. Once he had thought her face expressive. Now her expressions seemed to be donned like masks.

Maud rose. 'I must go and see how Nanny is getting on with the children's costumes. They are so excited about tonight. It is most kind of Lady St Devereux to have included Roddy and Bea in the invitation, but they all ought to rest this afternoon. Don't you think Bea is looking peaky?' she appealed to Emily.

'She has my fair skin,' Emily said.

It's to be hoped that's all of you she's inherited, Maud thought with asperity. Thank God there would be trains to London tomorrow, and the fancy dress ball would see them through tonight.

It was already uppermost in the minds of the children. Alice and Rose could not be kept from trying on their fancy dresses, white with blue stars and sashes, and, in Rose's case, wings. Wings were deemed unsuitable for Alice, who had a way of making such things look ridiculous, but her dress had long, full, pleated sleeves, and when she raised her wand and declaimed the fairy's speech from *A Midsummer Night's Dream*, instilled into her, together with the dates of Shakespeare's birth and death, by Miss Evans, Bea was quite prepared to believe that she could 'wander everywhere, Swifter than the moon's sphere' and to number her dark-haired cousin among the spirits believed in by the Indian servants, because she might at will transport herself to Cossipore or Simla, or anywhere else on earth.

She and Roddy wore pierrot and pierrette costumes, extracted from the dressing-up box and hastily refurbished. Roddy's did not exactly fit, but he was reconciled to it by being told that it had once been Uncle Jimmy's and by Rose's enthusiasm. She stroked the black pompoms down the front, admired the ruff (which tickled), and insisted on trying on the hat. It came down over her ears, and Roddy reclaimed it amid shrieks of laughter in which even Nanny joined. Bea herself fared better – Alice had worn the dress last year, and though it was a little short and the sleeves were tight, the effect was pretty. If only her head didn't ache!

She had wakened feeling heavy and listless, not exactly ill but certainly not well. Nanny had placed an enquiring hand on her forehead, but she wasn't feverish. It was just that everything was more trouble than usual – her limbs seemed made of lead. She had sat on the edge of her bed half dressed long after Roddy had gone down to breakfast, seeing Mary Bottrall's face, hearing her accusing voice. Could the things she said be true? Was Uncle Jimmy really responsible for Hector Bottrall's death? He hadn't killed him; that much was certain; so where did responsibility begin and end? Roddy and Rose were in some way responsible for the unhappiness at Amberley that was sending Mama, Aunt Poppy and Uncle Jimmy back to London as soon as the trains could get through. Aunt Poppy had kept to the second-best spare room all day yesterday, and the maids were grumbling at having to take up so much coal, but since then she had come into the nursery and played board games this morning, and declared her intention of visiting Grandmama in the afternoon.

Would Grandmama tell her about Mary Bottrall? What would Aunt Poppy say? Whatever it was, her view would be different from Mama's and Aunt Maud's – if they knew. Bea, sworn to secrecy by Alice, felt the weight of silence on her head. Which perhaps explained the nagging headache that made the day seem long. The fancy dress ball loomed like a penance; she did not want to go. But an invitation, even casually given, must be honoured once accepted, except in case of dire calamity. And the original St Devereux invitation, which had pride of place in the edge of the morning-room mirror, was like a royal command.

'Mama and Papa are thrilled to be invited,' Alice had explained when showing it. 'The St Devereuxs don't ask everyone, you know.' For all her scathing comments on convenience, even Alice's voice had a tinge of pride in it as she took down the engraved card. On its crested face Lady St Devereux requested the pleasure of Colonel and Mrs North's company at a fancy dress ball to be held at Mawby Hall on Thursday, December 27th, at half past eight o'clock, supper at ten and carriages at half past midnight. And on the back she had written in a dashing, violet-inked hand: 'And do bring Alice and Rose.' 'There are children staying there for Christmas,' Alice explained, 'so we're to have our own small dance, Mama said, and if we get tired we're to curl up on one of the big sofas until it's time to go home.'

The bit about curling up on a sofa sounded all right and Bea smiled wanly. 'I've never been to a fancy dress ball, have you?'

'Not a ball,' Alice admitted, 'only a children's party. This will be much grander. Papa is going as a pirate and Mama as a gipsy.'

'What about Uncle Jimmy and Aunt Poppy?'

'They'll come, but not in fancy dress. At least, they will if they've made up their quarrel.'

'Oh, why is everyone so unhappy?' Bea burst out. 'Your parents are looking wretched. Mama is angry inside, I can tell. Uncle Jimmy and Aunt Poppy aren't speaking. And this is Christmas, the season of goodwill.'

'I suppose,' Alice said cautiously, 'it's because we're human. We're never happy for very long. However hard we try to behave nicely, something always takes over and makes it all go wrong.'

Secretly she was beginning to wonder if this was what Mr Woodward, the rector, meant by Original Sin. What they acknowledged and confessed in church when they said 'there is no health in us.' What we do is marred by what we are. But she said nothing of this to Bea, who was herself looking thoroughly miserable. Instead she said: 'You look pretty in my pierrette dress, Trix.' And added graciously: 'Prettier than I did.'

Bea cheered up a little. 'Mama will be pleased. She's always wanting me to look pretty. I wish I looked like her.'

It was Roddy who had their mother's looks, though he had his father's eyes. Bea did not resemble her mother, a sore point with Emily. She would have liked to show off her daughter; it would enhance her own good looks if people could say, 'That pretty child is the image of her mother.' Unfortunately it was not the case.

But Emily had things more important than Bea's appearance to consider. As she smoothed the velvet folds of her Mary Queen of Scots costume and wondered if the stand-up collar needed pressing yet again before the ball, her mind was busily at work.

There could be no questions now of George writing to Harry about her infidelity. His own indiscretion had seen to that. He would not care for Maud to know of his liaison with Mary Bottrall, for Emily had no doubt but that that was what it was. She had already constructed an entire scenario and was in danger of believing it. That they claimed not to like each other was one of the oldest of deceptions, designed to fool no one but the claimants and a poor unsuspecting ninny like Maud.

After lunch she had again gone to George's study, well knowing he was within. There had been no 'Come in' in answer to her knock, but suddenly the door was wrenched open and George confronted her.

'What do you want?'

'George dear!' A delicate protest. 'A minute of your time, that's all. The hall is so public . . .' She allowed her voice to trail away discreetly and walked past him through the open door.

'What do you want?' he repeated.

'I don't want anything,' Emily said, 'except to make sure that we understand each other. We are birds of a feather, wouldn't you say?'

'Well?'

'I should hate to have to warn Maud of what Madam's pet pupil teacher is up to. Fortunately there will be no need. If I can be discreet, I'm sure you can be even more so.'

'You can't think I'd tell Maud!'

'No, George. But it would be a pity, when Harry is so far away, if distorted and exaggerated stories reached him about my friendship with his younger brother. These things are so easily misunderstood.'

When George didn't answer, she went on: 'I'm sure you agree with me that family loyalty is important –'

George made a choking sound but did not speak.

'– so you can be sure I shall say nothing. So long as nothing is said.'

Blackmail, George thought. This is blackmail. He moved to open the door for her, but still she stood her ground.

'May I have your word that you will say nothing? I will gladly give you mine.'

She held out her hand but he made no move.

'It will take time for a letter to reach Harry,

but Maud could know this afternoon.'

Over the teacups. Pouring poison. Tea sweetened with false sympathy.

'She is a good woman,' Emily went on. 'Such high standards. That vicarage background, of course. If she were more worldly . . .' She shrugged. 'So you'll give me your word, won't you?'

'You bitch!'

'Your word, George.'

After a struggle he said: 'You have it.' And turned to the window.

'Thank you.'

Emily let herself out.

Back in her own room, she congratulated herself on a successful manoeuvre. George's silence was assured. And so far as she was concerned, he could deflower every damsel in the village. It would take the pressure off poor old Maud. Properly speaking, Maud ought to be grateful. After all, it was what whores were for. But Emily doubted if she would be. Her innocence was obstinate. And obsolete.

It was matched by Poppy's, Jimmy might have thought, when at last he cornered her in the hall as she set out, pale but determined, to pay her promised call on Madam, spine rigid and head held high.

He called her name, but she hurried all the

faster towards the front door and was struggling with the bolt, Jarvis being occupied in the kitchen, when Jimmy caught up with her, pinning her with his arms.

'Poppy, you've got to listen to me.'

She gave a hunted look round the hall, and the foxes' masks and stags' heads gazed glassily back at her, deprived by the Norths of life. Yesterday we, today thee. Then, seeing that there was no escape, she went limp and bowed her head before the inevitable, leaving Jimmy to address the crown of her hat.

'I love you, Poppy,' he declared, heedless of who might be within earshot, though in fact nobody was. 'I'd never do anything to hurt you. But that business with Emily was before I knew you. It couldn't happen now because you fill my heart.'

The crown of the hat was unmoved, unmoving.

'Of course there've been other women,' Jimmy went on. 'I'm only human. But I've never felt for them what I feel for you. I never wanted to marry any of them.' He remembered Jacoba. 'Well, only one –'

'The South African!'

'What do you know of her?' Jimmy was startled. Had Emily been telling tales?

'Nothing, except that she existed. When you

came into Edelstein's –' the hat was becoming agitated – 'it was to ask about a picture called "The African Farm". It wasn't a good picture, you'd never heard of the artist, but it meant something special to you. In the picture there was a woman sitting on the verandah, the stoep, you'd call it. There was a woman in South Africa, wasn't there?'

'What if there was?' Jimmy's voice was rougher than he intended. There had been other things in South Africa . . .

'Oh, nothing – now.'

Jimmy seized her chin and lifted her face towards him. The crown of the hat was replaced by the brim and two brimming eyes.

'Poppy, I swear to you this is different. You must believe me. You must! Promise me you'll still marry me.'

He would have kissed her, but she turned her head away.

'I'll never forgive myself for what happened with Emily,' he went on. 'I owed Harry something better than that. But if you knew what torment it is just to remember that it happened, you'd forgive me, dearest. What's between us is too good to spoil.'

'There is nothing between us.'

It was as if she had struck him.

'I don't want to see you again.'

He dropped his arms. 'Do you mean it's all over?'

'It ought never to have begun. I knew that as soon as I came here and saw your family. I could never be one of the Norths.'

'We'll go away,' he said eagerly. 'We needn't see them.'

'No, Jimmy.' She shook her head. 'You're one of them, you see things their way – that's the trouble. We come from different worlds.'

Mum and Dad had accepted Jimmy, but had he really accepted them? She had assumed it because she wanted to believe it, but what if the assumptions were false? 'A nice young fellow,' Dad had called him. She did not know what he had called Dad. Suppose he had laughed at him with that easy condescension that came so naturally to his voice? And what had he made of Mum, who read with difficulty and introduced unorthodox variants into the spelling of her own name?

'You're my world,' Jimmy was saying.

'No,' she said, 'that can't be. Your world isn't mine. I don't belong here any more than you belong in Jubilee Terrace. Surely you can see that?'

'I can see only your face, your hair, your eyes flashing when you ordered me not to touch you.

Believe me when I say there'll be no other woman –'

'Oh,' she said, 'if it were only that!'

'Then what is it?'

'If you can't see it, you can't. And that's just the trouble: you *can't* see it and nothing I can say will make you understand. We're strangers, Jimmy, and you can't marry a stranger.'

'We'd get to know each other,' he said. 'If you prefer, we can have a longer engagement, wait until you're really sure.'

'I'm sure now.'

'Well, then . . .'

He could no longer keep his hands at his sides. They reached out hungrily but she evaded him.

'I mean I'm sure a marriage between us wouldn't work. I dare say I could fit into Amberley if I wanted to, but Jubilee Terrace can't.' The thought flitted through her mind that it would fit very well into the space of the hall and dining-room; at any other time she might have smiled, but Jimmy's miserable eyes forbade it. How could two eyes hold so much pain?

'Leave Jubilee Terrace out of it. It's you I'm marrying.'

'Can you leave out Amberley?'

'Yes,' he said. 'I can. Besides, George is going

to have to sell it. You won't need to come here any more.'

For a second hope flared in her. Then she saw his expression.

'You mind, don't you?' she said.

'It's been our home for generations.'

Our home! Not hers and his. He carried it on his back like a snail, and without it he was nothing. A soft, helpless creature without a shell.

'It's no good, Jimmy,' she said. "I can't marry you. Here.' She gave him back his ring, which had once again slid round so that only the plain gold band was visible. Magically, her hand was free again.

So was her spirit. With a sudden lightness she recognized the fetters at her feet. Ever since she had crossed this threshold the gyves of Northdom had laid about her. Now she was her own woman once again.

This time when she tried the front door it opened easily. The cold air was sweet on her lips. It would be hard telling Madam, but not so hard as going through with the marriage. She dared not look at Jimmy's face.

'Poppy . . .'

From the house she heard his voice call despairingly. From the house. From the accursed house. But he did not come after her as she picked her way across the turning-circle of gravel swept by the gardener that morning, and she did not look back until she heard the front door close.

In the hall Jimmy stood stupidly, her ring glittering in his palm with iridescent fires. She had rejected him. Rejected him not for himself but for what he represented, just as Piet Botha had rejected him all those years ago.

The injustice of it rose up in him like bile.

Boer could not marry Briton.

Even in infinity, it seemed, there were parallel lines that could not, would not, meet.

CHAPTER 9

George was out walking, moving over the land with the long, easy stride which he knew would carry him for miles. The gun nestled in the crook of his arm like a lover. Rooks flapped overhead. Underfoot the thin snow had the delicate crispness of dry toast.

All over Christmas he had been promising himself this: the solace of solitude in the landscape he loved. He had not planned it for this afternoon, but the need to escape from the house, above all from his study, had driven him forth like a hunted fox. One part of his mind took in with a countryman's pleasure the small curled clouds in the sky, the air's keen stillness, the pattern of ploughland and pasture, the blueness of distant hills. The winter sun levelled shafts of light at him, burnishing the boles of trees, intermittently blinding him as he made for Weston Wood. He had chosen it because it lay on high ground along Amberley's western boundary, and from there on a day as clear as this the view would be superb. He wanted very much to fill his eyes with it, imprint it on his retinas for life. For death, rather. Certain it was that we brought nothing into this world, but if we took anything out of it, it would surely be some last loved sight or sound.

This is the day of my death. The thought gave an extra sharpness to outlines, to colours an added depth. Every cell of his body cried out to him that it existed, witnessed, lived. Before setting out he had stood for a moment in his study and tried to imagine what it would be like not to be, but it was no use: everything around him was part of him. When he vanished from the scene, the scene would vanish too. Carefully he wound his gold hunter: it would tick on after he was dead but he could not comprehend it, any more than he could comprehend the sale of Amberley.

By order of the executors . . . desirable property . . . comprising house, extensive parkland, lodge extended and modernized . . . three farms at present let . . . four hundred acres . . . various messuages in the village of Croft Amberley . . . He could picture the sale notices, their heavy black type like mourning but not the sale's reality. Without him, all this was nothing. Without it, he was rather less. The destruction he was about to unleash was infinitely greater than the effect of one shotgun blast on his head.

He had decided against the revolver. Too obvious a suicide and Maud would lose even the mitigation of insurance; it had to look like accident. And it had to be well away from the house so that, whoever found him, it would not be Alice or any other child. He had settled on Weston Wood not only for the view from its summit, but because it would be easy to postulate a fall: a tree-root, a loose stone, inexplicable carelessness with the safety-catch on the part of an experienced and enthusiastic sportsman – the verdict would not be in doubt. He could not spare Maud the loss of her home, but at least he could save her the stigma of his suicide. Neither her dignity nor her piety need be affronted by the manner of his death.

He had not known he would choose today. When he awoke that morning it had been a day like all its recent predecessors, grey with worry but not yet black with despair. It was only when he had stood in the study after his visit to Reuben that the impact had begun to come home. He could neither save his house nor leave it. This was where he belonged. The earth that clung to his boots was his earth, the dead leaves had fallen from his trees. In any other existence I shall be a ghost, George thought; my heart is buried here. Into his mind there crept a vision of the Rev. Stephen Hunsdon, whose heart too had died before him and been buried in a narrow grave under a cross with a trail of marble ivy upon it. *Eheu, filia dilectissime.*

The Rev. Stephen Hunsdon had been a quiet man. He said little, smiled a rare, sweet smile, and divided his time between pastoral visits and the classical authors he loved. When his eyes lighted on Lilias, which they did often, his lips remained unmoved but his face glowed as though his skin were ancient alabaster illuminated from within. So when one bright January morning Lilias Hunsdon rode out alone; and when later Farmer Lewis's black hunter returned lathered and riderless with one boot still in the stirrup, and a frightened search-party set out; and when they found the muddied, bloodied bundle of torn dead flesh and clothing that was Lilias after her horse had dragged her a hundred yards, the Rev. Stephen Hunsdon said no word. He did not cry out, nor rail against his fate, nor curse God, though his voice quavered as he read the Order for the Burial of the Dead, and it broke briefly altogether when he committed his daughter to the earth. But the alabaster had become clay, the light had gone out. For George too the light had been extinguished, and despite the brightness of the day, the world was dark.

A particular darkness lay over the village of Croft Amberley and over the Bottralls' cottage home. If George had believed in witchcraft, he would have said that Mary Bottrall was a witch. How could he have been betrayed into embracing her against his conscious will? If it became known it would hurt Maud more than the loss of Amberley and her diminished status. Mary Bottrall and her grandmother would have to go. Perhaps she could be found a place as pupil teacher in a neighbouring village, or one even further away. Old Annie, of course, wouldn't like it. He could imagine the scene: 'You wouldn't turn us away, sir, would you, from the church with our Hector's memorial brass . . . I said to Mary, the Colonel will understand, seeing as how he's a military man himself, I said. You can be sure he'll see us right. We've spent all our lives in Croft Amberley. We couldn't live anywhere else . . .'

Perhaps old Annie couldn't, but her granddaughter certainly could. She'd have to. The village had contracted; there was no longer room in it for both the Bottralls and the Norths. It was only then that George remembered that there would soon be no more Norths. It was not for him to make decisions about the rent-free cottage and the pupil teacher's post. Death meant an end to decisions. With an amazing lightness of spirit and body, he breasted the next low ridge.

Ahead of him the land rose steadily but his even pace was maintained, spine straight, body resting in the basin of the hips, legs moving rhythmically, independent now of mind or will. Time was measured by his progress over the land and by that of the sun in the heavens, but time was meaningless. Life stretched, like his shadow, behind him; before him was only the brightness of the west.

He might have weathered the humiliation of Reuben's duplicity, the shame of the encounter with Mary Bottrall, but it was Emily's blackmail that had decided him to make an end today. *Am I intruding?* He could still hear her sugar-soft voice. *Birds of a feather* . . . No! He shook himself violently, breaking his even stride. There was no way he would be bracketed with Harry's wife – poor Harry! – nor risk her distressing Maud. A man who had sunk to the point where he was prey to his own passions, to Emily and Reuben, was better out of the way. A swift, sure death – he avoided calling it a clean one – had more to commend it than the grimy toils of life.

After Emily had gone he had made his way to the lobby between the kitchen and the back door where mackintoshes and boots, walking sticks and game bags, huddled in glorious disarray. He had told Maud before lunch he might try to bag a pheasant, but now he was after bigger game.

Seeing him with his gun, Mrs. Roberts called out from the kitchen, 'Going shooting, are we, sir?'

'Yes, got to replenish the larder,' George responded.

'That's right. It's a fine day, and you've a couple of hours still of light.'

And then the everlasting dark . . .

'I'll try for a brace of pheasants,' George promised.

Back came the answer: 'They'll do fine for next week.'

Next week . . . Next week, George thought, the household will be in mourning. Black had never suited Maud. Alice . . . He shied away from thoughts of his eldest daughter. Today week might be his funeral. 'Suddenly, the result of an accident' – he saw the black-edged mourning cards – 'George John North, eldest son of the late John North of Amberley, and of Fanny North; dear husband of Maud and father of Alice, Rose and Louisa.' And of John, George and Humphrey North, those three non-beings with whom he would soon be united in that squared-off plot of churchyard cordoned with low iron chains. *Requiscat in pace.* But first dying was necessary. George heard himself muttering: 'May I die in peace.'

He had seen death, death in bed and death in battle, but no man lived to tell the tale of that ultimate experience. Each death was individual and complete. When he reached Weston Wood he would seek out a favourite tree-stump on which he sometimes perched as on a shooting-stick to enjoy the view, rest the gun between his knees, muzzle uppermost, open his mouth and accept its lethal kiss. The double-barrelled metal tongue would be a last lover's, his hand on the trigger a final caressing embrace. And the view – perhaps that at least he would take with him, for at this spot where the scarp escaped from the woodland the view was breathtaking. To the west, the sea and the Severn, and beyond that the faint hills of Wales; to the north, the humps of the Malverns bisecting the arc of sky; to the east, the railway line snaking to London; to the south, the lowlands declining steadily into Salisbury Plain. All his life he had come here to draw strength from that vision, feet planted firmly on his own ground. Now that ground was cut away, though its earth would soon receive him. Now there remained only the taking of farewell.

He had avoided his family. There would be no goodbyes seen later as meaningful. Only to Rastus had he said the word. At sight of the gun the dog had bounded up eagerly and stood panting and wagging his tail.

George shook his head. 'Not this time, old fellow.'

The tail continued to wag.

'No.'

The tail slowed like rundown clockwork. The trustful eyes gazed at him, hurt.

George patted the dog's head and the tail started up again with vigour.

George said: 'No. I told you, you can't come.'

And because he could no longer bear that look of troubled, helpless love, he said, 'Goodbye, old fellow,' and shut the door upon a pleading whine.

He crossed the garden, tended well by Hector Bottrall's successor, and went out by the wicket gate which was the short cut into the paddock where in summer the horses grazed. A glance back at the house, foursquare in the winter sunlight, and he was striding out, squire for the last time of his domain. The trees rained a few late leaves upon him, the light wind lingered on his cheek. Goodbye, house and inmates and garden. Goodbye, trees whose new leaves he would not see.

At the end of the paddock he skirted a ploughed field. The autumn ploughing had gone well that year. Under the moist earth the winter wheat was already germinating – to be harvested by whom? He must tell them when they ploughed the forty-acre that he wanted that too under wheat. Tell them? He would not be here to tell them. Goodbye, wheatfields, goodbye.

In the lane he encountered Dick Sparrow from the smithy.

‘ ’Afternoon, sir. Not out for a spin?’

‘Mustn’t lose the use of my legs,’ George riposted. He would lose it soon enough.

‘Motor-car going all right?’

‘Never better.’

‘Ah.’

George sensed the lad’s disappointment. He was fascinated by the car, and would have spent every spare moment on it, buffing its leather upholstery, polishing its brass lamps, if he could find nothing mechanical that needed doing.

‘Don’t suppose a check-up would hurt it,’ George suggested.

Dick grinned broadly. 'I'll be along, sir.'

'Right,' George said, moving on. 'Up to you.'

He wondered if they would call Dick at the inquest as the last person to see him alive. As a person to testify that his thoughts were on practical matters, that he did not seem bent on suicide. He hoped Maud would have the sense to entrust the sale of the car to Dick Sparrow; he would know best what to do, where to sell and who might buy it. Goodbye, Dick. And car.

The lane dipped towards the woodlands. Already lambs' tails had formed on the hazel bushes in the hedgerow. The village children gathered nuts every year. Hazelnuts to eat and bright, shining horse-chestnuts that they baked to victorious hardness for the game of conkers. One year, the year he was ten, as old as Roddy, he had beaten all comers with a conker baked bullet hard. Another year he had been marbles champion of the village, and, already respected as the young squire, had glowed with pride at the village lads' acceptance of him as one possessing expertise in his own right. They had clapped him on the back in easy comradeship. Surely no later accolade had meant so much. But no son of his would ever know that pleasure. A goodbye to childhood.

In the woods in spring were wild daffodils,

tinged with the greensickness of girls. He had gathered them one year with Lilias. He had never come here with Maud. Lilias had taken off her hat in the warm spring sunshine and the March breeze had ruffled her hair. He had put out a hand, removed a vital pin, and all at once it cascaded about her shoulders and he was drowning in its soft waves. He would know that scent even on the other side of the tomb. Would he have the chance to know it? Would Lilias be waiting there? No. Either he was nothing or he would be everlastingly barred from her by the sin of suicide. Yet some memory of that scent had stirred in him that morning as he took Mary Bottrall in his arms, some base note not unfamiliar . . . Goodbye, Lilias, a long goodbye.

The thing to do when contemplating one's own death, George decided, as he followed the path upwards through the trees, was to dissociate oneself, become a detached observer as if on a reconnaissance patrol. So: you were observing a man, well-built, healthy, in his forties, clad in Norfolk jacket, breeches and tweed cap, his gaiters polished to barrack-room brilliance, his gun at the approved angle, carried easily. Only the safety-catch was off and the gun was loaded – unforgivable carelessness – and the sportsman had shown no interest when he had flushed a pheasant. This man was all outward presence and inward absence, his mind in such a whirl that random thoughts spun off at tangents. Alice . . . how she would grieve. Lulu, his youngest – would she even remember him? Who would look after them now? Who would look after Nanny Cardew? Would his mother find her a new post? . . . The Mater . . . He ought to have called to enquire how she was after that scene with Mary Bottrall yesterday . . . Mary, silly girl, firing his ricks to no purpose. Mary of the pliant body, scented hair . . . That leak in her cottage roof – someone else would have to see to it . . . What about the leak at Amberley? How much would the new slates cost? If he sold the car would there be enough money to pay for it? But it would not be for him to sell the car . . .

This man's thoughts come back to himself like homing pigeons. He is self-centered, egocentric, as these psychoanalysts now say. New jargon for an age-old condition. There are a thousand blowflies buzzing in his head. And later round it? No, not in this weather. The frost will come again tonight, and with it weasels, foxes, the predators of Weston Wood. Who will find him? Farm hands? Jepson? Dick Sparrow, enlisted in the hunt? Who will tell

Maud? Will she not have guessed already when he fails to return at dusk? Lilias would have guessed, might even have prevented him. Alice . . . The man does not want to think about his child's distress.

So he steps out more briskly as the trees start to thin. You have to hurry to keep pace with him, your heart is pounding, and ahead of him is a lake of fire. Sun and clouds, refractions, reflections, winter sunset on the last day of the world. You know this man's thoughts as if you share them. You saw him note the tree-stump where he will sit. You know how he will position the gun, lean forward shyly as if embracing it.

But first he walks to the edge of the escarpment where the land falls away. You stand beside him, sharing his vision. You can hear him panting in the still air. This is his home, his fief, his kingdom. Like him, you know it can never pass away. Heaven and earth shall pass away but the unchangeable remaineth, and Now is the instant of eternity.

He turns. You turn. The ground is slippery on this exposed western slope where the snow lies unmelted by the late sunlight. He slips. You stumble. Recover. Stagger. Fall, you're falling. Suddenly the gun goes off. A cry. A flash – gunflash or dying sunset? Blackness or shadows of night? Death or life?

You know only that this man is about to discover . . .

A pheasant whirrs up in fright.

'You may get down now.'

Nanny Cardew's order of release was greeted with relief in the nursery. The children had not enjoyed their lunch: Bea because a low, nagging headache made her long only for peace and darkness; Alice because she was bored, caught in the lull between tonight's ball and its excitements and the outcome of Mary Bottrall's outburst yesterday. Could Uncle Jimmy really be responsible for the death of Hector and others? It seemed unlikely, but Mary Bottrall had sounded so very sure. What would become of her now that she had said aloud the unspeakable, had lifted her hand against Grandmama? It was difficult to decide whether her situation would be better helped by the proven truth or falsehood of her accusations. On the one hand, it was wicked to tell lies. On the other, the truth was more difficult to dispose of. Alice decided she would have to consult Papa. If he knew what had really happened in the cottage, as opposed to what she said had happened, surely he would find some way of dealing with the situation. Papa could deal with anything. Except Mama, of course, and her fiat against riding. Today would be a perfect day to be out, clear and sunny, with just that hint of frost and the going firm but not heavy. She leaned backwards, imagining the movement of a horse.

'Don't tilt your chair, dear, it's dangerous.'

'So is riding,' Alice said.

'Well, I'm glad we see that at last. Your mama knows what she's talking about, so just you remember it.'

'I shall ride,' Alice said confidently. 'Some day.'

'Yes, dear. They say pigs might fly.'

'I can fly,' Rose interrupted. 'I'm a fairy.'

'Not off that chair, dear, if you please.'

Really, the children were a handful. Miss Bea sickening for something by the looks of her; Miss Alice at her most obstreperous; Miss Rose over-excited, bless her heart. With those wings on her fairy costume, they'd have to watch she didn't launch herself down the stairs. As for that Master Roddy, sitting there so glum-faced, they'd be rid of him the day after tomorrow, and not a minute too soon. Not from what she could make out from the other servants. Up to shenanigans with Miss Rose, and her as innocent as a babe newborn and him as ought to be. It was disgusting, that was what it was. But what could you expect, brought up in India among all those heathens? Mr Harry was quite right to be sending him home to school. Meanwhile he'd not get near Miss Rose again, not if she could help it . . .

She said briskly, 'You'd all better have a nice rest this afternoon.'

Only Bea went unprotesting, but Nanny was not to be gainsaid. One by one they were bedded down and the Venetian blinds adjusted against the afternoon sun. Alice had secreted a book, so she was prepared to allow her spirited objections to be overcome, well knowing that once the obedient Rose was sleeping she could settle to the luxury of a good read. Only Roddy, less forethoughtful, less versed in subterfuge, found himself wide awake, unable to relax in even the semblance of torpor while the bright winter day beckoned outside.

Cautiously he dressed again and opened the door to the landing. Nanny Cardew was nowhere to be seen, having retired to the kitchen to discuss with Mrs Roberts the significance of Mary Bottrall's morning call. 'Mr Jarvis said she looked pinched when she came,' the cook informed her, 'but you should have seen her when she ran out of the house. Her face – well, scarlet wasn't the word for it. I never thought to see that one embarrassed, but my word! the Colonel must have told her off good and proper, and not before time, I say.'

'She'll not be able to stay at the school now,' Nanny said, accepting tea and a biscuit, 'but what's to become of her I don't know.'

'It's education what's done it,' Mrs Roberts averred with feeling. (She would have been flabbergasted to learn that Madam agreed with her.) 'Annie Bottrall's only herself to blame, wanting her grand-daughter to be a pupil teacher instead of putting her in service like everyone else. Here, you've only got a plain biscuit – try one of them fancies.'

Education, or the prospect of it, was at the root of Roddy's restlessness. On January 10th the spring term at Bradwell House opened. It was barely two weeks away. 'Pity you couldn't have started in the autumn,' his father had told him. 'There'd have been other new boys then. As it is, you'll have to make the best of being on your own. Stand up for yourself – don't let 'em bully you. You'll settle down soon enough.' It didn't sound like it. It sounded terrifying. And the visit to Bradwell House had been worse. The headmaster in tweeds, exuding horrendous avuncularity; the other masters, shiny suits concealed by gowns and indifference by politeness, except where a gleam of genuine interest showed through; the matron, female presumably in gender but otherwise distinguished only by her skirts; the chilly, chalk-dusted classrooms; the dining-room with its boiled cabbage smell; the other boys, of whom there seemed to be thousands, of every conceivable shape and size but individually indistinct, herd animals with all the suspiciousness of the herd. No one had smiled, though one or two had made faces behind the headmaster's back. Roddy, uncertain how to respond, had stared at the floorboards and tried to forget the high wall with spiked railings on top of it which circumnavigated the grounds. It seemed impossible that his father, Uncle George and Uncle Jimmy should ever have been incarcerated in this place, have known its rituals, partaken of its traditions, and emerged like their fellow pupils with the three Rs, some acquaintance with Latin declensions and conjugations, and a thorough grounding in cricket and deviousness.

It seemed impossible, yet as Roddy crept down the stairs, avoiding the creaking tread as Rose had taught him, he caught sight of Uncle Jimmy in the hall and was immediately struck by his uncle's dejected shoulders. He looked as lost as Roddy felt, gazing at the front door as though it were indeed the front door of Bradwell House imprisoning him, and he a new boy abandoned on his first day.

To Jimmy, the front door represented a full stop in his existence. It would open easily enough, but only on Poppy's retreating back, her firm indifference to any plea of his. He could not stand there and watch her walk away from him. He preferred to look at the door, at the letter-box with its glass window to reveal the presence of letters and the sliding wooden door above for their removal; at the double front door itself with its frosted glass panels, penny plain in the centre and twopence coloured round edge. He preferred to stand there and see Poppy imprinted upon it, as if, so long as he stood still, her image would remain, her voice echo.

Roddy's voice was the most unwelcome in the world.

'Good afternoon, Uncle.'

Jimmy turned to look down on his small betrayer.

'Good afternoon.'

'Are you going out?'

'Yes.'

'For a walk?

'Yes.'

'Can I come with you?'

'I'd rather be alone.'

'I wouldn't talk or anything. You could

pretend I wasn't there.'

'You don't listen, do you, Roddy. I said I wanted to be alone.'

The child withdrew to the foot of the staircase.

'Uncle Jimmy.'

'What?'

'What do they do to sneaks at Bradwell House?'

'They lock 'em in the coal hole with rats and spiders,' Jimmy began, inventing savagely before catching sight of Roddy's stricken face. 'No, that's not true,' he corrected himself. 'They don't do anything very much. There's no occasion to because nobody sneaks.'

'I didn't mean to.'

'I don't suppose you did.'

You don't even know what you've done, and there's no way I can tell you.

'If I were you,' Jimmy continued carefully, 'I'd keep my mouth shut in future about what I saw around me, especially anything between a man and a woman. Things aren't always what they seem.'

And sometimes they were. Poppy would no longer have him. The fact stood as a withered tree in a green landscape. She had returned his engagement ring. If he had only been able to take her in his arms, would she have yielded, or would the gulf that had opened between them have grown ten times as wide? Or had it always been as wide and he too blind to see it? Had old Piet been right when he said that Briton could not marry Boer?

'Are things as bad as they seem between you and Aunt Poppy?' Roddy enquired anxiously.

'What's that to do with you?'

'I like her,' Roddy said. 'We all do. Please marry her.'

'You'd do better to ask her to marry me.'

'I will if I see her.'

'No, for God's sake keep out of it. Don't meddle with what you don't understand.'

Roddy understood very well that his uncle was unhappy. He sought for something comforting to say.

'My father says Mama is as changeable as a weather-vane,' he offered. 'Perhaps Aunt Poppy will be too.'

'Perhaps.'

Poppy the steadfast, whose honest eyes were as incapable of dissimulation as they were of compromise? No, there was no hope there and no use dwelling upon it . . . He became aware that they were still in the hall, that Jarvis had begun to shuffle in the background.

'Shall we go for that walk?' he said.

Once outside, Roddy set off eagerly down

the drive but Jimmy checked him.

'Not that way. We'll go up through the woods.'

Roddy loped after him obediently, unaware that they were thus avoiding the Dower House.

'This was my favourite walk when I was your age,' Jimmy told him. 'There was always so much to see.'

The first bluebells; the green flash of a woodpecker; the almost audible rising of the sap, plumping buds and unclenching leafy fingers; a squirrel's spiral ascent and splayed leap from trunk to trunk. Each year the miracles were renewed, no less miraculous for being expected, no less satisfying when found. The Easter holidays were one long voyage of discovery and rediscovery. Roddy would never make that voyage.

Looking down at his nephew trudging beside him, Jimmy said, 'You mustn't judge it now. In a few months' time it'll all look different.'

Even though it won't be ours to roam . . .

'Like when the monsoon comes.'

When the brown dust was laid by the first downpours and grass sprouted overnight on the maidan; when Mama who had complained about the dry heat complained about the humidity, and Papa said it was time they left for the hills. Everything in the hills was different:

the sharp, pine-scented air, the freshness of the early morning, the sudden surge of energy which made expeditions by pony imperative, attended by parents, syces, bearers, picnic hampers and other paraphernalia of exploration. Roddy had revelled in every minute, every second. It was a far, far cry from this.

'Do you remember when we went riding in Simla?' he asked his uncle.

'Yes, of course. It was good fun, wasn't it?'

Especially knowing that in the afternoon there would be a rendezvous with Emily in the swing on the verandah . . .

'Do you suppose they'll let me ride here in the Easter holidays?'

'Why shouldn't they?'

'Aunt Maud doesn't like it. She won't let Rose and Alice ride.'

Of course. That sister of hers who'd been killed. George's fiancée. What would it have been like at Amberley if he'd married her instead of Maud?

'A lot of things will have changed by Easter.'

'Do you think so?'

'I'm sure of it.'

You won't be coming here, for one thing. There'll be no ponies to ride. We're about to take a step downwards in the English social system and see how things look from the other side.

'It's a long time till Easter, isn't it?'

'A little over three months.'

Twelve weeks. Ten of them at Bradwell House. It was a life sentence.

'Uncle, did you like it at school?'

'Yes,' Jimmy said, truthfully. 'And unless I'm much mistaken, so will you. You enjoyed *Stalky and Co.*, didn't you?'

The Kipling volume had been his last birthday present to the boy.

Roddy quoted, grinning, ' "I cat, thou cattest, he cats." '

'Yes, well, we hope you won't throw up, but Stalky and his friends Beetle and M'Turk aren't so very different from Roddy North and *his* friends, and you'll have similar fun. You'll learn the secret language – all schools have one, though I expect Bradwell's has changed since my day – and you'll take part in all sorts of new activities, make new friends, and then go to a bigger school where you'll do the same thing all over again from the bottom.'

'And then go into the Army.'

And do the same thing all over again from the bottom. It seemed the ultimate in futility.

'If that's what you want to do.'

'I want to serve the King – Emperor, like my father.'

'The King, perhaps. Not the Emperor.'

'But they're the same!'

'Not inseparably. Have you ever thought what we mean when we talk about a country being red on the map?'

'We mean it's a British possession.'

'Which means it's red with blood.'

'Whose?'

'Ours and theirs.'

We have that much in common. The debt of Empire is always written in red.

'My father says our native troops are some of the best in the world,' Roddy said proudly.

'Is that a reason why they should die for us and our causes which have nothing to do with them?'

'They wouldn't die. We'd win.'

If might is right, and so long as we don't encounter a foe with similar convictions and superior firepower. Or one where right breeds might. Like the Boer farmers, who hadn't been a warlike tribe but peaceable, hardworking settlers until driven to take up arms. 'What benefit have you brought this land but bloodshed?' Piet Botha had demanded. 'What legacy do you leave but bitterness?' Sickened by both, Jimmy had not attempted an answer, but had sailed for yet another cornerstone of that Empire on which the sun never set.

'We won in South Africa,' Roddy reminded him.

'Did we?'

'You know we did. You were in the war.'

Which is to say I have deaths on my conscience. One in particular.

'It must have been fun, fighting battles.'

No, it wasn't fun. I was scared, and so were most of the men, Hector in particular. His teeth were chattering with fright, and I thought what a fool I'd been to let him follow me because of some faithful retainer nonsense. I should have made him go back to his beloved garden. Hector grew things – he didn't kill. Until that last mad outburst when he ran amok for my sake and has his name engraved on a brass tablet in the church as a result.

'I hate fighting battles,' Jimmy said.

'Cousin Alice says Miss Bottrall's brother was killed in a battle in South Africa.'

'He was. I saw him die.'

'I've never seen anyone die.'

'You will if you go into the Army.'

And it won't be like you think. Not everyone dies cleanly from a bullet. Some of them take days to die. And some aren't recognizable afterwards. Like Hector.

'Was Miss Bottrall's brother very brave?'

'Yes, he deserved a VC if ever a man did.'

'Why didn't he get one?'

'I don't know.'

'It's unfair.'

'Of course it is. There are brave men in all ranks. And on both sides.'

'But the British are bravest.'

'If you think so.'

If bravery has anything to do with winning wars. In South Africa it had been a matter of supplies, logistics. To begin with, the Boers had had the upper hand, living off the land, masters of the terrain, accustomed to the climate, while the British, red-coated, red-faced (how appropriate was that derisive nickname *rooineks*, rednecks) had blundered about in their close formations like unwieldy dinosaurs. And their big guns, for all the powerful new explosive lyddite, were useless against scattered farms, Boer laagers which could shift under cover of darkness, an enemy who too often announced his presence in ambush by a volley of whistling death. But in the end money – Kimberley's diamonds, the goldmines of the Rand – had bought in supplies of food and weapons while the Boers' supplies were diminishing of both. In vain their women and children worked the farms, carried food and messages to their menfolk, warned them of troop movements, of trainloads of supplies.

The British merely rounded up these dangerous auxiliaries and concentrated them in barbed wire camps.

'My father says the British never butcher women and children.'

'Your father is absolutely right.'

But there are other ways of letting them die: neglect, starvation, inadequate medical facilities. Many women and children had died through maladministration in the British concentration camps, Piet Botha's sister among them – a fact he flung in Jimmy's face.

'Do you think I'll see you marry her daughter,' the old man had shouted, 'when your countrymen murdered her?'

'Not murdered, surely.'

'Yes, murdered. What else is it to let a woman die of cold and filth and typhus and British indifference?'

'I accept the charge of neglect, but not of murder.'

'Save your hypocrisy, Englishman. I tell you, you have unleashed an evil on the world and you will live to rue the day your concentration camps were ever invented. My Anneke's Jacoba is not for you or the likes of you.'

And indeed the tear-sodden Jacoba had been sent hastily to a nearby farm until the representative of the murderous race of rednecks had been banished to whence he came. 'Tell me about her . . .' Emily's voice in the afternoon stillness had been seductive, inviting, but there was really nothing to tell. A kiss, a tenderness, a memory gently fading. Whereas the loss of Poppy was like tearing out his heart.

Roddy, tiring of the subject of warfare, decided to take his uncle into his confidence on other matters.

'When I grow up,' he informed him, 'I'm going to marry Rose.'

It certainly looked as if you were that way inclined on the dining-room window-seat, Jimmy reflected. Aloud he said, 'Does she know?'

'I expect so. I haven't actually asked her.'

'Girls usually know these things.'

'They're nice, aren't they? Girls, I mean.'

'Most boys think so.'

'I think I like Rose better than Bea.'

'Not better, Roddy. Differently.'

'Bea's all right for a sister, but with Rose it's as if I'd already told her everything about me, even things I never have.'

'I know the feeling.'

Acceptance. Of being loved for what you are. So that you want to do only what is worthy to be accepted, while knowing acceptance is there for whatsoever you do. Or you thought it was, until the moment of awakening and the bitter closing of a front door, when you discover the acceptance was not of you but of a false god made in your image and now thrown violently down.

'Of course,' Roddy went on, 'it will be ages before I can marry Rose. I shall have to grow up, become an officer . . .'

'How far ahead are you thinking?'

Roddy extended his mind to infinity.

'Oh, another ten years.'

A decade hence. 1917. What would England be like then? Jimmy shaded his eyes as if peering into the future, but it was against the brightness of the sun. Their path, which climbed the escarpment, had left the woods behind. The sunset tinged everything with transient glory but mortal eyes were unable to accommodate to such splendour. They were bedazzled. Doited. Blind.

'In 1917,' Jimmy said, 'you'll be twenty and I'll be forty-two.'

'If you hurry up and marry Aunt Poppy, you could have a son who'd be as old as I am now.'

'So I could. I hadn't thought of it.'

In 1917 what shall I teach my son? But I dare not think that far ahead. Let me get through today, the journey to London tomorrow, the last sight of Poppy as she walks out of my life. At that first sight of her in Edelstein's Gallery I was struck by her graceful movements and the swing of her hips as she walked. It will be the last thing I shall see as I watch her retreating figure hastening towards the exit at Paddington.

'Rose and I are going to have lots of children,' Roddy stated.

'I'm glad to hear it,' Jimmy said. Though I can't see the boy beside me grown into a solid citizen and paterfamilias.

'You can be godfather to one of them, if you like.'

'Thank you. May I think about it?'

Roddy nodded his head in an airy, dismissive gesture, and at that moment a shot rang out.

Both froze as the echoes ricocheted across the valley.

'Someone out shooting,' Jimmy said.

Indeed a pheasant had flapped into headlong flight but no second or third shot followed. Surely that had been a cry?

'It came from up there,' Roddy said, pointing to the ridge above them, confirming Jimmy's fears.

'That's Weston Wood. So whoever it is who's out shooting is shooting over Amberley land.'

The silence was suddenly sinister.

Jimmy said, 'I think I ought to go and see if

– if he's all right. You stay here, Roddy.'

The boy shook his head vigorously. Nothing would have induced him to stay alone in the gathering darkness which clawed upwards from the valley floor. At least the hilltops were still bathed in the golden light of evening, tinged now with sunset's blood.

'I'm coming with you,' he said. But Jimmy had already started, striking out diagonally and forsaking the path.

Higher up the slope there was a patch of darkness which resolved itself into the figure of a man. Jimmy felt himself sweating. I have been here before. It is not the first time I have seen a body sprawled on a hillside, lying so very still. Nearer. He must go nearer. This time there were no grenades. Hector had been unrecognizable, but this was only one shot. He could see the back of a Norfolk jacket, and breeched and gaitered legs . . .

Norfolk jacket . . . breeches . . . gaiters . . .

Suddenly he heard his own voice crying, 'George!'

'What is it?' Roddy called, panting and scrambling behind him.

Careful. Don't let the boy see it. He's never seen anyone die.

Jimmy moved to block Roddy's progress. 'Uncle George has had an accident.'

His mind moved with exceeding slowness but the natural world was slower: a leaf sank earthwards from a tree and in that time his thought had encompassed present, past and future: the causes and effects of tragedy.

He put a hand on Roddy's shoulder and spun the boy around.

'Run home as fast as you can, and tell –' he faltered, seeking a henchman – 'tell Jarvis the Colonel has had an accident with his gun. An accident,' he repeated. 'He should send Jepson to fetch Dr Paget and come himself at once, with two men from the village to carry the Colonel home. Tell them to bring a hurdle, or something similar.' And as the boy still hesitated: 'Go on, Roddy, run!'

He gave him a shove, and thus impelled, the young dispatch-runner sped off with the aim and swiftness of an arrow, leaving Jimmy to turn back to that patch of darkness which lay unmoving on the hillside, bathed now in sunset glow. Heart thudding, a taste of bile in his throat, slipping, sliding on ice and stumbling over tree-roots, he set off to where George, his own brother, lay face downwards in reddening snow.

CHAPTER 10

'No, Patterson, I told you to use the best china.'

Fanny North surveyed her afternoon tea-table with a frown. Beside her, Patterson frowned also: it looked good enough to her. The Coalport was very pretty and was always used when Mrs George came to tea (Mrs Harry was never there to be invited), so what was special about today? Not the guest, for gossip from Amberley had it that Mr Jimmy's young lady was pleasant enough, no side to her, not like Mrs Harry, but not quality. Why use the best tea-service for her?

Fanny could not have explained, but she sensed this afternoon's visit was important. She was entertaining a daughter – something she had not done since Lilias had died. So the Crown Derby, which she had brought with her to Amberley all those years ago and which normally reposed in a china cupboard and was taken out and washed twice a year, was to be used as an outward expression of something inwardly significant. It would grace the best afternoon tea-cloth with its six-inch edge of crochet lace. Its wide, shallow cups would hold tea, Indian or China, and its doilied plates a selection of postage-stamp-sized sandwiches and a good Madeira cake – none of those ridiculous choux buns and squares of Genoese pastry that Maud went in for at her At Homes; Fanny believed in a cake you could cut and come again. The wrought-iron tea-kettle stand beside her chair was already filled with methylated spirit which Patterson would light when she brought in the kettle of hot water; the silver knives and pocket-handkerchief napkins were posed beside each plate. With a sigh, Patterson now prepared to dismantle this setting, reflecting that Madam was on edge today.

It was true, and Fanny knew it, the edginess occasioned both by Poppy's visit and by a brief return of the pain. It had been no more than a knife-thrust twice or thrice repeated, but it was an unwelcome reminder that though she had won a battle, the war was still to win. But not this afternoon. This afternoon was reserved for an alliance, not for hostilities. This afternoon Poppy was coming to tea.

Fanny allowed herself to linger over the name: Poppy – it was ridiculous. The vogue for flower names had been long-lasting, but among the Violets, Roses, Mays, Ivys, even the occasional Myrtles and Olives, Poppy was a rank outsider. A weed. Fanny's lips twitched at the thought, for this Poppy was no outsider. Patterson noted the twitch with relief. Perhaps Madam was relaxing. Perhaps she'd enjoy her tea. She'd eaten little enough of her dinner, and the fact was worrying.

At the Dower House the midday meal was still called dinner and was the main meal of the day, since Madam disliked eating in the evening, maintaining that it kept her awake. Well, it wasn't food that had kept her awake last night, for she'd not had any. Once she'd stepped out of her stained clothes and commanded Patterson to burn them, she'd come down only for a little while and then retired early. Patterson had taken up hot milk and brandy, which she'd sipped sitting up in bed. 'That wicked girl,' she repeated at intervals. 'That wicked, lying girl.' Patterson didn't know where the lying came in, and was not sure either that she considered Mary Bottrall wicked, but she'd pay dearly for what she'd done to Madam, that was beyond a doubt. She'd called at the Dower House this morning asking to see Madam and Patterson had sent her away. If she was wanting to apologize she could wait till later. Patterson wasn't going to have her mistress needlessly disturbed.

She had been with Madam ever since she moved to the Dower House, and before that at Amberley, and regarded her by now almost as an item of personal property, to be kept furbished and in pristine condition in much the same way as she kept the contents of the house. To any talk of women's suffrage and female exploitation such as Mary Bottrall indulged in, Patterson turned a stone-deaf ear. She knew her place and considered that place a good one. Why question the natural order of things?

'When Madam dies you haven't got a home to go to,' Mary had once pointed out.

'Who says she's going to die?'

'It's bound to happen sometime.'

Patterson folded her hands in comfortable piety. 'Doubtless the Lord will provide.'

What she meant, and they both knew it, was that Colonel North would provide. The Colonel was a good employer and in Croft Amberley he was esteemed as such. Except by Mary, who felt his very virtues shored up a system she was out to undermine. Or had been, for by now she was in such confusion she no longer knew what she thought.

It was not so much that when George had

reached out to her in the study she had become suddenly conscious of woman's power, as opposed to the chatteldom she was always deploring, as that her realization of man's weakness had flowered. The tenderness that had overwhelmed her for this defeated, broken man was a new sensation, very different from the impatient, rallying affection that weakness had aroused in her hitherto. She no longer knew what was strength and what was weakness, nor in whom they lay, any more than she knew where power would lie in the future. She knew only that she was subject to that power.

To escape it, she had to get away from Croft Amberley. But where was she to go? Without qualifications or references, how was she to find another post? She could go to London, lose herself in the big city, perhaps find work of a sort, but what of her grandmother? The spectre of the workhouse, that misnomer which leered over every old and unemployed shoulder, had taken a menacing stop nearer. The Colonel would never evict her grandmother, especially if the sympathies of the village were on her side. But the Colonel was not staying. There would be no more Norths at Amberley. And who knew how a new landlord would regard a rent-free cottage, a new school governor her continuance at the school?

Mary shook her head as if trying to see through the fog of doubt and fear that now engulfed her. Perhaps Mr Jimmy's fiancée would help. Of course they had not met, but she lived in London, had a job, must know how one set about finding one. Would it be worth asking her? Or would she be too shocked by that scene in the cottage (for by now everyone at Amberley would know of it) to want anything to do with such an ingrate? Oh, why had she not kept her temper yesterday?

It was a question Annie Bottrall was continually asking.

'What did you want to go and behave like that for, and Madam always so good? I'm sure I don't know where you learnt your manners. Certainly not from me. Madam never forgets to come and see me each September on the day our Hector was killed, but you take no notice of the day. I said to Madam, "Mary never remembers," but Madam defends you, says it's natural in one your age.'

Never remembers, Mary thought bitterly, when the date is engraved on my heart; when it's the day I chose for firing those ricks, though no one realized the significance. Never remembers? If only I could forget. If only I could forget yesterday, blot out the past, step into a new, blank future armed with present knowledge. But where in the world shall I find a future? Her problems pounded at her, her head was throbbing. In the privacy of her bedroom with the stained wallpaper and the leaky roof, Mary Bottrall laid her head on her arms and – unaccustomedly – wept.

Poppy too was experiencing unaccustomed emotions as she covered the short distance to the Dower House. Now that the prospect loomed of a return home tomorrow, this city-bred girl began to understand the country's charms. She had never seen such clean snow or such clear winter air, for even in residential Battersea the smoke from a myriad firesides flecked snow, faces, washing, curtains, and hung in a haze above the rooftops so that the sun was seldom bright. Paved streets were fine in summer, but in winter they were slippery with liquid mud and horse dung, and even if you ventured only where the crossing-sweepers had been at work, the traffic sprayed skirts and trouser-legs with the black, foul-smelling slime. For those who travelled by cab and carriage London was a fine metropolis; but it was a filthy one for those who travelled by train or horse-bus or the new, rather frightening Underground. Here in the country even the mud and slush of partly melted snow were manageable so long as you picked your way, and Poppy was intent on doing just that when a figure stepped out in front of her and she heard someone say her name.

'Miss Richards?'

Poppy looked at the girl before her, a girl of about her own age, neat and shabby, her skin blotched with cold or crying.

'I'm sorry, I –'

'I'm Mary Bottrall,' the girl said.

The name meant nothing to Poppy, but Mary had no idea of that.

'May I have a word with you?'

'Of course.'

'I was wondering if you could help me get a job in London.'

Poppy looked at her in astonishment. 'What sort of a job?'

'Anything – anything at all.'

'I don't see how I can help. I'm not an agency.'

'Nothing going where you work, I suppose?'

Poppy considered the applicant and thought of Edelstein's. No, there would be nothing there.

'You should go up to London and see one of the female employment agencies,' she counselled. 'They find girls places.' One of them had found her hers. 'But you must know what sort of a job you want. Something domestic?'

The girl said positively, 'Something where

I can use my mind.'

A female mind was not nearly such a marketable commodity as a pair of female hands.

'Secretarial, perhaps?' Poppy said doubtfully. 'You have shorthand? Typing?'

'No.'

'Then I must tell you, most clerks are men.'

'I write a good hand.'

'Even so, men are preferred.'

'When are they not?'

'Is there no local work – perhaps in Barford?'

'I've got to get away.'

There was something desperate about the girl. Had some man seduced her? It was the only reason Poppy knew for such a state.

'You'd need somewhere to live, too,' she said. 'You'd have to find diggings.'

'Diggings?'

'Accommodation. Somewhere to stay.'

'How do you find that?'

'Oh, notices in newsagents' windows . . .' Poppy looked at her helplessly. 'I don't know. I live at home.'

And never had she been more thankful than at this moment for the security of Jubilee Terrace. London was no place for a girl alone, limited to the society of others of her kind, growing steadily older, driven in the end to accept the first proposal of marriage, however unsuitable, that she was lucky enough to have come her way.

'Don't do it,' Poppy said impulsively. 'You're better off in Croft Amberley.'

The girl looked at her. 'Much you know.'

I know that, at least, Poppy was thinking, though I didn't till I came here.

'It's all very well for you,' the girl went on, 'marrying into the gentry –'

Poppy bit back the words 'I'm not.'

'– going to call on Madam, taking lessons on how to look down on the rest of us –'

Anger and loyalty caused Poppy to say, 'I think I should leave you.'

'So do I,' the girl said fiercely. 'You weren't born into this trap. Stay out of it.'

Stung, Poppy retorted, 'I'll make my own mind up on that.'

'At least you've a choice.' The girl's voice broke suddenly. 'And thanks for nothing. You've been a great help – like all your kind.'

She was gone as swiftly as she had materialized. Poppy gazed after her. Mary Bottrall. She must ask Madam who she was, why she was so anxious to leave Croft Amberley, why so bitter. And so frightened. These thoughts disturbed and occupied her as far as the Dower House.

Madam rose from the fireside to greet her as Patterson showed her in.

'I am so glad you've come.'

'I should have been here sooner, but one of the village girls waylaid me in the park.'

'Waylaid you?'

'Yes. She wanted advice on getting a job in London. But she had no qualifications. I told her I thought she'd be better off staying here.'

How wisely Poppy had dealt with the situation. 'Some of them have the most ridiculous notions,' Fanny said. 'I think they really do believe that London's streets are paved with gold.'

'The hems of my skirts tell a different story.'

'Ah, but what romantic ever wanted to know the truth? Sit down, my dear. Patterson will bring the hot water in a moment and we can settle to a nice long talk.'

Poppy looked at her surroundings with interest, well knowing how she would be quizzed about them back home. And since this was to be a once and for all visit, she must make the most of it. Not that there was anything remarkable about Madam's sitting-room. Over-stuffed Victorian was how she described it to herself, made dim despite the brilliance of the day by heavy curtains, portière, dark wood and dark upholstery; even the wallpaper seemed dark – or what was visible, for much of it was hidden by paintings, more family portraits and gloomy landscapes in gilt frames, indistinguishable in the murky atmosphere but contributing to the oppressiveness. Only the fire had brightness, and the oil lamp by Madam's chair, throwing into relief the planes of her face, deepening the hollows in jaw and eye-sockets and at temples, making of her a graven image in flesh. Which was how she was seen, Poppy reflected. As local deity rather than woman, least of all as suffering woman. She shivered, recognizing that she was about to inflict a cruel blow. Briefly, the face had had the look of a death mask.

'I am so pleased you and Jimmy are to be married,' Madam said when Patterson had departed. 'His life has not run smoothly, as I am sure you know. It is time he had a little happiness – Indian or China? You take milk and sugar? – and I am certain you will know how to give it. And wherever you decide to live in London, I hope you will always look on Amberley as your centre, since it is the family home.'

She doesn't know, Poppy thought, accepting her tea – she preferred Indian. They haven't told her they'll have to sell it. She's going to have a double blow. She transferred a sandwich from the plate Madam was offering to her own plate, and said abruptly, 'Mrs North, I am not going to marry your son.'

Fanny's eyes went at once to the ringless fingers. No nonsense here about keeping on her gloves.

Poppy saw the direction of her gaze. 'I have broken off our engagement.'

Fanny North put down the plate of sandwiches.

'But why?'

Why indeed? Because in the last three days I have discovered we are a different species, come from entirely separate worlds. No embrace, however close, is going to hold us against the forces driving us apart.

'I don't think our marriage would work,' she told Fanny.

'But you haven't ceased to love him.'

Perceptive. And unfair.

'My feelings have changed somewhat towards Jimmy. In any case, I can't marry all of you.'

'You're not being asked to.'

'Yes,' Poppy said. 'I am. It's your ways, your traditions, that will be imposed on me. I'm not to have any of my own.'

'Has Jimmy ever said so?'

'No, but you're all too strong. Even if you didn't have Amberley –' which was as near as she dared go to telling Madam they wouldn't have it much longer – 'you're still a close-knit family, and it's not one where I belong.'

'Isn't that for us to decide? If we accept you –'

'That's right. If, after trying me out, you decide I'm a suitable acquisition, all well and good. What happens if you don't?'

'I was going to say that if we accept you, your breaking the engagement can only mean that you're rejecting us.'

'Yes.'

'Even though we're a part of Jimmy, the man you agreed to wed?'

'When I met Jimmy he was an individual. I didn't know anything about his family, his background, any more than he did about mine.'

'But he's accepted your family.'

'Yes.' There seemed no doubt of that. Jimmy and Dad got on famously. Dad had even taken him round to the Spotted Dog, introduced him to his cronies as 'our Poppy's intended'. Mum thought the world of him once she'd decided he was to be trusted. Sister Daisy was envious. 'Hasn't he got an air about him?' she said wistfully. 'Not that I'd change my Fred, but you'd walk tall by the side of that one, wouldn't you?' Brother Denis said he was a swell. And Jimmy seemed perfectly at home in Jubilee Terrace, even had his own special chair, an upright one which he'd appropriated and in which he contrived to look at ease.

'Do you think it was easy for him?' Fanny asked shrewdly.

Poppy flushed. 'You mean, to go slumming.'

'I mean your family's different from his. It sounds as if he's more adaptable than you are. Perhaps there's something to be said for his background after all.'

'He has all the advantages. I can't live up to them.'

'I haven't noticed you trying very hard. In fact, you're giving up before you've even started. I'm disappointed. I thought you'd more spirit than that.'

Poppy was silent.

'Let me give you some more tea – that's gone cold,' Fanny interposed. 'And you're not eating.'

Poppy managed a bleak smile. 'Nor are you.'

It was true, but Fanny hadn't noticed. Her attention was concentrated as if through a narrow funnel on the girl before her. She scarcely felt the twinge of pain that uncoiled within her vitals and curled itself up again.

'I'm not hungry,' Fanny said, 'but young people can always eat if they're healthy.'

And this girl was healthy. She would bear Jimmy sons. Must bear him sons. She could not be allowed to vanish. Or, as she thought of it, to escape.

Poppy's smile flashed out in all its brilliance

this time. 'I've heard my mum say that.'

'There you are. Your mother and I have much in common.'

Poppy wondered if Mum would agree. But the sandwiches were good and she was hungry. She had eaten little all day. It was necessary to remember to take several bites, for the tiny triangles were no more than mouthfuls, but this was not a difficult adaptation to Amberley ways.

'Even if we had nothing in common,' Madam went on, busying herself among the teacups, 'would it be right to make Jimmy suffer for what we are?'

'He'll suffer more if we find we're unsuited after marriage.'

'Why should you be?'

'We see things such different ways.'

'What things?'

Poppy looked down at her plate, already empty.

'Do you mean other women?' Fanny guessed.

The girl's sudden stillness was an answer.

'In South Africa,' Fanny said, as if she'd always known it.

'Yes, and in India.'

'India!' But Jimmy hadn't been there long, had stayed only with Harry in Cossipore and Simla, though some of the time Harry had been away . . . A sudden recollection ran through

Fanny of Emily's face and voice as she demanded to know if Jimmy were coming for Christmas.

'You mean Emily, don't you?' she said.

How right she'd been to dislike Emily Fanshaw, she thought as Poppy nodded, but she wasn't going to let her win. And win she would if because of her they lost Poppy. Fanny put down the teapot carefully.

'Listen, my dear,' she said. 'You find my son attractive. Do you think in that you're unique?'

A small shake of the head.

'And you haven't been in love before, have you?'

The shake was definite.

'But you have not been without admirers, so you know what it is like to attract. And you know that attractive people can't help being attractive. Are we to blame them for that?"

'He didn't have to – to –'

'Give in to temptation?' Fanny suggested. 'Of course you're perfectly right. I imagine there were many occasions when he didn't. But if he was attracted too . . .'

'She was married. Married to his brother.'

'I'm not defending him –' I am, of course – 'but no man's perfect. If you don't find that out with Jimmy, you will with someone else. Besides, it wasn't Jimmy who was married.'

'Do you call that an excuse?'

Fanny checked a gasp as the pain surged through her, but she said steadily enough: 'Most men will take what's offered. May I help you to a slice of cake?'

'No, I couldn't. Really.'

Fanny cut a generous slice and transferred it, unnoticed, to the girl's plate. It was not only men who took what was offered because it was offered.

'I appreciate,' she said carefully, controlling her breath against the pain, 'that you love – loved – my son, but are you sure it was Jimmy you were in love with, not just your idea of him?'

'I don't understand.'

'He is handsome, attractive – I believe his mother may allow as much – and you are on your own admission . . . inexperienced, shall we say? What more natural than that you should think the outward perfection mirrors an inner one? Now that you know it is merely the cloak for a man like many others, you are blaming him for your disillusion, whereas in fact you should blame yourself.'

'I can never respect him again,' Poppy said. She had begun absently to eat the cake.

'Perhaps not, but can you still love him?'

'For me, the two are one.'

'You mean your love has rigid limits. Yet it has just contracted, has it not? Which proves, at least, that it is capable of adaptation. By the same token, it can expand again.'

'No.'

'You can of course refuse to let it, but that is to refuse to love. Are you telling me that you, an attractive young woman, are refusing the very thing for which you were created? I call that blasphemy.'

Poppy looked up at her. 'How dare you!'

'At my age it is astonishing what one dares.' Especially in the interests of gaining a daughter . . . 'Tell me: do you intend never to marry?'

'I hadn't considered . . . No.'

'So you will some day face these problems with someone else. Shall I tell you what I think?'

Poppy sat silent, waiting, noting the silken sheen of sweat on Madam's face. Was it really so hot in the room? She had not noticed. Idly she chased the last few cake crumbs round her plate.

'I think you never loved my son,' Fanny said. 'You merely liked him.'

'How can you know what I feel?'

'How can any of us know another's feelings, except by what they say and what they do?'

In that case you must be ill, Poppy thought. Your face is as grey as your dress. She half rose, but Madam was speaking.

'You like people for what they are,' she said with difficulty, 'but you love them in spite of what they are. Until you know that, you know nothing of loving, and I tell you, you have never loved my son.'

'No!'

Poppy's denial was of her own as much as Madam's weakness, as Fanny North slumped in her chair. Poppy was kneeling beside her in an instant.

'Madam dear, what is it? You're ill.'

'A passing faintness,' Fanny managed, the admission wrung out of her.

'A glass of water, smelling salts . . . Let me ring for Patterson.'

'No need.' Fanny sought and grasped her hand, such a strong, warm, capable hand. A daughter's hand. 'It will pass. It's just that girl, she upset me so yesterday with her dreadful, wicked lies. I can't forget it, can't –'

She gasped, and her hand tightened in Poppy's, for this admission was more shaming than that of pain.

'What girl? What lies, dear?' Could Madam be delirious?

'Her lies about Jimmy,' Fanny said. She

closed her eyes against Mary's angry face and its accusation, whose cruelty lay in the fact that it might conceivably be true.

Beside her, Poppy said more urgently, 'What lies about Jimmy? What girl?'

If he had seduced one of the village girls, 'been attracted to her', as Madam would no doubt say . . .

She shook the cold hands in hers. 'What girl? Who are you talking about?'

'Mary Bottrall,' Fanny said.

The girl in the park. The girl who wanted a job in London. Poppy heard the despairing voice: 'I've got to get away.' Understandably, if she had indeed been seduced by the young master. London absorbed its share of such. You saw them in West End doorways, sheltering, sometimes cheaply smart, sometimes . . . But no decent woman looked at them, though here and there a face stood out, bold or terrified, occasionally good-looking, sometimes still with the bloom of youth and health. And some of them were started on this path by men as casual, as careless as Jimmy.

She said bitterly, 'I might have known it.'

Fanny roused herself. 'What do you know? Has he talked about it to you?'

'Never.' Did Madam think she would permit such conversation, even had Jimmy dared?

'Nor to me, though I thought he'd told me everything when he told me how Hector died.'

What was she talking of? 'Hector?'

'Mary's brother. He enlisted to be with Jimmy and was killed in South Africa.'

Poppy's relief was so great that she almost proclaimed it, but she said instead, 'What is Jimmy supposed to have done?'

'Mistimed the attack in which his men died, including Hector.'

'An error,' Poppy said, 'not a crime.'

'A disgrace.' Fanny's strength was returning, the pain receding. Her voice had something of its old ring. 'He was responsible. They trusted him and he failed them.'

'How does Mary Bottrall know?'

'She had a letter. From one of Hector's friends.'

'Who might have been mistaken.'

'Perhaps, but we shall never know.'

'Then give Jimmy the benefit of the doubt.'

'Oh, I do, my dear. What mother wouldn't? It's the slur when that wicked girl makes it known. And she will. I know her – she has always hated us. Even if it is untrue, we shall never be able to live it down.'

'We! Us! Your precious family. You can think of nothing else. What about Jimmy? Is he a disgrace to the lordly race of Norths because he's made an all too human error and has to live with its results?'

'I was so proud of him . . .'

'Were you? Or were you proud of your idea of him? Surely it's *your* love that has rigid limits and can't adapt to love him as he is. You love people in spite of what they are. Until you know that, you know nothing of loving –' Poppy swept relentlessly on. 'That's what you said and I believed you. Now tell me: by that same reckoning, do you truly love your son?'

'Yes,' Fanny said. 'As much as you do.'

Across the tea-table they faced each other, adversaries yet allied. Poppy was the first to look away, and they sat silent in the sunset light which shone full on the western window, filling the dusky room with gold. Without apology, Poppy rose and, standing in the window's embrasure, watched Roddy running through the park, stopping now and then to clutch the stitch in his side and catch his breath, intent on heaven knew what secret game of childhood. So would her own son run, hers and Jimmy's, though never through Amberley's park. Somehow it no longer mattered.

'What are you looking at?' Fanny asked.

The future . . .

'Only Roddy running towards the house. Are you feeling better? Shall I help you up to bed?'

'No, my dear, Patterson will do it. Be good enough to ring for her and she will show you out.'

Poppy moved towards the tasselled bell-rope by the fireplace and Fanny heard her suddenly catch her breath.

'What is it?'

'That painting.'

Fanny shifted in her chair and the pain shifted with her. Cautiously she turned her head. Sunlight lit the picture in question as if for exhibition, making it stand out from all the others in the room.

'I've always liked that portrait,' Fanny said softly. 'I brought it from Amberley when I moved here. I used to imagine the girl in it was my daughter. Somehow, she has a look of you.'

Poppy saw no resemblance between herself and the dark-eyed girl holding a beribboned hat in the picture, but she saw several other things. She had not spent three years at Edelstein's without acquiring some knowledge of painting.

'May I have a closer look?' she said.

She picked her way between the crowded furniture and peered with an attentive eye.

'Who is she?'

'Some eighteenth-century ancestress of my husband's.'

'Don't you know who it's by?'

You must do. You can't possess a treasure like that and not know it. Or rather, I suppose you can if you're a North.

Fanny confirmed this view. 'We have so many pictures. I'm glad my favourite pleases you.'

'Pleases me! Madam dear, don't you realize what you've got?'

The name of the painter at last meant something to Fanny. A trace of colour stained her cheeks. Or was it the sunset's reflection?

'Do you mean it's valuable?' she asked.

'Valuable! You'd have to have it authenticated, get an expert to assess it. I'll ask Mr Edelstein – he'll know what to do.'

Poppy's words were tumbling over each other in her excitement. The salvation of Amberley lay ahead. Under their noses, on their walls, in their midst, unnoticed, unregarded.

'If I'm right, it's worth a fortune,' she said.

Maud went very slowly up Amberley's wide, shallow staircase, as if she scaled a mountain peak. The house was eerily still. Sounds from below stairs or the nursery seldom penetrated the thick walls and stout doors that interposed between them and the family's living quarters, but one was always conscious of the hidden life behind them. Now Amberley was a house of the dead.

She was tired, so tired that each step was an effort. Since Roddy had come running in, panting, gasping out his message to Jarvis, wide-eyed with the thrill and horror of it all, her mind had functioned on two separate levels: one purely practical – hot water, brandy, linen for bandages, hot-water bottles; the other cut off as effectively as below stairs and the nursery by even thicker walls and stouter doors, behind which thoughts, prayers, feelings were concentrated in a single syllable: George.

She had stood like a statue at the foot of this same staircase as the men came in carrying the hurdle, hearing herself give orders, hearing the words of others, hearing and not hearing them. Waiting for Dr Paget's gig; the lathered horse, flanks heaving; the stairs taken two at a time. Only when she heard his voice pronouncing did she begin to believe, to accept what in her heart she knew.

The curtains were drawn on the landing, so often forgotten. The maids had done a good job, anxious to please in this hour of crisis. She parted them and looked out at the stars. Cold and remote, these dead worlds sparkled down on her: Orion's sword and belt, the Great and Little Bear, the Pole Star, which her father had taught her to identify. Of course Lilias had identified them more quickly, named more constellations, but it had not availed her in the end. On the night of her death they had gathered undimmed in the heavens. In January it would be sixteen years since Lilias had died.

She let the curtain fall and crossed the landing, hesitating at the door of the room in which George lay. Silence mantled the house, the hall, the stairs, the bedroom. Noiselessly she opened the door.

A shaft of light from the small oil lamp she carried lanced the dimness. On the pillow she could see George's head. He lay as if asleep, but the light had roused him. He turned to her.

'Come in, m'dear,' he said.

She entered quietly, closing the door behind her, hastening to turn up the light, to examine him, reassure herself yet again of what Dr Paget had told her: 'He's going to be all right.'

The fall which had caused the gun to go off had slewed George sideways. He fell heavily, striking his head, while the blast of the shotgun almost missed his foot, and even there, its fullest force deflected, the heavy boot and gaiter had spared him the worst effect.

George too had heard the doctor's pronouncement, but from a distance. A part of him was still outside himself, looking down on the bloodstained body about which they were all so busy, which Paget was repeating was going to be all right. From the moment he had heard Jimmy's voice on the hillside, felt his hand on his shoulder, he had known that he had failed. Even in the ultimate admission of failure he had not been successful. He who should have been dead was very much alive.

'George, old fellow! Are you all right? Can you hear me?'

Dazedly he murmured. ' 'S'nothing ... tripped ...'

'What the devil were you doing carrying a gun with the safety-catch off?' In his relief Jimmy scolded like a woman.

'Don't know ... thinking of other things ...'

Amberley. He was thinking of Amberley. Jimmy knew it as if it had been said aloud. That damned estate had cost him Poppy; it had almost cost him his brother. Anxiously he said, 'Can you move?'

The blend of dark and light which made up George's vision began to cohere into shapes. Jimmy's face. A patch of sky. A patch of snow. A tree-root. He put up his hand. 'My head ...'

'You knocked yourself out in falling. Let's have a look at your foot.'

Jimmy was busy unbuckling George's gaiter, unlacing his boot, stanching blood.

'I don't think it's too bad,' he reported. 'I've sent Roddy to get help. Lucky you didn't blow your foot off. Lucky you didn't kill yourself, come to that.'

'Unlucky . . .'

'What's that?'

'I said unlucky . . .' Briefly the blackness came back. When it cleared, Jimmy was bending anxiously above him.

'George, you didn't mean to . . .'

'No.' The lie came out quite clearly. George winced as he tried to shake his head. 'My fault. Tripped. Should have been more careful. Maud mustn't think . . .' He identified a distant throbbing as his right foot. 'Bloody silly,' he said, and closed his eyes.

Maud mustn't think it was anything but an accident, Jimmy silently completed. So it had been a suicide attempt. Poor old George. And he, Jimmy, had been so absorbed in his own affairs that he had never noticed his brother's desperation. Could he have prevented this?

'Look,' he said awkwardly, 'you can have my share of the Amberley income.' He wouldn't be needing it now that Poppy had said no. 'And I'm sure Harry'll chip in with something. We'll save the place somehow. You'll see.'

He had no idea if they could, but it was worth saying. Behind closed eyelids George smiled. 'Decent of you . . .'

They were decent, his brothers, Maud, the

Mater, that girl of Jimmy's. It was only Emily . . . But Emily would be going back to India, back to Harry. And Mary Bottrall would be going – where?

'That girl,' he said suddenly. 'That Bottrall girl. She'll have to go.'

'All right, old man. Take it easy. If you say so, go she shall.'

Jimmy had no idea what George was talking about, but it seemed a soothing reply, although whatever she had done, he was already resolving to intercede for Mary. As Hector would have wanted him to. For a moment the English hillside was a dusty kopje strewn with corpses, bright not with sunset but with dawn. Then he heard the voices of the rescue party, and went to meet them thankfully.

Lying in bed after Paget had gone, George too was conscious of a deep thankfulness that all he had surrendered had been given back to him. For a few days, at least. He lay in the familiar double bedroom, even though the double bed had been less familiar to him of late. The shadows cast by the furniture were known and reassuring. His wife's profile equally so.

'Have they gone?' he asked.

'Nearly an hour ago,' Maud answered. 'They should be there by now.'

After hasty consultation it had been decided

that all but Maud and George would attend Lady St Devereux's fancy dress ball as planned. It would be good to keep the children occupied, better to ensure the quietness of the house, best of all to give the lie to any exaggerated stories of the seriousness of George's condition or the nature of his accident.

'Papa has had an accident,' Maud said firmly in the nursery. 'He tripped and his gun went off and shot him in the foot. Of course he should have had the safety-catch on, but even an experienced sportsman like Papa can be careless. We must be thankful the results aren't serious.'

Brief though the speech was, she found she was addressing it more and more to Alice, whose scepticism shone in her eyes. Why could the child never believe what she was told? Did she think her mother would lie to her? For I am not lying, Maud insisted to herself. This is what George and Jimmy both say happened. Am I, like Alice, doubting what I am told?

'Can I see Papa?' Alice demanded.

'Tomorrow,' Maud temporized.

'Is that a promise?'

'Yes.' She would have to see him sometime. Alice appeared satisfied.

'Are we still going to the ball?' Bea asked her.

'Yes, dear. It's a time for you all to get

dressed. Your mother is doing so already, and you and Roddy will go with her in one carriage. You two –' she eyed her own daughters – 'will go with Uncle Jimmy and Miss Richards who are going to wear Papa's and my costumes.'

Jimmy and George were much of a build – there would be no problem there. As for Poppy – she supposed she would have to get used to calling her that, since she and Jimmy seemed to have made it up in the aftermath of George's accident – her dark looks would be ideal for a gipsy. Better than mine, Maud conceded, knowing that looks had become irrelevant. Let Emily queen it as Scotland's Mary in fact as well as fancy. Let Poppy dance until her shoes wore thin. She, Maud, was the chatelaine of Amberley, the lynch-pin on which the whole household turned. Above all, she was George's wife, the woman at his side. If he fell, however briefly, it was she who stepped forward to take his place.

It was with a new confidence in her position that she waved the carriages off. 'Maud is amazing,' Poppy whispered to Jimmy, making it an excuse to draw his head down to her own. And Jimmy, seizing the chance to kiss her ear, responded, 'She always has been, but it's never showed.'

'Your mother is a wonderful lady,' Poppy said

warmly to the children as the carriage swayed along.

'Yes,' Alice said, surprising herself by the admission. 'She's better than Aunt Lilias would have been.'

'What do you mean, dear?'

'Papa wanted to marry Aunt Lilias, Mama's sister, but she died.'

'I see,' Poppy said, glancing at Jimmy for confirmation and indeed seeing many things for the first time.

'Aunt Lilias would have wanted to queen it,' Alice went on. 'Like Aunt Emily, only better, of course.'

Jimmy suppressed a smile. 'And you – don't you want to queen it?'

'I shall be like Aunt Lilias,' his niece informed him, 'only I shan't even have to try. People will pay me court in any case.'

They will too, Poppy thought without envy, watching the child's emphatic toss of the head. 'And what about you?' she asked Rose, anxious that there should not be another Maud, another Lilias. 'Are you going to queen it when you grow up?'

Rose smiled seraphically. 'I'm going to marry Roddy.'

Jimmy said with feeling, 'Lucky chap.'

'No, Uncle Jimmy, it's me that's lucky,' Rose

insisted. 'He mightn't have wanted me.'

'There'd be others.'

Rose shook her head. The gesture was oddly convincing. 'There's only Roddy for me.'

For an instant the shadowy carriage interior darkened.

'Don't be too exclusive,' Poppy warned.

Alice shivered. 'The way you talk, anyone would think you were older than me, Rosy-posy.'

'It's just that I'm more grown-up,' Rose said.

Above the children's heads Jimmy and Poppy exchanged glances. In a sense Rose's remark was true. Not for her the storms and tempests that would buffet her sister; she was as composed as a woman of forty, secure in the position she anticipated as hers. Poppy found herself praying that that anticipation would be fulfilled, for if it weren't, what would be left? A withered rosebud?

Abruptly she said to Jimmy, 'Did you tell George about the portrait?'

'I told Maud.' Who had not realized the significance of the news. What would George say when he heard? It should have a healing effect on mind and body, and it was all due to Poppy. Without her, they would never have known what treasure hung on Amberley's walls, or rather on those of the Dower House, though the painting belonged indisputably to George.

'Are you sure it's what you think it is?' Jimmy asked, still unable to believe it.

'I'm ninety-nine per cent sure. I'd like Mr Edelstein and his experts to verify it.'

'And will Edelstein take care of the sale?'

'Of course. Shall I ask him to waive his commission as a wedding present?' Poppy's eyes beneath the gipsy kerchief were dancing.

Jimmy kissed the tip of her nose. 'I love you,' he said boldly. To her, to the children, to the world.

It was not something Maud could ever imagine herself saying to George, however deeply she felt it, for George loved Lilias. Therefore he could never love her, though he was a good and faithful husband, deserving of her support and respect. She had not had to suffer those shaming liaisons, those temporary infidelities, which her father had discreetly referred to as 'lapses from virtue' when he tried to speak to her of marriage and what it might involve. Did involve, for she had sometimes suspected that in those around her adultery was the normal state. It was well known that Eddie St Devereux kept a mistress in London, to which Muriel turned a blind but resentful eye. The marriages that Madam arranged for erring village maidens were not always due to indiscretions with equals; their lords and masters were sometimes indiscreet. But George had kept himself free from any taint of scandal and her from any taint of shame, and she was grateful, all the more so because she had failed him in failing to produce an heir.

Looking at him now, sick and defeated, her heart was wrenched with pain. He prided himself on his skill as a sportsman. He must be ashamed of his own carelessness. And of course it *was* carelessness. No other thought could be entertained.

She asked gently, 'How do you feel?'

'Not so bad.'

'Is there anything I can get you?'

'No, m'dear. You could perhaps sit with me a bit.'

Maud hid her exultation at being wanted. 'I'll fetch some mending. Alice has torn her coat again. What that child does to her clothes I can't imagine. She'll need a new coat soon.'

Another expense . . . But such worries had receded from the precious limbo in which George was dwelling. Tomorrow or the day after he would have to face them, after Emily and her two had gone. When there was no more fear that some vengeful caprice might lead her, regardless of the forced bargain struck between them, to tell Maud of that moment when she had opened the study door. It was nothing, but Emily would make it sound something. And Maud would never understand. It would hurt her enough to lose her home and her position. Her pride at least was not going to be harmed. Not if he could help it. George stirred and winced.

In a moment Maud was at his side. 'What is it, dear? Are you in pain?'

'Only from my own clumsiness.'

'Dr Paget says you won't take long to mend.'

'Since when have you taken to believing Paget?'

'I always have. It's your mother who dismisses him. Which reminds me, George: I do not think she is looking well. On Christmas Day there was a greyness about her. I suspected something when she did not come to church.'

George was not given to questioning the mutability of living monuments.

'Oh, the Mater's good for years yet. She'll see us all out.'

She probably will, Maud thought. Mrs North. Madam. Eternal first lady of Croft Amberley.

She said, 'Perhaps it was my imagination.' And meant: my wishful thinking. But George had other things on his mind.

'Did I hear Jimmy'd made it up with

that nice girl of his?'

'Well, the pirate and the gipsy left hand in hand for the ball, chaperoned by Rose and Alice.'

'Decent of Muriel St D. to ask the children too.'

'Convenient.' Maud shared her eldest daughter's view of the lady's conduct, but as it happened, it was indeed convenient. Except that they would all be overtired tomorrow. But at least Emily and her brood would go. She would no longer have to suffer the presence of the heir to Amberley, that boy who was not her and George's son, who had been caught with Rose in a position saved only by innocence – George had assured her of that.

'Youngster had no idea of the significance of what he was doing,' he had said after interviewing Roddy. 'He thinks it's all a game. He's as innocent as our little Rosebud. Wonder how long that'll last after he gets to Bradwell House.'

Maud interpreted this as meaning that they must watch him in the future, especially as he seemed so fond of Rose. And she of him. But suppose in ten years' time . . . Rose would be eighteen then, and Roddy of age. Suppose in 1917 they married? Rose would be the next lady of Amberley.

Her matrimonial speculations were interrupted by George announcing, 'I'll come down tomorrow. See 'em off.'

'No, dear, you must rest. Dr Paget said at least until the weekend.'

'Nonsense. Jarvis'll give me a hand, and there's a stout stick in the hall belonged to m' father. I'm not staying up here in bed.'

Some start must be made on that chaos of papers in the study. He could handle that sitting down. He could handle it better if Maud were beside him. The thought came unbidden, and stayed. He looked at her under the lamplight, stitching at Alice's coat. This competent woman was far removed from the desolate girl he had married. It was the mark of her competence that it seldom showed, except as now, in time of crisis. Everything would be worse without Maud.

'I'm a lucky man,' he said.

She looked up, frowning. She needed glasses.

'Why do you say that?'

'I mean I'm lucky in the woman I married.'

Maud bowed her head to hide the start of tears. That he should say as much was more than she had ever dared to hope for. George loved Lilias.

'You've been a good wife to me,' he said.

His tone was tinged with farewell sadness, as though their life together were ending. As though he himself were near death.

Maud said briskly, intent on banishing such morbidity, 'Isn't it amazing that Miss Richards – Poppy – should have discovered that valuable painting hanging in the Dower House?'

George had been lying still, but his stillness now was absolute. He might have been an effigy on a tomb.

The effigy spoke. 'What painting?'

'The one Madam's always liked. That portrait of a girl, some eighteenth-century ancestress of yours. You allowed her to take it when she moved.'

'You mean the picture's mine?'

'Of course. Poppy came back wild with excitement about it. She thinks you'd be able to sell it for a very considerable sum.'

A very considerable sum. George savoured the words. 'Why didn't you tell me sooner?'

'My dear, she arrived back from visiting your mother just as the men were carrying you in. You'll agree it was hardly the moment. I gather she told Jimmy later on and that was when they made up their quarrel. It was only afterwards that Jimmy told me.'

'How soon will they know?'

'Know what?'

'If the picture's worth money.'

'Poppy is going to ask Mr Edelstein to come

down. No doubt he will bring his experts.'

'But we could sell it soon?'

'If you wish. I thought as it's an ancestress you might wish to keep it.'

'Bugger ancestry!' George said.

Maud dropped her sewing. That George should use such language! The blow to the head must be worse than they had thought. To her astonishment, he did not apologize and, glancing at him, she saw that his head was turned away from her and his shoulders shaking. It took her a moment to realize that he wept.

Gently she put a hand on his shoulder. 'Please, dear. I understand. It was a momentary lapse.'

Her words roused him. 'It's nothing of the sort,' he roared, struggling to sit upright, pain and weakness forgotten. 'It's the saving of Amberley.'

And then it all came tumbling out, the debts, the incessant struggle to meet them, the appeal to his brothers, the visits to Reuben. Maud listened to the catalogue, appalled. So much that her husband had never told her, that he had insisted on bearing alone.

'Why did you never say anything?' she asked when he paused, exhausted.

'I couldn't face telling you that I'd failed you,

that you were going to lose your home.'

'*Your* home. It's been your home for generations. Amberley means more to you than it does to me.'

'You mean you wouldn't have minded leaving it?'

'I didn't say that, but so long as I have you and the children . . . And how can you talk to me of failures when I've never given you an heir?'

George remembered vividly Maud's pregnancies: her sickness, the lank hair and bloated body, her uncomplainingness through it all, even when the end was the small, quiet burial of a small, quiet body in St Peter's churchyard. Yet she had given him Rose and Lulu; she had given him Alice, who was Lilias over again.

'Roddy'll do very well as an heir,' he said. 'I'd rather have my daughters – and my wife.'

'I'd rather have you than Amberley.' Such admissions gave Maud the courage to put her worst fear into words. 'George, tell me the truth: that accident with your gun was an accident, wasn't it?'

'Of course it was,' George lied.

What else could he say? The burden of secrecy was upon him, and on the whole it seemed a small price to pay.

His wife relaxed against him. 'If you'd been

killed and I'd discovered afterwards how worried you'd been, I don't think I could have borne knowing that you hadn't felt able to share it. I should have known then that I had truly failed.'

George put an awkward arm around her. He had never considered that in sparing Maud he might have inflicted the cruellest blow of all. Against his hand he felt her breast tauten. He moved his hand; she did not shy away. Very gently he unfastened the brooch at her throat, a big cameo that he had given her on Lulu's birth. If it had been a son, he was going to give her a bracelet. He remembered it now with shame. Six times Maud had risked her life for him, not counting miscarriages. How would he and the children have fared if she had died? St Peter's churchyard had its share of stones sacred to the memory of women who had died in childbed. The bed in which he lay, in which his children had been conceived and born, might easily have been Maud's deathbed. He had no right to risk her life again.

He made to withdraw his hand. To his surprise, he met resistance. Maud's hand held his in position while the other undid the buttons of her dress, pulled the pins from her hair which, thicker than it looked, fell loose about her shoulders, while the dress sank to the floor in a pool of folds. Maud, who was meticulous about hanging garments, left it lying. Her petticoat followed as she turned her back to him.

'Unlace me,' she commanded hoarsely.

His fingers fumbled with the lacing of her corset. 'My dear, are you sure you want me to . . .'

'Don't you want a son?'

'You know I do,' he said, recognizing that the prospect of saving Amberley had stimulated his desire.

'And do you think I don't? Do you think I don't want you?' Maud laid her head against him. 'Why, I wanted you the first time you came courting Lilias. I often used to wish her dead. If that shocks you, I can't help it, but I felt like a murderess when she was killed. And then when you turned to me and I inherited her happiness, her home, her husband, it was as though I were profiting from a crime. But I could never tell you how much I loved you because it was always Lilias you loved.' George made to speak, but she placed a finger to his lips and hurried on regardless. 'Oh, George, if you knew how I have ached for you these last months, and tonight – tonight is the first time . . .'

The first time, perhaps, in all our years of marriage that we have truly been man and wife,

George supplied; and stumbled into explanation.

'I didn't feel I could after what Paget said at the time of your last confinement.'

'What did Paget say?'

'That I should leave you alone . . . that you ought not to conceive again too quickly.'

'Much as I esteem Paget as a doctor, there are times when as a man he's nothing but a fool. I suspect that's true of most men.'

'What's this? Women's rights in the bedroom?'

'Only the right to love.'

The only one that matters, George thought as he drew her into his arms. He had his life, his wife, and please God he had Amberley if Poppy's assessment of the painting were confirmed, but the one that mattered most was the woman who lay beside him, whose mouth came seeking his. The very familiarity of her body was reassuring. He explored it like a traveller returning home. He reached over and turned out the lamp because he needed no light to guide him down these well-known, well-loved pathways.

In the darkness he heard his deepest self murmur, 'I love you,' and did not know which of them spoke.

CHAPTER 11

For the second time in a week Beatrix sat opposite her mother in a moving vehicle, only this time the vehicle was Madam's carriage with Wilkins on the box. They bowled smartly along the frost-gripped highways, keeping a respectable distance behind the Amberley carriage in which Uncle Jimmy and Aunt Poppy and her cousins rode. The stars glittered, the rime on the hedgerows glittered; in the carriage Mama's eyes glittered too. Bea pressed her aching forehead against the window and wished that instead of going to a fancy dress ball they were going home; home to the room she shared with Roddy in the comforting depths of Amberley. If only she could be seen into bed by Nanny Cardew, presented with hot milk and the command, 'Now, Miss Bea, I don't expect to see any of that left when I come back to put out the light.' If only Papa would come in, as he did every night in India when duty did not keep him, sit on the end of her bed and ask, 'How's my little girl?' – a question to which he expected no answer beyond the conventional assurance that she was very well.

Even tonight she supposed she would give it, although she felt – not ill exactly, but what Nanny would call 'out of sorts'. Her headache nagged but had not become insupportable; her listlessness had not mounted to feverishness. She had had no excuse not to don the pierrette costume and join the others for the ball, though the black stockings prickled and the conical hat, now on her lap, was painfully tight round her head. Beside her, Roddy swung his feet off the floor in a maddening rhythm until Mama said, 'Oh, do sit still!' with such controlled anger in her voice that Roddy's pompommed toes came to rest with absolute precision a neat six inches apart.

Like his sister, Roddy dreaded the ball, but for different reasons. Dressing up was all very well for girls, or even for grown-up men like Uncle Jimmy, but he didn't suppose any other fellow would be there in what felt like over-large rompers and with a pie-frill round his face. Before departure, Cook and the maids had gathered in the hall for a viewing; he had been referred to as 'quite the little toff'. Uncle Jimmy, a most gentlemanly pirate, had been gigglingly encouraged to display a leg. The girls had been applauded, Rose especially, and Aunt Poppy had stolen the show by banging her gipsy tambourine in a rhythm which everyone recognized as 'Ta-ra-ra-boom-de-ay' and performing the appropriate steps. Then Mama had appeared at the top of the stairs and they had all fallen silent as slowly, head held high, Mary Queen of Scots made her descent. The silence was broken by Cook saying loudly, 'What a pity Mr Harry can't see you now, mum.' Mama ignored her, gathered Roddy and Bea around her, and said to the others, 'Shall we go?' She swept out, but not before Roddy had seen Aunt Poppy make a face at Uncle Jimmy and heard Cook say, 'Stuck up ain't the word.'

He wished he could have ridden in the other carriage so that he could have been with Rose. Since Christmas night they had never been alone together, there had always been grown-ups around, even after that long and largely incomprehensible interview with Uncle George which had culminated in a clap on the shoulder and the injunction, 'Don't let me catch you doing anything like that again, young feller – now or at any other time.' When I'm grown up, Roddy promised himself, I shall do what I like, when I like, and where.

Now he merely said, 'No, sir,' and Uncle George said, 'Right. Guard – dismiss!'

As the carriage turned into the drive of Mawby Hall they slowed to a procession, for the horses had to pick their way through rutted mud and snow. The entrance steps were carpeted, grooms came forward to hold the horses, guests cast aside lap-robes and descended, dainty shoes preserved from slush and mud. Glancing back, Poppy saw a line of lamps like an unending London cab rank, the horses' breath steaming in the still air. Then Jimmy was handing her up the steps, maids led her aside to a room where her coat was taken from her just as though it were not shabby, and she rejoined Jimmy and Roddy in the hall. Rose, Alice and Beatrix were behind her, and behind them Emily, and the seven of them mounted a branching staircase to where a harem lady in gold spangles and Turkish slippers was waiting to greet them, flanked by a gentleman, presumably her husband, resplendent in hunting pink. Music was playing, half drowned by laughter and many voices. She heard Jimmy explain, 'My brother . . . a slight accident . . .' Then he was introducing her: 'My fiancée, Miss Richards . . .' Murmurs of 'Delighted . . . delighted . . .' 'And my sister-in-law, the Queen of Scots – or should I say the Queen of Hearts?

– otherwise Mrs Harry North.' Then they were in the ballroom. Someone gave her a mask and a dance programme, which Jimmy appropriated at once, handing it back with assurance, 'I've given myself all the best dances, including this first one,' and she was floating, floating in his arms.

The ballroom was a whirl of colour, whiffs of scents, eddies of conversation. 'Last Season was so dull' . . . 'My cousin, whom you may have heard me mention' . . . 'Who's that attractive filly over there?' The masks did not conceal, but they lent a mystery to eyes, an invitation to glances, sometimes intentional and sometimes not. Some couples had eyes only for each other; some danced unconventionally close; some danced well and others were clumsy; some gazed anywhere but at their partners, exchanging with others smiles of acknowledgement, ardour, assignation, for where better than at a ball? There were a number of men in hunting pink, several pirates, two jesters, one tall and one tubby, a couple of bewigged eighteenth-century ladies, at least one other gipsy, but no second Mary Queen of Scots. Poppy glimpsed Emily surrounded by courtiers, and guessed she was enjoying herself. Let her. Tomorrow she would be gone; she would sail for India and it would be three years before Harry's next home leave. Meanwhile Jimmy was beside her, his arm circling her waist. He was whispering, 'Take off your mask. I want to see you,' and Poppy happily obliged.

Jimmy looked down at the smiling face which he had feared was lost to him. Poppy had been in the hall, still in outdoor clothes, when the men had carried George in – he had been aware of her even then. As Maud took over, she slid towards him.

'What's happened?'

'George tripped and shot himself in the foot.'

'Is it serious?'

'I don't think so.' He had seen far worse on the battlefield.

'Thank goodness. Did Roddy see it?'

'No, I sent him back with a message.'

'That was clever of you,' she approved.

They were talking without constraint, their quarrel forgotten.

'Did you enjoy taking tea with the Mater?' he asked.

'Yes.' Poppy wondered whether to tell him of Madam's faintness and decided against causing further anxiety; she had other, more momentous news. 'Jimmy, there's a painting in the Dower House that I'm sure is worth a fortune and no one's ever realized it.'

Jimmy heard her out with mounting excitement. If it were true, it was a double mercy George had been spared. He put an arm round Amberley's saviour. 'Poppy to the rescue,' he said.

'You sure make me sound like a girls' school story.'

'No, just the heroine of the most romantic novel I know. Shall we call it *The Saving of Amberley*?'

'I'd rather it was *Poppy and Jimmy*,' she said.

'Much better,' he agreed, 'and the opening chapters are excellent. But won't readers find fifty years of happiness dull?'

She laid a finger to his lips. 'Don't talk like that. Who knows what's lying in wait in the future? There might be another war.'

If there was, Jimmy thought, I should not be in it. I've learnt my lesson. I should not enlist. But plenty would, of course. The rush to the colours. He had seen it all in 1899. Now, glancing round the ballroom at Mawby Hall, he could almost pick out those who would unthinkingly answer the call and as carelessly throw their lives away in the name of glory. To him, glory had a hollow sound.

'Is this next dance yours too?' Poppy was asking.

'No, our host has claimed you.'

'Then kiss me now. No one will notice.'

Jimmy bent his head, and her hands went up to draw him closer, the diamond half-hoop, restored to her finger, glinting for all the world to see. He wanted to grow old with Poppy, but would he? Not for the first time, he was thankful he could not foresee.

Poppy was wrong in thinking no one would see that swift, secret embrace. Chatting brightly to her partner – she did not lack for partners – Emily watched the pair of them weave in and out of the throng. There was no mistaking the intentness of sexual attraction – she would recognize it anywhere. Somehow they had made it up and the thought did not please her. Her mask could not conceal her frown.

'Is Your Majesty displeased?'

She raised practised eyes to her partner. 'Not with present company.'

'Not fair to offend the fair.' Her partner was already a trifle fuddled. 'Who's that fast gipsy piece?'

Emily was about to say 'My brother-in-law's fiancée' when she saw that his gaze was directed elsewhere. Another gipsy in nearly identical costume was moulded to her partner. Almost it might have been Poppy: the hair showing beneath the kerchief was dark; they were much of a height, and her features were obscured by the mask; but this girl was a stranger.

She looked away and answered, 'I don't know.'

'Too bad. I was hoping for an introduction. She doesn't exactly hold back.'

'I'm afraid I haven't been watching,' Emily said stiffly as her partner drew her to him in attempted emulation.

'Oh, come now, Your Majesty, your eyes are everywhere. They've certainly not been gazing into mine.'

His were slightly bloodshot, Emily reflected, as she hastened to assure him, 'I'm just enjoying the ball.'

Part of her was. She loved to dance, to feel her body sway to rhythms not her own. The orchestra, though small, was lively and performed its share of the latest hits. *The Merry Widow* provided much of the music – she had hoped that Jimmy would take her to see it, but no – and as her eyes raked the room yet again in search of him and Poppy, she wondered in how many couples the words of the waltz song aroused response. 'Though I say not what I may not let you hear, Yet the swaying dance is saying, "Love me, dear . . ." ' Instinctively she pressed herself a little closer to her enthusiastic partner. It was unthinkable that Jimmy should marry that girl. If he couldn't see it, surely Madam could; yet Madam, who had frosted Emily from the day Harry had first brought her home, had not only gone out of her way to be gracious to this weed, this Poppy, but she had specifically invited her to tea. Emily had hoped that it might be to discomfort her in the privacy of the Dower House, but Poppy had returned ebullient; even the alarm over George's accident had not dampened her spirits. Whatever rift there might have been between her and Jimmy seemed to have been speedily mended. Emily's chagrin was complete, especially when she caught sight of them, a pirate and a gipsy, dancing in their own private, impenetrable world.

Emily could not have said when the plan first formed in her head. Not that it formed; it was no more than a determination to separate them and a shadowy perception of how it might be done. But it depended on so many things: the right place, the right time, her own guile, and it was only on the last of these that she felt she could rely. Of course it would not bring Jimmy back to her – that was more than she dared hope – but she was beyond the point of considering personal advantage; as with the destruction of Harry's letter to

George, she craved only the loser's taste of power. Straitened circumstances in Cossipore would be more bearable if they were accompanied by Amberley's downfall; the loss of Jimmy was endurable if Poppy lost him too.

'You know, you're a very fine dancer.' Her partner's voice brought her back.

'Thank you. It helps when a man knows how to lead.'

'And when a woman knows how to follow.' The arm tightened about her waist.

This time she did not resist, and her partner was heard to say later that that Mary Queen of Scots was a damned attractive woman, and those stiff, stand-offish skirts were deceiving, by Gad they were.

'Ladies and gentlemen, your partners, please, for a veleta.'

The Master of Ceremonies was already becoming hoarse. Half the county seemed packed into the Mawby Hall ballroom, and there was another impromptu ball for the servants downstairs. Bea was dancing with Alice, Rose and Roddy having been whisked away by the harem lady with gold spangles, their hostess, Lady St Devereux. Alice was a natural dancer; Bea knew only too well that she was not. She was the despair of her mother, and even strained the saintly patience of Madame Vee, the tiny, exquisite, dark-haired lady who earned a meagre living by trying to instruct the young sahibs and memsahibs of Cossipore in the rudiments of rhythm and grace.

'One and two and point your toe,' she murmured to herself.

'You're out of step,' Alice hissed.

'Sorry.'

Bea's dances were punctuated with apologies, her partner's gallant, her own embarrassed. 'I never seem to get it right,' she would say tearfully to Madame Vee.

'Don't cry, little one,' Madame Vee would comfort in her soft accent, and regardless of the fact that Beatrix was as tall as she. 'It is not the whole of life, to dance. For you there will be other things.'

Bea certainly hoped so as she stumbled yet again and another apology rose to her lips.

'Don't keep saying sorry,' Alice instructed. 'You only make everything worse.'

'Sorry,' Bea said automatically, and felt herself begin to blush.

If only she could move with the grace of Madame Vee, who was like a small cat and had in addition the feline characteristic of never appearing to perspire. She was the most beautiful and romantic person Bea had ever seen, the Vee being short for Varvara because she was half Russian, as she had once confided; her late father had been an officer of the Tsar.

'An officer, perhaps,' Mama said when Bea reported this at the dinner table. 'Did she tell you what her mother was?'

'Why would she?'

'She'd have every reason not to. Varvara indeed! More likely her name is Vijaya.'

'But that's an Indian name.'

'Precisely,' Major North said from the head of the table. 'The girl's a chee-chee.'

'What's that?'

'Your mother will explain.'

But Mama never had, beyond saying something about mixed blood. And what was wrong with that? Yet there must be something, when the most beautiful woman in Cossipore – even more beautiful than Mama, Bea admitted – was not invited to anyone's dinner parties and was barely acknowledged in the street.

As the tempo of the dance quickened, Bea reflected that even Madame Vee would surely perspire in the Mawby Hall ballroom. Her palms were moist, she felt as though she had a moustache of tiny dewdrops, she was warm and sticky below the waist. Worse still, her feet were more than ever reluctant to obey instructions, or even to keep time.

'What *is* the matter?' Alice asked in irritation.

'I don't feel very well.'

'Then you'd better sit down,' said practical Alice. 'There's a sofa over there.'

'I think I need the ladies' cloakroom.'

'Why? Are you going to be sick?'

'I don't know.'

'Would you like me to find Aunt Emily?'

Bea had had experience before now of Mama's reaction if her pleasures were interrupted. 'I'd rather you came with me,' she said.

If only Ayah were here. Or even Nanny, with a brisk 'Feeling a bit poorly, are we? Never mind, we'll soon have you right.' Even so, there was something comforting about Alice's presence as her cousin put an arm about her waist and said, 'Poor old Trix.'

No one in the ballroom noticed their departure, but someone outside it did. Nose pressed against the glass of a small side window, Mary Bottrall witnessed a kaleidoscopic fragment of all that was going on. Faintly she could hear the music. Her eyes picked out a dozen details of costumes as they danced by: a Dolly Varden hat, a spyglass, braid on a collar, a bosom daringly displayed. Oh, to be part of it, to dance to that music, to lose oneself in the alluring anonymity of fancy dress! Where was the fairy godmother who should have waved a wand and dispatched her to the ball? Only give her the chance and she could have been the belle, the charmer of Prince Charming, who must surely exist within that close-packed throng.

When she had left the cottage and her grandmother's unending lamentations, Mary had had no intention of coming to Mawby Hall. All she wanted was fresh clean air rather than a room in which the fire was smoking, and a chance to give her strong young body exercise. Her boots rang out sharply down the village high street. She was aware of curtains twitching as she went by. But 'Only Mary' the villagers would have murmured, well knowing her love of night-walking, and adding meaningly, 'She's got something to be walking off tonight.' Then, thankful that they were not in those neat black boots whose uppers were always polished, regardless of the state of their soles, they would return to their fires, to the last of the Christmas beef and poultry, and the enveloping ordinariness of everyday.

Mary was light on her feet; the night excited her. It was as though her feet had wings, like those of the god Mercury whom she had seen pictured in books from the library; she seemed to skim the ground. On a night as moonbright as this there was no need for caution; besides, she knew every rut of every lane for miles around. When the first carriage overtook her she had shrunk back against the rime of the hedgerow; with the second and its successors she had boldly stood her ground, feeling the brush of air as they passed her, breathing in the swift horse scent. Some of the coachmen knew her and saluted; others speculated why this young woman should walk abroad so late and guessed she was on her way to help in Mawby Hall kitchens, where there was always plenty of work after a ball.

Mary had forgotten about the ball until the carriages reminded her. Now, impulsively, she resolved to have a look at how the gentry disported themselves. After all, she might not have another chance if she and Gran were to be evicted . . . She avoided wondering what would become of them. Her first thought of escaping to London had had to be abandoned after her meeting with Poppy in the park. Clearly there was nothing there for a girl who lacked the qualifications of a lady typewriter, and a factory worker's wage would not keep her, away from home. But if the Norths were forced to leave, to sell Amberley, surely for the Bottralls that would mean reprieve? Unless the Colonel acted hastily because of that episode this morning in his study . . . But only Mrs Harry knew of it, and Mrs Harry was not here for long. She was even cutting short her visit, Sam Jepson reported, and returning to London next day. And Colonel North had other things on his mind. The loss of Amberley meant the heart was being torn out of him, leaving his straight shoulders slumped, his strong hands flaccid. The one she had held had been inert, like a dead man's hand.

Head high, Mary passed through Mawby Hall's crested gateway. Away to her left, through a stand of trees, the lake's sheath of ice glinted. There would be skating if the frost kept up, except at the end farthest from the house which never froze over because a stream flowed in. When the lake froze the St Devereuxs opened their grounds to all and sundry, and a rope was stretched across the lake midway, with notices beyond saying 'Danger', which tempted the foolhardy to stray. One year the ice had broken and a young man had fallen in. He was quickly pulled out, but Mary remembered the warning creaks, the loud crack, the blackness of the water which lay evil and still despite the trickling of the stream, so different from its summer self edged with buttercups and water-crowfoot, its surface swallow-skimmed.

Once inside the gates of the Hall, Mary veered away from the drive and its line of carriages and slid like an eel through darkness round to the back of the house. The ballroom windows shone out above her, too high for her to see in. Except for one, beneath which there was an outhouse with a sloping roof from which the snow had cascaded. Cautiously she scaled the slates and pulled herself upright, gripping the window-ledge.

The first face she saw whirling past was Mr Jimmy's, alight with happiness. She stuck out her tongue at him. What right had he to happiness when he was responsible for Hector's death? Unless . . . unless Madam was right and Hector's friend had misunderstood, had blamed him unjustly. It was a possibility Mary had never considered before, but since this morning she had looked on the Norths differently. If Colonel North was vulnerable, fallible, so perhaps were they all. Even Madam. Her visit had been kindly intentioned; she was old; she could not help her manner; she had not been looking well . . .

Lady St Devereux floated by, all veils and gold spangles, her teeth bared in something that passed for a smile. Other faces, unfamiliar beneath wigs and head-dresses; Mrs Harry, the most regal of them all. Briefly Mary watched

Alice and Beatrix dancing, saw them falter, then hurry from the room. Her hands were numb; so were her feet, she discovered. She slithered down the outhouse roof and dropped to the ground. At that moment the kitchen door opened. A familiar voice cried, 'Mary! What are you doing here?' Jepson and another servant were carrying out an armful of empty bottles. He looked at her in astonishment.

Mary said, with a touch of her usual defiance, 'I came to see the ball.'

'Then come on in. We're having a bit of a ball ourselves downstairs and I need a partner. No one'll mind so long as I vouch for you.'

Mary hesitated. A guest at the servants' ball when she was too proud to be a servant? But neither was she a guest at the ball upstairs. For a moment she hated ballroom and servants' hall in equal measure.

Watching her, Jepson said, 'No obligation, of course,' and turned away. That was all you ever got for trying to be decent to Mary, the stupid, stuck-up cow. Then he felt his arm grasped and looked down at her.

'Thanks, Sam. I'd like to come.'

The whole of Mawby Hall was full of balls within balls, embraces within embraces, tomorrow's intrigues crystallizing tonight as surely as the water of the lake was crystallizing, building up and damming even the stream-fed entrance which still flowed. The supper-dance was coming up and most of the guests had already contrived to take a peep at the vast collation spread out in the supper-room. The Mawby Hall indoor servants were lined up and waiting – no ball until later for them – and the butler was giving last-minute instructions. Of Lady St Devereux there was no sign.

'Her ladyship has already checked everything,' the butler said with bland half-truth, for her ladyship had been in and out of the room constantly, as the level in a wine-bottle showed. And now she was seated in the room set aside as the ladies' cloakroom, bright-eyed, loud-voiced, surrounded by anxious friends concerned to forestall possible scandal. There was nothing in life so bad it could not be hushed up.

Lady St Devereux had lit a cigarette and was waving it rather than smoking it.

'The bastard's leavin' me,' she said.

'Muriel, dear!' said one of the ladies in shocked protest.

'Wha'ssa matter? You think my language is too plain?'

'You're drunk,' said an older woman.

Muriel St Devereux regarded her narrowly. 'So what if I am? Didn't you hear me say

Eddie's quittin'? For good this time. Goin' up to London tomorrow by the fast train.'

'He'll be back,' another woman predicted confidently.

Muriel blew smoke. 'Who says I want him back?'

'Dear, we all know it's not the ideal marriage, but surely you're not thinking of divorce?'

'I'm thinkin' of freedom.'

'But your reputation!'

'*My* reputation! *I'll* be divorcing *him*. And about time too. He's never been faithful, except perhaps on our honeymoon.'

'You're not the only woman in that position,' another voice said crisply. 'Most of us learn to cope.'

'I'm sick of copin'. Why do you think I chose to dress up like some whore in a harem? It's what I've been all my married life.'

She began to cry, noisy, gulping sobs. Someone took the cigarette from her. One lady, sharper-eyed than the rest, murmured, 'Control yourself. Or at least lower your voice. Two little girls have just gone into the far cubicle.'

Muriel said, 'Oh God, I'm going to throw up.'

Consternation.

The older woman said authoritatively, 'It's

the best thing. She'll be better after this.'

'But it's the supper-dance. She'll be missed.'

'A headache. Indisposition.'

The ladies nodded understandingly and scattered to spread the word, leaving only two as guardians.

'She can't divorce him,' said the elder. 'However innocent you are when you go into court, you come out sullied. Divorce is social death for a woman.'

The other said hesitantly, 'That hardly seems quite fair.'

'Who said anything about being fair? You take life and twist it. It's surprising how much you can wring out of it if you try.'

'By unfair means.'

'My dear girl, what do you expect? Equality? Anyone would think you were a Suffragette.'

'I wouldn't be anything so unladylike. All the same, I sometimes think they have a point . . .'

'Then don't let me hear you say so. By the way, I hope those children have gone?'

'Oh yes, I think so. I believe I saw them going.'

'Thank heaven. Now, Muriel –' to their emerging, whitefaced hostess – 'let's see what we can do to make you presentable again.'

Presentability was in Poppy's mind too as Jimmy whirled her around the floor to strains of Strauss.

'My hair's coming down,' she whispered.

'Let it. I'd love to see it.'

'This isn't the place or time.'

'Perhaps not,' he conceded. 'Do you want to go and tidy?'

'Where do I go?'

'To where you left your coat.' He sensed her hesitation, and led her out of the ballroom to the gallery above the main staircase and the entrance to the supper-room. Several smaller rooms opened off it and had been furnished with tables and chairs so that those ladies who wished for peace and quietness, or simply to rest their feet, could wait while their escorts besieged the buffet. Jimmy pointed to the first small room opposite the right-hand branch of the staircase.

'You'll find me waiting in here. There'll be other ladies coming out in a minute, but if you go now you'll beat the rush when the supper-dance is ended.'

He pointed her in the right direction and she departed, her kerchief awry and dark hair escaping over her shoulders with a truly abandoned, gipsyish air. Down the stairs – how small she looked – and through the door to the right, where he could no longer see her. He turned back to the little room to wait.

Once out of his sight, uncertainty overwhelmed Poppy. What was she doing here in the house of these titled people, decked out in clothes that were not even her own? Lord St Devereux had been charming when he danced with her; other people too had been kind; Jimmy could not have been more attentive; but it was all a long, long way from Jubilee Terrace and the kind of ball she had attended in the past. Those were balls to which you bought a ticket (or had one bought for you), held in assembly rooms or halls, given by local clubs and trade associations, graced sometimes by the presence of the Mayor. The parties her family and friends made up were noisier, friendlier, than that which had set out from Amberley. They went in hired cabs, and coming home they were always joking and laughing and full of the good time they had had.

She was so full of remembrance of them that she was unprepared for the small, flying figure that suddenly flung itself into her arms, causing her to stagger, still further dislodging her kerchief, sending more of her hair tumbling down.

'Alice! What ever is the matter?'

'Oh, Aunt Poppy, Aunt Poppy—'

All her grave composure gone, Alice looked

suddenly very much a frightened child, Rose's elder sister, as she fought for coherence and breath.

'–Aunt Poppy, you must please come to Beatrix. She's ill and I don't know what's the matter with her, but I think–' Alice's gift for the dramatic asserted itself – 'I think she's bleeding to death.'

Of all the balls within balls held that evening, one of the smallest was that composed of Rose and Roddy and the two children staying at Mawby Hall.

When Lady St Devereux had swooped down on them, announcing in the kind of grown-up voice that brooked no gainsaying, 'I need you two to help me,' they had followed her meekly enough. So long as they were together . . . And here there was no one to pour scorn on them for holding hands, as even Nanny had taken to doing in the past two days: 'A big boy like you, Master Roddy. I should think you'd be ashamed.'

Lady St Devereux smelt of sweat and face powder, and violet cachous when she opened her mouth to speak.

'I've got two little people for you to play with . . . dance with,' she informed them. 'They're just the same age as you.'

In this she was mistaken, for of the two children sitting disconsolately in an alcove the boy was one year older than Roddy and the girl two years younger than Rose. Roddy saw with sinking heart that they were dressed in what his father would have called mufti. It seemed to give them an advantage from the start.

'There!' said Lady St Devereux, much as a conjuror might say Hey presto! 'Edgar and Stella. I know you're going to be friends.'

Her second statement seemed likely to prove as inaccurate as her first, but she did not linger to discover. With a bright 'Enjoy yourselves, chicks,' which momentarily united all four against her, she turned on a Turkish-slippered heel and was gone.

Edgar broke the silence. 'Is that fairy your sister?' he demanded, pointing at Rose.

'No, Rose is my cousin.'

'We live in Bayswater. Where do you live?'

'In India.'

'Seen any elephants?'

'Yes.'

'Ever ridden on one?'

'No.'

Edgar lost interest in India.

'My father's a stockbroker,' he announced.

'Mine's an army officer. And Rose –' Roddy drew her firmly into the conversation –

'Rose's father is Colonel George North of Amberley.'

'Where's that?'

'About two miles away.'

'Oh. I heard Lady St Devereux telling my mother that there was no decent society round here.'

'Perhaps she doesn't know many people,' Rose said politely. 'She hardly ever calls on Mama. Are you staying here?' she asked Stella.

'Yes.'

'Are you enjoying yourself?'

'No.'

Stella rarely said anything but yes and no, they were to discover. Edgar elaborated.

'The country's a dead bore. My father said so. He didn't want to come.'

'Then why did you?'

'Mother was keen.' This was evidently sufficient explanation. 'Personally I'll be glad to get home.'

'We're going back to London tomorrow.'

'So are we.'

'We might see you on the train.'

'Hardly. We have a reserved compartment. There are four of us and my mother's maid.'

'Did you have a nice Christmas?' Rose asked Stella.

'No.'

'So you're glad to be going home?'

'No.'

Rose looked to Roddy for assistance. He hurled himself into the breach.

'Do you go to a boarding school?' he asked Edgar.

'Yes, worse luck.'

'Don't you like it?'

'*Like* Bradwell House?' Edgar paused to consider the enormity of this suggestion. 'It's unfit for human consumption,' he pronounced.

Roddy hoped they couldn't hear his heart sinking. To him it felt like a stone.

'I'm going there next term.'

'My condolences. Of course,' Edgar continued, brightening, 'it gets better as it goes on. The new boys – squabs, we call 'em – always blub a lot at first. We rag 'em, you see. And then, they miss their mothers. Or their cousins,' he said, with a glance to Rose.

'I shall miss Rose,' Roddy admitted innocently, 'but I shall write to her every day.'

Edgar licked his lips, foreseeing future diversion. 'You're only allowed one letter a week. And it has to be to your parents. And old Beaky censors them.'

Roddy felt an urge to blub there and then. 'Who's old Beaky?'

'Mr. Thompson, the headmaster. He's

got a nose like a beak.'

Rose moved her hand in Roddy's. 'Never mind, Roddy. I'll write to you.'

'Sweethearts, sweethearts,' Edgar crackled. 'A squab with a sweetheart. That's new.'

Roddy would have liked to hit him, but he felt Rose's restraining hand. 'Perhaps we ought to dance,' she suggested. And to Stella with supreme self-sacrifice: 'Would you like to dance with Roddy?'

'No.'

'Why not?' Rose asked dangerously.

Stella abandoned monosyllables for a sentence. 'I don't like him.'

The sound of a slap rang through the room.

'How dare you!' Rose panted. 'He's worth three of your stupid brother.'

Stella seized Rose's golden curls. 'He's not!'

The thorns of Rose's fingernails were out instantly, and a smear of blood appeared on Stella's cheek.

'Here, North, call off your spitfire cousin. She's bigger than my sister.'

'She isn't. Your sister's fat. Like you,' Roddy added, assessing his opponent and neatly dodging the first blow.

'At least I'm not dressed up as if I belong to a pierhead concert-party. You wait till I tell 'em about this at school.'

The battle raged. A small chair was knocked over and went unnoticed in the mêlée until a cool voice said, 'What's going on here?' and the combatants pantingly drew apart.

Jimmy North surveyed his nephew, who had a bruise that might be going to be a black eye. His niece's fairy wings were askew. Edgar's nose was bleeding on to his shirt front. Stella's lace collar was torn.

'Have you no manners?' he asked, lips twitching. 'You are all four guests in this house.'

Roddy hung his head. 'I'm sorry.'

'He didn't start it, Uncle, I did,' Rose protested. 'And Edgar hit him first. He goes to Bradwell House, where Roddy's going, and he says it's awful.' Her blue eyes brimmed with tears.

Jimmy inspected Edgar. 'Been there long?' he asked.

'A term,' Edgar mumbled, blushing.

'Hardly long enough to judge, is it? My first term was awful too. Of course,' he added quickly, 'some boys take to it from the start. It makes a difference if you know someone there already, someone who'll show you the ropes.' He allowed an instant for the idea to penetrate their skulls, then said to Edgar, 'Got a clean shirt you can change into?'

'Yes, sir.'

'Then I suggest you cut along and do just that. As for you –' he turned to Roddy – 'I should bathe that eye in cold water. Edgar will show you where.'

He became aware that Rose and Stella had turned on him a trustful gaze.

'You're still in one piece, aren't you?' he asked, searching for inspiration what to do with them while trying unsuccessfully to straighten Rose's fairy wings.

They nodded like dutiful dolls.

'Then why don't you go down to the supper-room? The boys will join you. You can't keep a boy away from food.'

Still they hesitated.

'Go on. There's ice-cream,' Jimmy thankfully remembered. And as a final inducement: 'It's pink.'

After Rose and Stella had departed hand in hand, he returned to the room at the top of the stairs where he was to meet Poppy, apologies and explanations on his lips. 'You should have seen them . . . our little Rosebud began it, can you imagine? . . . Someone must have said something against Roddy, nothing else would make her go berserk . . .' He got no further with rehearsing his account of the incident, for

Poppy was not there. He looked around, willing one of the seated ladies to transform herself, then went to the head of the stairs. People were milling about everywhere, fetching and carrying food and drink; some were sitting on the steps. The hall below was a-swirl with colour. Talk and laughter floated up, occasionally shrill, but with an undertone of good humour. The ball was a huge success – something that would be long remembered after the St Devereux divorce had faded from the headlines and Mawby Hall was up for sale.

Now, however, Jimmy searched the crowd vainly for his colourful gipsy. She was nowhere to be seen. Of course, it might have taken him longer than he thought to deal with the children. What if she had come and gone? If she had returned and failed to find him, would she have gone to the supper-room? Or would her fragile confidence have crumbled, causing her to hide herself? Should he stay or go in search of her? Jimmy hovered distractedly. He was almost relieved when Emily appeared at his elbow.

'All alone?' she purred.

'Yes . . . No . . . I'm waiting for Poppy . . . I was called away . . . She seems to have been delayed. But you?' Jimmy recovered himself. 'You're not without a partner?'

'Oh no, Mr. Channing is looking after me.'

What a pity one could not say, 'The Honourable Geoffrey Channing'. Jimmy might not even realize that his sister-in-law had effectively removed from circulation one of the most eligible local bachelors, to the chagrin of several mamas who had been hoping that fancy dress would lend their daughters an attraction in the eyes of the Honourable Geoffrey which they had hitherto failed to possess.

'Oh, good.' Jimmy tried to concentrate on what he was saying while his eyes roved everywhere. 'Emily, Poppy went to the ladies' cloakroom. Do you think you could see if she's still there? She might have been taken ill or something.'

Emily went very still. 'Oh no,' she said softly, so softly. 'I don't think your Poppy is ill. Why, I believe I saw her quite recently.'

'Where?'

'In the room opposite the other branch of the staircase.'

'She must have come up the wrong side. Thanks, Emily.' Jimmy had already taken a step away from her when she laid a hand on his arm.

'Of course I wouldn't have left her alone,' she said gently, 'but you see, she wasn't alone. I thought she was with a partner and that was why you were on your own.'

The stricken look on his face was reward enough for what had been almost too easy. Never had she believed revenge could be so simple – or so sweet. As she passed the other room, which, being at the far end from the ballroom, was deserted, she had glimpsed a gipsy clasped in a man's arms. She paused, but it wasn't Poppy; she had been wishfully deceived. But if she could be mistaken, so could Jimmy.

She said, 'I think you ought to go and see.'

He moved like a blind man; she followed discreetly. He would never have noticed that there was another gipsy at the ball, and even if he realized that the girl so wantonly embracing was not Poppy, she herself could plead innocence. The close similarity of the costumes, the height, the colour of the hair, anyone could mistake the one for the other. She hoped the embracing couple were still there.

They were. From a few paces behind him, she saw Jimmy go very still and had a sudden fear that he might launch a physical assault upon the couple – a complication she had not foreseen. She moved forward protectively, but after one long look he merely turned away, almost colliding with her. She put out a hand to touch him.

'I am so sorry,' she said.

Jimmy looked down at this stranger in the pearl-encrusted cap and stand-up collar. Why was she trying to accost him when all he wanted was to get away? he wanted the farthest ocean, the remotest desert isle, the veldt even (though never India), anywhere where there was no Amberley, no family, no acquaintance however distant, above all no Poppy, to remind him of this shame.

She was getting her own back. A part of him did not blame her. She was demonstrating that what had been all right for him was equally so for her. He had shown her that for him other people's marriage vows did not matter. Could he reproach her for disregarding her own? And not even marriage vows. She was still a free agent. Engagements had been broken before now. Had she chosen this way of telling him that despite their seeming reconciliation, their relationship was no more?

It hardly mattered who the man was. No doubt she had chosen the first who came to hand, and there would be plenty willing to respond to such an invitation in the easy, relaxed atmosphere of the ball. 'Though I say not what I may not let you hear . . .' The words of *The Merry Widow* waltz song returned to mock him. There was nothing like a ball for stolen pleasure, and all the chaperones in the world had found no way of denying them. 'Every touch of fingers tells me what I know' – or what I delude myself into believing, for those same fingers can rest as lightly on another's arm; 'Seems to say 'tis true, 'tis true' – ah yes, that 'seems', that word slipped in which can invalidate all the others, especially the final phrase, the triumphant 'You love me so,' when the music crescendoes to its climax and the dancers draw apart from theirs. 'You love me so' – not 'so much', but 'so', meaning this way, meaning no way at all. Jimmy shook his head and realized Emily was confronting him, had just spoken.

'I am sorry,' she said.

Was it the first or second time she had said it? He neither knew nor cared.

'The man is – notorious,' she ventured. A little fuel to flame could do no harm.

But her fuel was ill chosen. It did not matter to Jimmy whether the man was notorious or not, whether Poppy had sought him out or he had waylaid her, for this was no casual kiss. It was a demonstration of sexual attraction for all the world to see. The unworthy thought sneaked in that it might be the kind of thing she was used to in the circles in which she moved.

'Come.' Emily was leading him back towards the supper-room. A gentleman hovering with two plates greeted her appearance with relief.

'Mr Channing – my brother-in-law . . .' Emily made the introductions. She had a chance to say 'The Honourable Geoffrey Channing' after all.

Jimmy's response was dazed but courteous. Emily was wondering what next to say when she noticed swift movement in the crowd below them and saw Poppy hurrying up the stairs. Yes, there was no doubt: the two gipsies were easily mistaken. Emily was preparing to exclaim, apologize, explain, her sweet, short moment of triumph over, when she realized Poppy was hastening not to Jimmy's side but to hers. And Poppy, more relieved to single out the Queen of Scots than she would ever have believed possible, was drawing her aside, anxiety and concern radiating from her.

'Your daughter needs you,' she said.

The Honourable Geoffrey Channing's hands wavered. He would have flapped them had they not been full. 'Sounds nasty, what?'

'I don't think so,' Poppy assured him, never taking her eyes off Emily. 'She's being looked after in the ladies' cloakroom, but it's her mother Beatrix needs.'

Emily calculated swiftly how to deal with

this unwelcome development. If she went at once, all maternal solicitude, she would appear the perfect mother and men always approved of that. But what they really preferred was the independent, mature, untrammelled woman, particularly one whose husband was far away.

She made a little gesture of resignation and apology to her partner. 'Do excuse me. I'll be back as soon as I can. Meanwhile, I'm sure Miss Richards is hungry. It would be a kindness to give her my plate.'

She turned to go, only to find Jimmy confronting her.

'You knew,' he said in a low voice.

'Knew what?' She was alarmed by his intensity.

'You knew that other gipsy wasn't Poppy.'

Emily's chin came up as far as her stand-up collar would allow it. 'Indeed I didn't,' she lied.

'You did,' Jimmy insisted. 'You'd had plenty of time to check. You were out to make trouble between us.'

'Why should I want to do that?'

'God knows. Jealousy, I suppose. The old, old story of a woman well and truly scorned.' The scorn was in his voice as he looked at Emily's stiff skirts spread winningly, the glowing velvet of her dress.

Emily put out a hand. 'Jimmy, I didn't mean to –'

'I'd rather not hear.'

'That's unfair.'

'Unfair? Coming from you, that's rich. Shall I tell you something? You're shabby, Emily. You're the shabbiest woman I know.'

Picking her way down the stairs between those sitting out, Emily felt her face flaming. He had said it so unnecessarily loud that the Honourable Geoffrey Channing must have heard him; so must Poppy and others standing by. Shabby. She, Emily North, the belle of Cossipore, was shabby. Whatever was wrong with Beatrix, her mother decided, it would provide the perfect excuse to get away. They would leave this scene of humiliation, and tomorrow they would all leave Amberley. After that she would leave England as soon as she could get a berth. The SS *Jaipur* with its handsome second officer did not sail till February, but there were other boats. There were always others . . .

Her quick footsteps pattered across the hall. She pushed open the door of the ladies' cloakroom and Beatrix, sobbing, flung herself into her mother's arms.

Emily's decision to leave early had its repercussions in the servants' hall, where the impromptu ball in progress was every bit as spirited as its official counterpart above stairs. It consisted mostly of the outdoor servants, plus visiting coachmen and grooms, but the presence of the kitchen staff whose task of washing up did not begin till later, and of housemaids whose task of cleaning came later still, was not sufficient to secure equal numbers. Sam Jepson had done well to acquire a partner when he could. Music was provided by an elderly upright piano on which an under-footman thumped with the forte pedal held firmly to the floor, while one or two cronies assisted him in keeping time by banging beer bottles on the lid.

To the regret of the dancers, the hall was not big enough for the lancers or a cotillion, but the waltz, the polka and the barn dance were enthusiastically performed. If the words were known, everyone sang them, while the piano-player, avoiding subtleties of syncopation, concentrated on the beat. The housekeeper, Mrs Beales, to whom Jepson had presented Mary, kept a prudent eye on what was going on, but when the butler descended briefly and led her on to the floor, the dancers drew back to enjoy an exhibition of faultless footwork which would have done credit to any of the couples in the ballroom above.

Mary flung herself into the gaiety. She was a wilder, freer dancer than Mrs Beales, and tonight desperation lent an extra emancipation to her movements which Jepson appreciated. Mary was good fun when she chose to be, better than anyone else he knew; and he hadn't half admired her for telling off Madam, though along with the rest of the village he feared the consequences for her might be grave.

'Has the Colonel said anything to you?' he whispered.

Mary moved her head back. 'What about?'

'About you and your gran – what's happening to you.'

'No,' Mary said, 'nor he won't.'

The broken man who had held her that morning would take no action, she had almost convinced herself of that. As for the new owner of Amberley, whoever he was, why should he evict them? He would not be buying grudges with the ground.

Jepson swung her round in the barn dance and there was a thunder of stamping feet, as much from the spectators as from the dancers. As they returned to their places, Wilkins lumbered across.

'Got to go now,' he informed Jepson, wiping his beer moustache with the back of his hand.

'What, both of us?' Jepson asked, dismayed.

'What's the matter?'

'No,' Wilkins said, 'only me. Mrs Harry's got to leave early. One of the little girls isn't well.'

'That'll please her,' Jepson opined

'Yes, she's mad as a hornet. One to be sorry for is the child, if you ask me.'

'Which one is it?' Jepson asked, hoping it wasn't Alice.

'Miss Beatrix. She and her mother and Miss Alice are to go, and you're to stay on for Mr Jimmy and that Miss Richards and the two little 'uns.'

Jepson said, 'Right you are. Suits me.'

It suited him very well. He was enjoying himself, and so was Mary. Her cheeks were becomingly flushed. One or two of the other men were giving him glances of envy or admiration, and that suited Jepson too.

'Can I get you some refreshment?' he offered Mary. There was tea and lemonade for the maids, with Mrs Beales keeping watch to make sure the beer bottles marshalled at one end of the big servants' hall table were reserved exclusively for males.

'Thank you,' Mary said. 'I'd like a lemonade.'

'Quite a day,' he remarked conversationally. 'What with the Colonel's accident . . .'

The whole village knew of that. Even old

Annie Bottrall had briefly abandoned lamentation on her own behalf in favour of her benefactor's and had, as usual, found adequate cause for alarm.

'You mark my words, Mary, the Colonel's like to lose his leg. The gangrene'll set in and that'll be the end of him. Unless he survives, of course.' She paused to contemplate this possibility, more unwelcome to her granddaughter than she knew. 'He might, I suppose,' she conceded. 'I was saying only the other day the Norths are a lucky family. Apart from Mrs George's poor sister, that is. I remember when they laid her out they had to turn her head to one side in the coffin to hide what had happened to her face. So young she was. There's nothing like the death of a young 'un for making you feel your age. Not that I shall live long. I shall end my days in the workhouse, thanks to you and your wicked tongue. And Madam always so good to us . . .'

The monologue wandered on. Mary had said mechanically, 'Oh, Gran, do be quiet,' but neither content nor volume decreased. In desperation, she had seized her coat, closed the cottage door behind her, and escaped into the night.

'How is the Colonel?' she asked Jepson now, feeling the enquiry was expected.

'Dr Paget says he'll be as right as rain in a week or two, and of course he's all the better for Miss Richards's good news.'

'What's that?'

'Why, it seems there's a valuable picture in the Dower House which'll fetch a fortune if they sell.'

Mary's face was so expressionless that Jepson thought she had not taken in this statement. 'The Family's short of the ready,' he explained. 'Or so Mr Jarvis was telling us. The picture's a real windfall, like.'

The Norths are a lucky family. Mary heard her grandmother's voice.

'So the Colonel won't have to sell Amberley,' she said tightly.

'Sell Amberley? I don't know about that. Who told you he was going to?'

'I heard it.'

'Ah, you hear a lot of things. You don't want to take no notice. The Norths 'ud never sell Amberley.'

'No,' Mary said. Not if they could help it. Not if there was a fortune hanging on their walls. They would stay, and she and Gran . . . *I shall end my days in the workhouse.*

She asked Jepson, 'Are you getting me that lemonade?'

Jepson went. Despite the hot room, Mary

shivered. Amberley was not to be sold. There would be no new owner, no wiping the slate clean, as the children did in school. She and Gran would have to leave their cottage. Gran homeless at her age . . . *I shall end my days in the workhouse.*

'No,' Mary said faintly.

A girl near her asked, 'Are you all right?'

The question was echoed by Jepson, returning with the lemonade. Mary looked so white that he wondered whether to fetch Mrs Beales, but she glared at him with eyes that made him think of a trapped animal defying with its last breath the trapper, and insisted there was nothing wrong. 'Except,' she added in a small voice that was unlike her, 'if you don't mind, Sam, I'll change my mind and have a cup of tea.'

Jepson obligingly made his way back to the table. When he returned with the tea, Mary was gone.

'Your friend wasn't feeling none too good,' a maid informed him. 'She asked me to say as she's gone home.'

Blast her, Jepson thought savagely, spoiling a good evening without so much as troubling to explain. She had been all right until five minutes ago, he was certain. It must have been something he said, but he could think of nothing in their brief exchange that could have upset her. He set down the cup of tea. 'You should see me dance the polka,' pounded the pianist. Jepson turned to the hopeful housemaid beside him.

'Would you like to dance?' he said.

Out in the grounds Mary Bottrall walked unseeing. A million stars were gathered overhead. A million points of light were glittering on the hedges, on grass crisply coated with frost. An owl floated from one tree to another. More distantly, one hooted in the wood. She could hear a carriage horse stamping, the chink of harness. There was a sudden upsurge of music from the ball.

The supper interval must be over. 'Ladies and gentlemen, take your partners for a waltz.' Mary paused to listen. It was *The Skaters*, one of her favourites. For a moment she stood with head thrown back and eyes closed, drinking in the music and the night.

The sound of an approaching carriage roused her. That would be Mrs Harry and the girls. Yes, Wilkins was on the box, but he did not raise his whip in greeting. Madam's servants loyally took Madam's part. And if her servants did, how much more would her family. No, the Colonel would have no mercy on her if he stayed. And stay he would, for had not Jepson revealed that Amberley was safe for another generation? The Norths were a lucky family indeed.

Unlike the Bottralls, Mary thought bitterly. Her parents and Hector dead. Private Hector Bottrall killed in action. Private Hector Bottrall killed . . . Oh, the unfairness of it all. This time tomorrow the eviction order might have been served and a week later Gran could be in the workhouse, unless the Colonel took pity on her. As he might on an old woman left alone and helpless, whose sole fault lay in her grand-daughter. If she could only have gone to London, leaving Gran at the Colonel's mercy, might not that mercy have been shown? But conversation with Miss Richards had made it clear that the metropolis offered no solution. Whichever way she turned, there was no escape.

Her next thought caused Mary to draw in a breath of cold air so sharply that she choked, a rasping gurgle that rattled in her throat. She gave a little cry, unheard by any except the patrolling owl, and half turned back towards the Hall with its lights and music, vibrant with laughter and life. But for her the ball was over. The Master of Ceremonies could call in vain, 'Your sets for the lancers, please.' Cinderella would not answer. For the rest of them, there would be carriages at half past midnight, and all revellers abed before the moon went down.

Mary shivered in her thin coat. Surely the air had turned colder, or was it someone walking over her grave, as Gran called the uncontrollable shudder that passed through her? She knew now what she was going to do. It would take courage, but Hector had demonstrated that the Bottralls did not lack courage. It would be unpleasant, but the thought did not make her shrink. If it was the only way left, then she would take it, just as Hector had done, and with as little thought of sacrifice.

Against the fading music from the ball she set off, walking briskly, the sound of her neat black polished boots with their varnished soles ringing out like drumbeats on the hard surface of the driveway, and throbbing like muffled drumbeats as she turned aside through the wood.

CHAPTER 12

'. . . And so, dearest, I am coming home.'

Emily hesitated and then underlined the word 'home' with a flourish. Harry was not a subtle man.

'We have had a pleasant Christmas,' she wrote (what was another lie more or less?), 'enlivened by the news of Jimmy's engagement, of which he will no doubt tell you himself.'

He had better. She wasn't going to. She could not bring herself to write about Miss Poppy Richards and her triumphs, except the one that most affected them.

'His fiancée is connected with the art world,' she elaborated, 'and I am sure you will be relieved to know that she has identified a family portrait as being of great value, thus relieving George's financial distress. He will not need to sell Amberley, so I have destroyed your letter on the subject, with which, needless to say, I agreed. It was like you to be so unselfish, but the situation does not arise. I expect you will be as thankful as I am that we are not called on to make such sacrifice.

'The children are well,' she continued, 'and looking forward to their schools. Roddy has met a boy who goes to Bradwell House, so he already has a friend.'

She paused, looking at her sleeping daughter, and added, 'Beatrix is quite the little woman now.'

Would Harry understand? It didn't matter. What mattered was that it was true. Her daughter was no longer a child, and she herself felt older and in some way threatened by this entrance into womanhood. The candle on her dressing-table guttered. The carriage clock showed seven a.m. She was on the threshold of a new day, a new era, in which Jimmy had called her shabby and the candlelight in the mirror showed her an ageing face. The contents of her dressing-case, artfully applied, would present a different picture by the time she went downstairs, but in this chill room, as yet untouched by dawn or by maids bringing up hot water, she and truth were face to face.

It was time for retreat, what Harry would have called a strategic withdrawal to a position already prepared, the preparation being this letter which she was composing so carefully. Emily sucked her pen; composition did not come easily, but her husband had to know not only that she was sailing earlier than intended, as soon as Cox's and King's could find her a berth, but also the reason why. Which of course had nothing to do with Jimmy. Thank God she had opened George's study door when she did and found him with that Bottrall girl. He would hold his peace, she was sure of it, and see to it that Maud held hers.

'All these events,' she wrote, 'underline the fact that I have been away far too long from my Harry. I miss you, dearest, every day. So I have decided, once the children are in school, to cut short my visit and sail for home without delay.'

Harry would at least appreciate that neat reversal, for in India England was 'home'. How good for him to feel that 'home' to her was where he was.

Behind her, Beatrix stirred.

'Mama . . .'

'Yes, dear.'

'This is your room.'

'Of course. You can't share with Roddy any more.' And it no longer matters that you share with me, for Jimmy will not come. He belongs to Poppy, and I must sail for India, Harry, and 'home'.

Beatrix sat up. 'Who are you writing to?'

'Papa, naturally. Shall I send him your love?'

'Yes, and tell him – tell him I miss him more than I ever did.'

It was true. Mama had said that what had happened to her was never mentioned between ladies and gentlemen. 'Except to doctors,' Mama said, 'and –' with a half-smile – 'husbands.'

'Not to brothers?'

'Roddy is much too young.'

'Nor fathers?'

'Papa would not wish to know.'

He probably wouldn't, Beatrix reflected. Papa expected children to cause no trouble, and trouble included being ill. Or 'indisposed', as Mama put it, though 'having a headache' would apparently do just as well. Of course other ladies would know, would in their turn tell her when they were 'indisposed', which happened once a month –

'For the rest of your life?' Beatrix asked in horror.

No, Mama said, but until you were quite old.

'But why?'

Mama shrugged. It was part of being a woman. Beatrix would understand better by and by.

But all Beatrix understood was that she was now cut off from her father and brother, the two people who meant most to her in the world.

With Mama it was different. She loved her mother, but she found she could face their impending separation with equanimity, and even with fortitude. For something had happened to Mama last night, as apparently momentous as what had happened to her. Looking at her now in the unflattering light of the candle, Beatrix thought: She's not beautiful any more.

It was not candlelight that illumined Maud's face in the mirror, for the sickroom rated a paraffin lamp. Perhaps they might even be able to extend gas lighting to the upper storeys, Maud speculated, if the news about the portrait were true. Oh, let it be true, she prayed, with a glance at George sleeping beside her. We could neither of us bear it if it were not. Some miracle has saved George from the worst consequences of his accident. Don't let that miracle be in vain.

In repose George's face looked younger, the lines of strain erased. The stubble on his chin gave him an unexpectedly raffish appearance, not at all like that of the stolid squire. He could grow into that later in the morning, and during all the days, months, years that were to come, when he would still be squire of Amberley and she would bear his son.

For I shall have a son, Maud thought. He was

conceived last night. I know it, as surely as I know my own name. With the harvest this year will come my harvest: Maud, wife of George North of Amberley – of a son. And this time he will live. There will be no more nephews for Lilias. My son will live and Lilias is dead. She had a sudden vivid memory of the last sight of her sister, lying waxen-white in her coffin, her ruined face turned to one side. That was how she had lain ever since in the churchyard, looking towards Amberley. Her eyes were fixed in death, and it seemed to Maud that not six feet of earth nor a stout oak coffin with brass handles could divert her gaze from the future that should have been hers.

Her future, but my present. The thought grew and blossomed in Maud's mind. She slipped out of bed and drew back the curtains to reveal dawn red in the east. Shepherd's warning, perhaps, but when had the future not threatened, and not all its threats came true. There would still be Norths at Amberley, she was certain, and her son, not Emily's, would be the heir. Mrs George North of Amberley. She savoured the title with pride, and, glancing round the room, caught herself wondering if there might now be enough money to have it redecorated to her own taste instead of Madam's, Madam having hastily had the room done over to welcome her as a second-best bride. She raised her arms and stretched luxuriously towards this day of new life, dawn of marriage. George watched her from the bed through half-closed eyes, still pretending slumber, pleasurably reminding himself that this was Maud, not Lilias. Maud was his wife, his life, his present and his future. Lilias was the past. She was dead.

Only in speech had Maud ever reminded him of her sister. She had the same light, musical voice. Sometimes in the dark he had allowed himself to believe it was Lilias speaking, hating the moment when the illusion must be dispelled by light. Now, watching his wife silhouetted against the window, her nightgown fallen back from her arms, her hair loose about her shoulders, he saw for the first time that there was a likeness. The same small, straight nose, firm chin, and slender neck below it, the same swift turn of the head as she heard him move, saw him hold out his arms towards her.

She ran to him, light of heart and foot yet already heavy with the child she knew she carried.

'Oh, my love, my love, my love,' he said.

Later, as she descended the stairs, returning the maids' greetings, responding to enquiries about her husband, Mrs George North of

Amberley was conscious of a new ease. Her orders had always been readily obeyed, her justice and reasonableness respected, but now she felt free to take decisions without reference to George, to Madam, to the shade of Lilias.

So it was arranged – smoothly, without anyone becoming aware of the organization – that young Dick Sparrow from the smithy would drive Jimmy and Poppy to the station in George's motor-car. Emily, the children and the luggage would travel more conventionally in the brake. Maud glanced at the clock in the dining-room. In another two hours they would all be gone, and instead of the eggs, bacon and sausage, grilled kidneys and cold ham arranged on the sideboard there would be congealing fat and dirty plates. As there would be long before if someone did not come and eat them. She turned to sound a summons on the hall gong that was used only on rare occasions, and encountered her eldest daughter at the door.

Alice's head was thrown back with a touch of bravado or defiance. We are going to have a scene, Maud thought, noting automatically as she said, 'Good morning, Alice,' that her daughter's stockings were askew.

'Good morning, Mama. When can I see Papa?'

So that was it. Last night's promise was being claimed.

'You may go up when you've had your breakfast.'

'Isn't he coming down?'

'No, he will have a tray in his room. I dare say he will come down later to see our visitors depart.'

'Is Trix all right?'

'If you mean Beatrix, I am sure she is.' As well she might be after the upheaval last night, with Emily rousing the household although it was unnecessary: she had only to take Beatrix into her bed. No wonder Alice had looked frightened. 'It's quite natural, you know,' Maud added awkwardly. 'It happens to all girls in time.'

'Is it going to happen to me?'

'Of course. I'm glad you've had this advance notice.'

'I won't let it happen!' Alice cried, repelled and sickened by what she had witnessed.

'You'll have to get used to being a woman.'

'I'd rather be a man.'

Lilias had once said much the same, had vowed she would not be a woman. Sighing, Maud took her place behind the tea and coffee pots, the small extra pot of China tea for Emily, hot milk, cold milk, an expanse of waiting cups. 'I'm afraid there are some things you can't choose,' she informed her daughter.

Lilias had never accepted that and she had. Yet Lilias, for all her brilliance, her charm, her classical education and steely will-power, had ended in a mess of mud and blood. Whereas she, Maud, was the inheritor. The meek shall inherit the earth. And when they did, they had no further use for meekness and no need to fear Lilias.

She looked at the young Lilias before her and said carefully, 'Now that you're older – and more responsible,' she added quickly, 'Papa and I have been wondering' (only George did not know he had been wondering yet) '– wondering,' she went on more firmly, 'if it is not time you learned to ride.'

'Mama!'

'Gently, dearest. I have only just put my hair up. Oh, be careful –' as the milk jug nearly went flying. 'You must not be so impetuous, you know.'

'No, Mama. You're right. I won't be.' Alice went skipping round the room and just escaped colliding with Emily. 'Aunt Emily, I'm going to learn to ride.'

'How nice,' Emily said dully, wondering what the excitement was about. Riding was an over-rated pastime, though there were few garments more flattering to the female figure that a well-cut riding habit – a fact she had early found out.

'Trix, I'm going to learn to ride.'

Bea hugged her. 'It's what you've always wanted, isn't it? We'll be able to go riding together in the holidays. When are you going to start?'

'I thought Jepson might take you out on the leading rein this afternoon,' Maud answered. It would get Alice out of the way. And Rose could stay in the nursery with Nanny and Lulu, giving her and George a chance to get to grips with those papers in the study. She checked the still empty places at the table and asked Alice, 'Where is Rose?'

'Saying goodbye to Roddy.'

'Where?' Mama's voice was sharp.

'Out in the hall,' Jimmy said, entering with Poppy.

Maud and her sister-in-law relaxed.

'They appear to be exchanging love-tokens,' Jimmy said with a smile, thinking of the little pair who had sat opposite him and Poppy on the way home from the ball. Hand in hand and half asleep, Rose's head on Roddy's shoulder, as the carriage swayed along. Later, Poppy's head had sunk gratefully against his shoulder as he reached out and captured her hand.

The second half of the ball had passed in a

blur of bliss as dance succeeded dance, his hand on Poppy's waist exerting gentle pressure while hers lay like a sleeping kitten on his arm, his ring on her fourth finger emitting reassurance with every wink and flash of faceted fire. His left hand clasped her fingers – how fortunate that fancy dress precluded gloves, and the subtle pressure of each reiterated the message of her eyes – 'I love you', reminding him cruelly of his doubt. Never again, he promised, glancing down at her kerchiefed head. He had been about to throw away his happiness when chance or fate, or whatever Poppy's apposite return might be termed, had handed it back to him with a mocking bow – 'You dropped this, sir' – and he saw that it was still unblemished and unharmed. So must George have felt when life was handed back to him.

'Did you tell George about the painting?' he asked Maud.

'Yes.'

'Did he get up and dance a jig around the bedroom?'

'No,' Maud said, 'but he was very glad.'

She did not intend to describe George's reception of the news in detail, that would be to reveal too much; but her face told Jimmy all he wanted to know.

He touched her briefly. 'I'm glad too. I hope

you both know that.'

Rose, who had come in looking subdued, followed by Roddy, was chasing food around her plate.

'Eat up,' Maud encouraged her. 'Grandmama will be here soon.'

'What's she coming for?'

'To see everybody off.' The line was clear, the trains were getting through. Soon Amberley would return to normal. From the hall came sounds of luggage being brought down. 'We'll assemble at the door to give you a good send-off,' she told Poppy. 'The servants will be there too.'

How feudal, Poppy thought. Across the table she caught and held Jimmy's eye. He shook his head – say nothing; and winked – I know how you feel. Perhaps after all visits to Amberley might be endurable so long as she and Jimmy were as one. So long as there was Madam – Madam would always be worth visiting. She might even come and stay with them some day?

At that moment, when Jimmy was helping Poppy to grilled kidneys and Maud was buttering a slice of toast, when Emily was protesting that she wanted nothing but a cup of China tea, thank you, and Rose was finding swallowing difficult because of the lump in her throat, Fanny North was lying on the floor of her bedroom, willing herself to rise. She had slid from her chair when a spasm of pain ended in faintness and now found her eyes level with the valance of the chair, with the fender and the gap between door and floor through which a cold draught whistled, chilling her even as consciousness returned. She sat up. Her breakfast cup had rolled and broken, carried by the impetus of her fall, and a trail of tea-leaves adorned the wet patch on the carpet. They had the shape of a skull. They tell fortunes from tea-leaves, Fanny thought wildly. What did that woman say when I was a girl – that I should die when I had a daughter? She was wrong: it was my daughter who died. If she had lived she would be married now, with children, or else living here with me, instead of gazing at me from an eighteenth-century portrait which Poppy Richards, who looks uncannily like her, says George must sell to save Amberley.

As her head cleared events came back more coherently. She had not felt well last night, had retired to bed as soon as Poppy had departed, and then lain wide awake. That wicked Bottrall girl . . . Jimmy . . . the need to protect him from her lies . . . Poppy . . . they must not scare her away, she would be good for him . . . The thoughts went endlessly round. The first stab of pain caught her in the midst of envisaging

Jimmy's wedding: not here at Amberley like all the others, but in some London church, newish suburban gothic, with hardly any flowers. Whereas St Peter's was always a bower; flowers in the church-yard too; on John's grave and the graves of the three little boys . . . pity Maud couldn't manage an heir, but now at least there was Roddy . . . not his fault that he was Emily's son.

The pain surged, overwhelmed her, and receded, leaving her breathless and faint as she felt the next wave gather. Her daughter's birth had been like this. She could not remember the boys' births, except that she had been tired and triumphant, with everyone, especially John, congratulating her, telling her she'd done well. But her daughter's birth had been different: she had not been in control. The midwife's instructions, the doctor's ministrations, bore no relation to the pain that gripped and tore. It was a living thing and she its victim; her daughter a dead thing at the end. As I shall be, Fanny caught herself thinking. Except that I won't let it happen. I'm only sixty-five. With a magnificent effort she had pulled herself upright in bed and struggled across the room to her usual chair. When Patterson brought in her breakfast, there was nothing obviously amiss. She could not eat, but some she hid and the rest she fed to the birds. Wilkins could drive her the short distance to Amberley. She must at all costs keep up until the visitors had gone. Till she had said goodbye to Poppy Richards – soon to be Poppy North. Till George had dealt by eviction with that lying Bottrall girl. When she felt the carpet against her cheek she almost gave up the struggle, but somehow she got to her knees. She must dress, but perhaps Patterson could do her hair – she was always asking. And for once a little rouge could do no harm.

So the Fanny who descended from her carriage, immaculate, upright, unbowed, was almost the Fanny everyone knew, though there was a haunting difference of which nearly everyone was aware. 'She's looking older,' Mrs Roberts murmured to a housemaid. I never expected to see her use paint, Emily thought. She's as stiff as a ramrod, Wilkins noted as he held the carriage door for her; Patterson must have laced her too tight. 'Have you got rheumatism, Grandmama?' Rose asked sympathetically. 'No, child,' Fanny replied with truth. Further enquiries were drowned in the roar and splutter of Dick Sparrow bringing the motor-car round to the front door.

The bright yellow machine halted, quivering as if with ague. Dick touched an imaginary chauffeur's cap. This was the life. A smart livery to equal that of Wilkins or Jepson and the power of twelve horses at his command. He threw open the door with a flourish and officiously dusted the leather seats. Not for him if he could help it the work of the smithy, the round of horseshoes, broken axles, and the iron wheelrims of carts. That belonged to the past; the petrol-driven engine was the future. He might even run a garage some day if a few more gentlemen would follow the Colonel's example and invest in a motor-car. Mr Jimmy didn't know how lucky he was to be driven to the station in style, with his fiancée from London (who knew all about pictures) perched up beside him, she holding on to her hat because the girls always did, and he, if he knew what was good for him, holding on to her tiny waist.

Although the motor-car travelled faster than the brake, it had been decided that Poppy and Jimmy should leave first because the narrow country roads offered few opportunities for overtaking, and a motor-car rattling and snorting behind them was enough to make the quietest horses bolt. Besides, there was a comfortable waiting-room at Barford station, the long seats upholstered in black horsehair with deep-buttoned backs and wooden arms, and a roaring fire kept burning in the steel grate at all times, fed with the railway company's own coal.

The young couple might even have a little time together before other passengers arrived. Jimmy and Poppy were not dismayed by this prospect as they set about making their farewells.

The servants first. 'Thank you for everything.' 'Best of luck, sir . . . miss . . . Happy New Year . . . One with wedding bells in it . . . Thank you, sir, very good of you . . . A pleasure to have you with us, miss.'

Then the children. Alice had vanished, but Rose was present, standing with Roddy hand in hand. 'Goodbye, Uncle, thank you for the golliwog.' She had tactfully remembered to bring it with her. 'Goodbye, Aunt Poppy, I'm so glad you're going to marry Uncle Jimmy because that means he'll bring you again, and I hope . . . I hope . . .' She searched for a grown-up expression. 'I hope you'll be as happy as Roddy and me.'

Everyone laughed at this and no one spoke.

'And Alice – where is Alice?'

'Alice is with her father,' Maud said, realizing suddenly that she was no longer jealous of her daughter. Was not she, Maud, carrying George's son?

'We'll see her when we go up to say goodbye to George, then.'

'I think he's coming down.'

'No matter. Mater, it's been great to see you.

Bet you never guessed what my surprise was going to be.'

'I couldn't have guessed anything so delightful,' Fanny said, smiling at Poppy. The smile was genuine, but it had to be kept in place. 'Come again, my dear, and come soon,' she said, kissing her. Only Poppy noted the emphasis on the 'soon'.

'I will,' she promised. 'Perhaps with Mr Edelstein.'

'Oh, of course. The picture.'

'As if you'd forgotten it,' Poppy teased.

But Fanny had forgotten it, for what was canvas compared to living flesh and blood? The girl in the picture stood before her, garbed differently but essentially the same. Jimmy's bride-to-be. Mrs James North of the future. My daughter-in-love, Fanny thought.

'In any case I shall see you at our wedding in April,' Poppy insisted. 'You'll come, won't you, even though it isn't going to be here?'

Jimmy, the best beloved, the only one not to be married in Croft Amberley . . .

'I shall come if I can,' Fanny said.

What was that prophecy in the tea-leaves – you will die when you have a daughter? Well, I have a daughter, but I am not going to die, Fanny maintained, drawing in her breath as the pain lanced through her.

Poppy heard the indrawn breath. 'Can I do anything?' Her voice was pitched very low.

'No, dear.' Fanny's voice was equally low. 'Only – take care of Jimmy for me. That girl and her wicked lies . . .'

She was not going to die, but she was handing on a trust to Poppy just as if death were really at hand. I, Frances Anne North, do give and bequeath unto my dear daughter-in-love Poppy Richards the care and cherishing of my best beloved son . . .

Poppy was laughing. 'She can't hurt Jimmy. Let her talk if it gives her relief. She has so little in her life –'

And will have less if I can do anything about it, Fanny promised.

'– and she must have adored her brother. We ought to pity the poor thing.'

A touch of the old Fanny came back. She snorted. 'In a minute you'll be wanting us to reinstate her at the school.'

'Well, why not?'

'Over my dead body.' But perhaps it would be. 'I think,' Fanny said, straightening herself and trying to breathe evenly, 'it's time that you and Jimmy left.'

Poppy flung her arms around her. Everyone was careful not to look startled. No one had ever done that to Madam before. And Madam was responding, holding the girl to her as if, Mrs Roberts said later, that Miss Richards was her own flesh and blood.

'Goodbye, Madam dear. Maud –' Poppy turned impulsively to her almost sister-in-law, using Maud's name for the first time – 'you will look after her, won't you? Madam dear, take care.'

Fanny made no promises. What you promised you had to perform, and she would not begin this new and precious relationship with a piecrust promise.

'Goodbye, daughter,' she said.

On the landing outside George's room Jimmy and Poppy encountered Alice, looking solemn and important.

'We nearly missed you,' Poppy cried.

'I'm sorry, Aunt Poppy, I was with my father.'

'Who has entrusted the management of the estate to you,' Jimmy suggested, 'to judge from your careworn look.'

Alice smiled because it was expected.

'Perhaps you've been prescribing for him,' Poppy said. 'Didn't I hear you say you wanted to be a doctor?'

'I don't now. I'm going to be a teacher instead.'

Since last night Alice had become less than enthusiastic about the idea of stanching blood, whereas a teacher like Miss Bottrall was someone who stood up to Grandmama whom not even Papa dared to contradict. Doctor of Physic no longer seemed so attractive. Certificated – that was what teachers were. They went to training colleges, unless they were too poor like Miss Bottrall; and if she, uncertificated, could outface Grandmama, a certificated teacher could probably stand up even to God.

As soon as she had finished her breakfast, Alice had sped to her father's room. Mama said nothing, but then this morning Mama was different. Mama had said she could learn to ride. What Mama had actually said was, 'Papa and I have been wondering if it is not time you learned to ride.' It was the 'Papa and I' that worried Alice. Had Mama really discussed it with Papa?

She found her father in his dressing-gown, looking pale but otherwise himself, and sitting in a chair by the window with his bandaged foot resting on a stool. She kissed him. He had not yet shaved and the bristles on his chin were rough and pleasant.

'Good morning, Papa. Are you feeling better today?'

'Much better. Soon be back to normal.'

Alice decided this was probably true. It was only now that she saw him looking much as usual that she could bring herself to admit she had been frightened lest he die suddenly in the night.

'I'm so glad.' First fear dismissed, she proceeded to tackle the second. 'Mama says you've decided I can learn to ride.'

'Does she, by Jove!' So she hadn't discussed it with him. 'You want to, don't you?'

'I've wanted to for a long, long time.'

'Yes, well, your mother . . . It's understandable, in view of your Aunt Lilias.' Who looked much as you do at this moment, except that you're alive and Lilias is sixteen years dead. 'Anyway, your mother has withdrawn her objections.'

'And you – have you withdrawn yours?'

'I never had any. I shall enjoy riding round the estate with my daughter.'

'Even though I'm not a boy?'

'What's that got to do with it?'

'I can't inherit.'

'Who'd want to inherit the headache of Amberley? Do you realize if your Aunt Poppy hadn't spotted that picture hanging in the Dower House we'd be bankrupt?'

Alice wasn't sure what bankrupt meant, but it was evidently serious. 'Is that why you've been so worried?' she asked.

'What do you know about my worries?'

'I know you go to bed late and get up early and shut yourself in your study and you don't want anyone to see the post. And on Christmas Eve in Barford you didn't want us to see you. Who were you visiting in Dunstan Street?'

'A business acquaintance.' Mary Bottrall, and now Alice. How many others had witnessed that shaming visit? George added, 'I shan't need to go there again.'

But Alice's attention had turned to her next anxiety. 'Papa, are you going to let the Bottralls stay?'

The unexpectedness of it caused George to say, 'You want to learn to mind your own business, young woman.'

'Mama says the tenants *are* our concern.'

'Then since you ask, I haven't decided. What do you think I should do?'

'Let them stay. Miss Bottrall's right. Why should they be servile and grateful because Grandmama decided to take them some soup?'

'Hey, hey – what's this? Jack's as good as his master?'

'He might be better sometimes. In South Africa Uncle Jimmy got the timing of the attack wrong and Hector Bottrall saved it.'

George drew a deep breath. 'Is that what Mary Bottrall says?'

'Yes.'

No wonder Jimmy had written interceding for Hector's grandmother and sister, even though the details had never come out. How the Bottralls knew of it George could not imagine. Would it look as if he were being blackmailed if he now allowed them to stay? Faintly his nostrils remembered the scent of cheap soap in Mary's hair. She had shown courage, he supposed, in coming to him, apologizing, confessing; it was not her fault if he had been overtaken by desire . . .

He said to Alice, 'She fired my ricks last summer. What do you say to that?'

'She shouldn't have fired your ricks. She should have fired someone else's.'

In spite of himself, George laughed.

Alice pressed home her advantage. 'You'll let them stay, won't you, Papa?'

'We'll see. There's your grandmother to consider.'

'She needn't take them soup next year.'

Nor any other year, George calculated, if Maud was right in saying the Mater wasn't up to snuff. He hadn't noticed, but women were quicker to detect these things. She might be failing. Impossible to think of Amberley without her, but it was bound to happen sometime . . .

Satisfied that her father would relent, Alice

proceeded to her final question, designed to lay the most terrifying fear of all. Not wanting to see his face when she posed it, she gazed fixedly at the window and said, 'Can I ask you something, Papa?'

'Ask away.'

'You were out shooting yesterday, weren't you, when you tripped and your gun went off?'

Behind her she felt him go still. His voice was neutral. 'You know I was,' he said.

'If you were going shooting,' Alice said carefully, 'why didn't you take Rastus?'

The dog. Oh God, I forgot about the dog.

'I had other things on my mind,' George said equally carefully.

Alice turned, and her eyes fastened upon him as if they could see into his soul. 'It's easy to forget a dog, isn't it?' she said softly. 'When you're going out shooting, I mean.'

'Very easy,' George agreed.

'So that answers that.'

'Yes.'

But nothing was answered. Or rather, everything was.

'I shan't mention Rastus,' Alice assured him, 'and Mama will never think of him.'

'Thank you.'

They regarded each other while the realization of conspiracy seeped into them. George was the first to look away.

'If I'm to get dressed and come downstairs, you'd better leave me,' he suggested.

Alice fought to control her voice. 'Of course, Papa. But oh –' she flung herself upon him, making him wince – 'you don't know how thankful I am you didn't shoot yourself seriously. Suppose instead of your foot it had been your head!'

Suppose it had been, George thought later, as he stood on the front step with Maud beside him, leaning heavily on his father's stick. The motor-car bearing Jimmy and Poppy had departed with a series of backfires that had so startled the horses that Jepson had had difficulty in controlling them. But now the quiet bustle of departure was familiar, apart from the scuffed gravel which the gardeners would rake later and the sickly smell of petrol hanging in the air. George had leisure to reflect that if everything had gone as he intended, it might have been a hearse standing there.

Roddy and Beatrix were making their farewells – 'Not long till we see you again at Easter, miss', 'Now, Master Roddy, you mind and behave nicely at school' – when George was aware of a slight commotion on the edge of the group, where a man from the village had come hurrying up. Jarvis moved swiftly to intercept him, but as he listened the butler's face grew grave. With a sinking heart, George recalled that the last time there had been such an irruption it was because the village hall was on fire. A tablet on the new village hall recorded that it had been rebuilt through the generosity of Lord St Devereux and Colonel George North of Amberley.

Rose watched the man arrive with chill indifference, saw without seeing Jarvis move towards Papa with what looked like tidings of heavy import. Whatever they were, they could not worsen the present. Roddy was going away for ten whole weeks. How was she to endure ten Sundays in church without him, fifty days of lessons with Miss Evans, seventy nights of brushing her hair one hundred times, ten occasions when she could perhaps write to him (although he had explained he would not be able to answer), and still maintain a smile on her face? 'Miss Rose is like the sunshine,' Cook said fondly. 'It does me good to see her, she's as much a tonic as the spring.' When Roddy returned the snow would be gone and the drive would have a frill of daffodils, but where in her sad little soul in the meantime was she to harbour spring?

Her fingers closed over the curious brown

pebble in her pocket. 'It's from the garden at home,' Roddy had said as he gave it her a bare half-hour ago in the long narrow space under the stairs where Jarvis kept the trolley which was used only when Mama had ladies to tea. 'Mrs George North. At home.' The engraved cards were ordered by the boxful, so that only the date needed to be filled in. Sometimes Alice was asked to help, but Alice had inky fingers and too often the smudged results had to be thrown away. 'Rose is much neater,' said her mother. 'She's going to be such a help to me one day.' Rose burgeoned with pride, for she loved being helpful, but even the idea of helpfulness palled when she thought of the ten long weeks ahead of her. Would Roddy be the same when he returned?

In exchange for the Indian pebble she had given him the pink sugar mouse saved from the toe of her Christmas stocking, and they had gone in to breakfast with their treasures cunningly concealed in pockets where they could fondle them in secret. Indeed, Roddy had fingered the pink sugar mouse so often that already it was growing slightly soft. Would it be all right to take the mouse to school with him, he wondered. He remembered what his father had said about his teddy-bear. The thought of Edgar's mocking face was not encouraging, even though by the time the ball was over they had vowed to be friends next term. Would he see Edgar on Barford station? Would Edgar speak to him before getting into that reserved compartment which sounded so dauntingly grand? He had departed last night with a nonchalant 'See you next term, North' – and next term was terrifyingly near. Roddy wished with all his heart that he could stay at Amberley in the gentle company of Rose, and of Uncle George who looked so like his father. Ten weeks was an eternity to be away. Ten weeks ago he had been on Cossipore station, looking down from the tall iron train into his father's up-turned face.

'Goodbye, son. Quite an adventure, this, isn't it?'

'Yes, it is rather.'

'Don't worry. You'll be all right. Chip off the old block, and so on.'

'Yes, Father. Will you write?'

'Every week,' Major North promised.

Roddy relaxed slightly. His father's promises were kept.

'Though you'll have to allow for delays in the mails. This damn train's late already and if the mails miss a sailing . . . Of course it'll be the same for us in reverse.'

Roddy nodded. The distance between

India and England was incomprehensible, and there was a speck of dust in his eye, which must have been why it kept watering. There seemed to be a speck in his father's eye, too.

'George'll see you right,' the Major assured him. 'He's a good sort. Maud's all right too. Don't think George appreciates her –' He broke off. 'Right, son. Better let your mother come to the window.'

He reached up. Roddy reached down and they exchanged a manly handclasp.

Back in the gloom of the compartment, Roddy set about removing the speck of dust from his eye.

Now, once again, there were protracted departures, and already it was getting late. Roddy, who had his father's sense of punctuality, knew that the brake should be leaving, but instead all the grown-ups, Mama included, were gathered in a huddle – Uncle George, Aunt Maud, Grandmama, Mr Jarvis, a man from the village. Solemn-faced, they were talking in hushed voices. Then Mama came across to them, with a determinedly cheerful air.

'We're going, Roddy.' (George had said, 'For God's sake get the children away.') 'Say goodbye to your cousins.'

Roddy said, 'Goodbye, Rose.'

'Goodbye, Roddy.' Her lips were trembling but her tears had not overflowed. For the first time in her life Rose controlled the floodgates. It was Roddy who, once again, was troubled by a speck of dust in his eye.

Beatrix, standing a little apart with Alice, watched them indulgently, but watched now from the far side of childhood. They were such infants – like a miniature Darby and Joan. Which meant they were very much a couple, like Uncle Jimmy and Aunt Poppy, or Uncle George and Aunt Maud. Not that she had at first thought of George and Maud as a couple: they had seemed distant, almost estranged. It was like Papa and Mama in India, who so often had nothing to say. Yet in both cases she had been wrong, for her aunt and uncle seemed inseparable this morning, and Mama was cutting short her visit to England simply to return and be with Papa.

Now Mama was coming towards them. 'Time to go, darling,' she said, over-bright.

'What's happened, Aunt Emily?' Alice asked.

Emily was flustered by her failure to convey that everything was normal. 'There's been an accident –'

'Uncle Jimmy!'

'No, not the motor-car. A young woman in the village. I don't think you know her –'

'Miss Bottrall!'

'Why, yes –'

Alice asked more urgently, 'What's happened?'

'I really don't know, dear –'

'Is she dead?'

'You'll have to ask your mother. Come along, Beatrix, Roddy. We don't want to miss our train.'

There was a final hug from the children for Nanny, who by holding Lulu in her arms avoided the delicate decision of whether it would be appropriate to hug them in return. Then they were in the brake, with the luggage piled around them and Jepson flicking the reins of the horses while his throat worked painfully. Mary Bottrall. He could not believe it, although neither could he believe that Colonel North would lie. He would not say she was drowned dead if she wasn't. Mary . . . Last night they had been dancing, laughing. She was at her best and, as always, fun to be with. This morning . . . A sob like a groan burst from him, and for a time it was as well the horses knew the way.

'Goodbye . . . goodbye . . .' The chorus of farewells swelled and receded. Roddy leaned over. 'Goodbye, Rose, I'll be back.' It was a promise he would make and keep many times until that day in 1917 near St Quentin when a young subaltern would fail to fulfil all his promise, and Rose would dwindle into lesser loves.

'Goodbye ... goodbye ...' Beatrix waved with her mother. Goodbye, Amberley, I'm so thankful I'm leaving. Goodbye, Amberley, I'm so thankful I'm coming back.

Alice suddenly turned and yelled, ''Bye, Trix.'

Whatever had happened to Miss Bottrall (and she was convinced that Alice was right and she was dead), this was an avowal of friendship and Beatrix's heart soared. In the Easter holidays they would go riding together, and with Alice she would discover the delights of an English spring. In the summer they would lie in the long grass of the orchard, just as her father had described doing with Uncle George, reading and munching early apples and talking as only best friends talk. In the autumn, perhaps, as with the riding lessons, Uncle George and Aunt Maud would undergo another transformation and allow Alice to join her at The Limes.

'Goodbye ... goodbye ...' Beatrix glanced at her mother, but Emily was gazing straight ahead as though she saw all that lay before her and did not like what she saw. For her, there would be the voyage out, monotonous this time; the falsely ecstatic reunion with Harry; the boredom of Cossipore; and then the growing certainty that the reunion was to have issue. Patricia Frances would be born the following year.

'Goodbye . . . goodbye . . .' Fanny managed to lift her hand as if in blessing, while leaning against a portico pillar for support. A little longer, and she could relax. A little longer, and Jimmy would be married to Poppy. (The brake was disappearing down the driveway . . .) A little longer, and Maud might yet give them an heir. And only a very little longer, and the pain would be no more. Already some part of it had receded with the news of Mary Bottrall's death. Jimmy was safe now, safe from her slanders, and it was no use Maud calling it an accident when remorse had so clearly been at work. Found drowned as a result of crossing the frozen lake at Mawby Hall in an attempt to take a short cut – that was what Maud was saying – but taking a short cut to where? Certainly not in the direction of the Bottralls' cottage, and Mary knew all about the dangers of the stream. No, if she had gone into that icy water, it must have been deliberately. Fanny's thoughts were untinged with pity, for she accepted that if they had been, Mary would have rejected it. Of course there was old Annie Bottrall; when she felt better she would have to call on her. Such gestures were appreciated, expected even, in

Croft Amberley. If only Mary had been able to recognize that. As it was, she had pitted herself against the system and the system had very properly prevailed. And would do for so long as she, Fanny, was there to uphold it – but for how much longer was that? The death that grew silently, invisibly, within all living creatures was in her about to be given birth. She noted, without surprise, that she no longer fought against it. Whatever courage Mary had shown in walking steadfastly into the lake's freezing water, Fanny North would emulate.

She staggered. George put out an arm to steady her and almost staggered himself.

'You all right, Mater?' God, she looked ghastly.

'It's nothing. A little dizziness, that's all.'

'You must come in and rest,' Maud said authoritatively, and made to take her arm.

(The brake was out of sight . . .)

'Thank you,' Fanny said, pride fighting a losing battle as she set foot in Amberley. For so long she had been mistress here, even from the Dower House, that to enter by Maud's invitation was an admission that she now took second place; though it was still she who commanded, 'You had better fetch Paget,' before collapsing on a chair in the hall. Then some further explanation seemed needed for the people who surged around her and she fought to give it, aware briefly of Alice's white, questing face. What should she say? I am ill – oh, never that; besides, she was not ill, she was dying – but at least: 'I am not well.'

There was no room for George in the hall. He sensed that Maud wanted him out of the way. At times of birth and death men were supernumeraries and women came into their own. Not that the Mater was dying: 'a little dizziness' – that was all; but she had never had any use for Paget, and it was unlike her to send for him. No doubt it was the shock of hearing about Mary. He admitted to feeling shaken himself. Who could have believed she would do anything so foolish when everyone knew that end of the lake was dangerous? At least, that was Maud's explanation, which he had already adopted. He approved the speed with which she had begun putting it about. If you repeated something loud enough and often, it was astonishing how it came to be believed. But not by him. He would go along with ensuring a scandal-free verdict and sparing old Mrs Bottrall further pain, would have a word with the coroner, with the police in Barford, but he did not believe it was Accidental Death. Any more than it would have been if he had not tripped in Weston Wood yesterday, thereby achieving accidental life. And if he had not achieved accidental life, if Poppy had not found that picture, would Mary be still alive? If fortune had not smiled suddenly on the Norths who had done nothing to deserve it, need Mary Bottrall have died?

George shivered. The water must have been so very cold, but the mud would still be unfrozen. He had a vision of that limp, drowned body, mud streaking the eyeballs, the black, no longer polished boots. Her hair would be hanging in rats' tails, no scent of cheap soap now. Had she really believed he would evict them from their cottage? Had anyone else, come to that? Was he about to be blamed by the village, the rector, as the indirect cause of her death?

He became aware of Alice standing beside him.

'Papa, you should go indoors. You mustn't catch cold. If Grandmama is going to be ill, Mama will have to look after her. She can't nurse you as well.'

'Quite right, m'dear.' George limped towards the door.

The sound of Lilias's voice – no, Maud's voice, her mother's voice – stopped him as Alice spoke again.

'Papa.'

'Yes, dear.'

'Miss Bottrall is dead, isn't she?'

'I'm afraid so.'

'What happened?'

'She was found drowned in the lake at Mawby Hall.'

'Did she drown herself on purpose?'

'No, no, the ice gave way. She must have been taking a short cut.' He heard his voice ring hollow, and Alice was not deceived.

'Did she do it because of us?'

The voice of the village . . .

'What do you mean?' Though he knew.

'Because she thought you were going to evict them. Because Grandmama wanted her dismissed from the school.'

'Neither of those things would have happened.'

'But perhaps she didn't know that.'

'She would still have been very foolish.'

As I was. As Alice alone knows I was.

'Is it really a sin for a person to take his own life?'

'The rector would say so.'

'Yes, but what do *you* say?'

George said, retreating shamefully, 'I say you should run along and stay out of the way until this upset is over. What have you done with Rose?'

'She's gone with Mrs Roberts to the kitchen.

They're going to make fudge cake.'

'Why don't you go too?'

Alice stamped her foot. 'Because I'm not a child any longer. Why won't people realize that?'

George looked at the passionate girl in child's clothing who stood before him, and said, 'Because we don't want to, I suppose. You mark the passing of time and we would rather it didn't hurry. Remember, as you grow up, we grow old.'

As you grow up. Become a woman. Like Trix. For it would happen, however much she rejected it. And by the same ruling her father would grow grey and stooped, would someday stagger and collapse on a chair in the hall as Grandmama had just done. Old people died, and Grandmama would die, would be buried in a hole in the ground, leaving a hole in their lives which would be filled more slowly, and in their memories not at all. But it was not only the old who died. Young people died too: Aunt Lilias, her three baby brothers, Hector and now Mary Bottrall. It was so random, so unfair.

She did not realize these last words were spoken aloud until her father answered her. 'Who says life's got to be fair? It never is, so if you want to be thought grown up you'd better start getting used to it.'

Then he added, as if speaking to himself, yet to her and to anyone else who would listen: 'And be thankful it isn't fair.'

Life is unfair, be thankful. The words reverberated in Alice's head as she made her way to Weston Wood. From the scarp above the wood she could watch the London train carry away the last of Christmas and wave to it unseen as it raced by.

Ever since she was a little girl and had been first taken there by her father, Alice had loved watching the trains. Trains were exciting. They could go anywhere. Not only to London, or to distant cities like Edinburgh and Truro, but to Holyhead for Kingstown across the Irish Sea, or from the Channel ports to Paris, Berlin, St Petersburg, to Rome, to Vienna and Budapest – all those capitals which Miss Evans insisted on her learning, that world which she would someday see.

It took five minutes from leaving Barford for an express to come pounding into view, tossing its mane of smoke and giving forth the distinctive rhythm which proclaimed it was approaching full speed. Da-da-da-dum, da-da-da-dum, as it headed for the black mouth of the tunnel, the final syllable savagely cut off; and an instant later the hills gave forth a mocking echo, a phantom da-da-da-dum.

'Life is unfair, life is unfair, be thankful.' Alice repeated the rhythm as she climbed. To be in time to see the London train she should have left when the brake did. Instead she had lingered, allowed herself to be delayed. But she had to know what had happened to Miss Bottrall. She could not have left without knowing that. And now that she knew she had difficulty in comprehending – not that Mary Bottrall was dead, but that she, so vital, so rebellious, had chosen death instead of life.

Life is unfair. Of course it was when you considered. That was what Miss Bottrall had protested about when she had hurled the soup at Grandmama and rejected charity. But unfair or not, it was still life, still a source of protest. There were no protests from the dead. And if life had been fair, perhaps it would have been Mary Bottrall who was still living and her own beloved father dead.

The train burst upon the landscape without warning just as she reached the scarp. One moment all was still and silent, the next the glistening locomotive and its attendant carriages were reverberant among the snow-streaked hills. In one of those carriages was Uncle Jimmy with Aunt Poppy beside him, Aunt Emily with Roddy and Trix; in another, those horrid children whom Rose and Roddy had met at the ball last night, together with their parents; in another, Lord St Devereux. Part of Alice's very self was being torn from her as the train progressed across the countryside from left to right. Yet the loss was compounded by excitement: it seemed as if another part of her must be aboard the train. So too were Mama and Papa, and Rose of course, and Nanny and Lulu, but the roll-call did not end with them. Jepson was there, with his tear-streaked face (but why was he crying?); Jarvis and Mrs Roberts; Grandmama sitting in a corner, no longer forceful; old Mrs Bottrall opposite. Mary was not there, for the dead did not travel; as well expect to find Aunt Lilias. But everyone still living was being borne onwards, onwards, over the gleaming rails.

Their destination scarcely mattered. What mattered was to travel, to be part of the ineluctable progression that led from birth to death, as surely as the main lines all over England converged on a terminus.

Alice raised her hand and saluted the train rattling and swaying into the future. Into the unknown. Into life.

The engine shrieked in despair as the tunnel engulfed it, but the echo came back loud and clear.

Life is unfair. Be thankful.

The season of goodwill was over. In three days' time it would be New Year.

THORNDIKE PRESS HOPES you have enjoyed this Large Print book. All our Large Print titles are designed for the easiest reading, and all our books are made to last. Other Thorndike Press Large Print books are available at your library, through selected bookstores, or directly from the publisher. For more information about current and upcoming titles, please call us, toll free, at 1-800-223-6121, or mail your name and address to:

THORNDIKE PRESS
P. O. BOX 159
THORNDIKE, MAINE 04986

There is no obligation, of course.